MOM BOSS

Hilary Grossman

Published, 2020

Cover Design by Hilary Grossman
Edited by Christina Boyd

This is a work of fiction. Names, characters, places, brands, media, and incidents are either the product of the author's imagination or are used fictitiously. Any resemblance to similarly named places or to persons living or deceased is unintentional.

PRINT ISBN

ISBN-10:

Library of Congress Control Number: _____

To all the heroes and essential workers – especially the moms who have been doing double duty…

PRAISE FOR HILARY GROSSMAN

"Liane Moriarty brought it back in Big Little Lies and Laurie Gelman made it laugh-out-loud funny in Class Mom. Hilary Grossman's new novel brings it center stage as the Forest River PTA dishes out more drama than you'd find in a Meryl Streep movie."
- *The Book Whisperer*

"Hilary Grossman knocked it out of the park with her fourth novel. Go On, Girl is filled with humor and heart.
- Meredith Schorr Best Selling Author

"Dangled Carat sparkles with humor and shines with wisdom. It is a gem of a book."
- *-Christina Baker Kline - New York Times & USA Today Best Selling Author of Orphan Train.*

"I don't think I could love this book any more than I do. A fantastic read that moms alike will be able to relate to. Grossman has you laughing, biting your nails, yelling at your e-reader, and rooting for the characters."
- Tracy Krimmer – Author of Lipstick & Lattes and Mistletoe Mishap

CHAPTER ONE
NOW
AUGUST
Almost Back to School

"JACKIE? JACKIE MARTIN is that you?"

I felt a gentle tap on my right shoulder. I quickly tucked my iPhone back into my Louis Vuitton hobo bag and took a deep breath. The email I had read only seconds ago from Principal Williams while standing in line at Paired, my favorite shoe store, had startled me to my core. "Startled" was probably a poor choice of words, I was so troubled by the confusing words I contemplated fleeing the store without purchasing the three pairs of Manolo Blahnik sandals I had found at twenty-five percent off. But I knew forgoing the shoes wouldn't magically shed any light on the situation, so why would I let a great shoe sale go to waste? There was no harm in shopping first and worrying later, right?

Even though all I wanted to do was hand the cashier my American Express card and make a mad dash home, I wasn't about to be rude. I plastered a bright smile on and took my time before I turned around. "Hi. Yes, I'm Jackie," I said, locking eyes with an unfamiliar, petite, Lululemon-clad, blonde woman.

She balanced two shoeboxes awkwardly against the left side of her hip and thrust out her free hand. "I thought so! Hi, I'm Colleen Drake." I shook her ice-cold hand. I was thankful I had opted for a shopping cart to hold my finds. I would have hated to risk dropping a box and causing a scene.

"My family and I just moved to Forest River from Ohio a couple of weeks ago. I have a son, Dylan, who will be entering fourth grade."

"How lovely. I am sure Dylan will love to have a seamless transition. And you will be extremely pleased with the education here. We're very fortunate to live in this town. We have wonderful schools."

Even though I was angry, frustrated, and confused about Principal Williams's email, there was no way I was about to let my personal feelings show. Ever since I orchestrated my way into the PTA years ago, I had been an avid supporter of all things Forest River Elementary School. My children followed in my footsteps. My oldest daughter, Hayley, had been a greeter for years. Her job was to help make new students feel comfortable.

"Oh, I know"—her eyes fluttered—"the schools' reputation was one of the main reasons we decided to move here when my husband was transferred to New York."

"You're not alone. Most people settle here for the same reason," I said, even though the stellar school system was the last thing on my mind when Scott and I moved to town, a little-known fact I'm now embarrassed to admit.

I added, "I'm sure you won't be disappointed." The people at the registers completed their purchases, and Colleen and I both took a few small steps forward. I hoped the movement would distract her and put an end to her jabbering. Normally, I could chatter on about the school for hours, but at the moment, the thought of making small talk with a stranger felt like a chore.

But this Colleen person seemed starved for conversation. "I know I won't be disappointed." Then with a slight squeal, she said, "I am so happy I bumped into you. I was dying to meet you before orientation day. I feel like I know you already."

"Excuse me?"

Her face flushed. "Oh, I'm sorry. I didn't mean to sound like a stalker or a crazy person. I joined the Forest River Moms and Dads Facebook page practically the moment after we signed the contract for our house. I wanted to get a lay of the land, so to speak. I used to be a research assistant before I became a stay-at-home-mom. I must have scrolled through every post since the inception of the group. I must say, I am extremely impressed with everything you've accomplished in such a short period. You are a remarkable woman."

She seemed like a woman after my own heart. Also, a compliment goes a long way. It was sad how many people don't realize this. During my tenure, I played an intricate part in the school's decision-making, especially concerning field trips, class celebrations, and fundraising efforts.

"Thank you. Everything I have done was truly a labor of love," I admitted mostly honestly. I tucked a strand of blonde hair behind my ear. "And I'm extremely fortunate. I have a wonderful team. Currently, all of the positions are filled, but we never turn anyone away. We're constantly on the look-out for parents to pitch in and help with our important work." I reached into my purse and pulled out a hot pink PTA business card that contained my contact information and handed it to the woman. "We'd love to have you join us. If you're interested, give me a call."

"Oh, thanks," she said as she tossed the card, without even a glance, into her oversized Prada bag. "I appreciate your offer. I'm sure you know how it is moving to a new town. I know I am going to be quite busy. I doubt I'd be able to offer much assistance now. But it was very kind of you to invite me."

"No worries," I said. "Volunteering and service isn't for everyone."

"So true. Jackie, I appreciate you giving me your contact info, though"—she grinned—"and since you are such a kind, giving person, if my son or I run into any issues getting situated, would it be okay if I called you?"

The cashier gestured for me to approach the register.

"Of course. Anytime."

Sure, part of me wanted to tell this nervy woman to buzz off, but I couldn't say that as a representative of the PTA. She knew an awful lot about me, and I knew almost nothing about her. Besides, she might not be ready or willing to participate in the PTA right now, but you never know what the future might bring. I crossed my fingers and hoped she'd prove to be supportive and helpful, as so many others had been over the years.

I learned the hard way in a town like Forest River, New York; you never can tell what to make of people. And keeping up appearances did come at a price.

CHAPTER TWO
NOW

To: *Jackie Martin*
From: Forest River Elementary School Principal, Harrison Owen Williams, Jr.
Date: 8/25 @ 10:04 AM

Subject: Meeting request

Salutations Jackie,

I hope the summer has treated the Martin family well and you have all enjoyed your much-needed holiday away from the demands of Forest River Elementary School.

Maybe it's me, but the breaks seem to fly by faster with each passing year. I am sure that both Cassidy and Hayley are excited to embrace another exciting term just like my staff and I are.

Unfortunately, I have had to make a change to Hayley's placement. She will no longer be in Mrs. Epstein's class, as initially indicated. Instead, she will spend her final year in Mr. Smithstien's fifth-grade class.

I'm sorry to inform you of this change at such a late juncture. I would love to meet with you in person to go over the motivation for this action. I will not be in the office or available by phone at all today. I know you'll be eager to discuss this matter, so I have cleared my calendar tomorrow and we can meet any time after 9:00 AM. Please let me know what time works best for you.

Send my regards to Scott and the girls.

Sincerely,
Harry

Harrison Owen Williams, Jr.
Principal, Forest River Elementary School

"This is unprecedented!" I bellowed into the phone as I paced around my expansive kitchen.

"Jackie, please," my husband, Scott, practically begged. The poor man. He had been trying unsuccessfully to get me off the phone for the past fifteen minutes, after I had read him the e-mail from my daughters' principal.

I knew I was a bit irrational, since I knew Scott had a meeting to go to, but I needed him too. I had to talk to someone! I tried to track down my best friend, Donna, but she was uncharacteristically missing in action, not answering my calls or texts.

"You must try to calm yourself down. I'm sure there is a logical reason for Harry's actions."

"Like what?" I demanded as I opened my SubZero refrigerator and pulled out a bottle of water. I must have re-read the principal's email at least forty-six times. No matter how many times I stared at his insouciant words, I couldn't decipher their meaning. "Never, in all of my years of service, have I seen a student get booted from a class line up before the semester started. This is unprecedented!"

"There is a first time for everything, honey."

I took a sip of my water. Instead of easing my mind, his gentle tone and nonchalant nature pushed me across the thin line between worry and panic, the place I tried to avoid visiting the most.

"Scott"—I exhaled deeply, struggling to keep my tone steady—"let me try this again. Don't you understand? Never in all of my years have I seen anything like this occur. Children aren't just removed from a class without a reason. All of Hayley's friends were placed in Mrs. Epstein's class. Now she will be all alone."

"Jackie, really? It's not like she's being sent to solitary confinement at the state penitentiary. She's the most popular kid in the grade. She'll be fine."

"But Scott—"

"I know you're upset, Jackie, but I don't know what else to say. I have faith you'll figure this all out. And we'll talk more when I get home, but I'm sorry. Unless I get my butt into the conference room right now, I'm going to have a mutiny on my hands. I don't have the bandwidth to deal with that on top of this mess." His voice softened slightly. "Hang in there, gorgeous. I'll make sure to catch an early train home tonight. Love you."

"I love you too," I said back, even though my husband had already disconnected the call.

I glanced at the clock once more. It barely moved since the last time I looked. Hayley and Cassidy wouldn't be home from day camp for another few hours. I felt like I was going to crawl out of my skin. Bursting with nervous energy, I changed into a ratty pair of sweatpants and oversized tee shirt I stole from Scott years ago and jumped on the treadmill. I tried calling Donna and was once again greeted by her voicemail. In all the years we've been friends, she never once ignored my calls. Sure, there were times when she was busy and couldn't speak, but she'd fire off a quick text as a response. If she hadn't just posted a selfie holding two bags outside of Paired to her Instagram story, I might have panicked that something terrible happened to her this morning.

If only I had more information about what prompted the principal's email, I would have been able to channel my energy into something productive. I lived by the old adage "proper planning prevents poor performance." I hated being unprepared, and unless I figured out what motivated Principal Harry Williams's actions, I had no hope of figuring out a way to fix the problem.

I had gone through every "what if" scenario I could think of, and no matter how much I wracked my brain, I couldn't fathom to guess what could have caused my daughter to be singled out. I was glad Harry wanted to meet in person to discuss, but it was cruel of him to drop this bomb on me this morning when he knew full well he'd be unavailable until tomorrow. Why couldn't he have waited until then to reach out to me? I had no doubt he knew I would be obsessing over this change of plans. Harry knew me better than most. Unlike most of my friends and my PTA colleagues, Principal Williams understood that underneath my strong, confident, and often bossy public persona, there was an anxiety-ridden mother who'd do anything to protect her daughters.

"Ugh," I said to no one but the house as I walked upstairs to my bathroom after completing a five-mile run. I stripped out of my sweaty workout wear and turned on the shower, full force. I exhaled slowly as I stared at my complexion in the mirror and cringed. My hair was a wild mess from anxiously raking my fingers through it, and my blue eyes looked bleak. It had been over five years since I had felt this way. I thought, based on everything I did then and the years that followed, I'd never feel this level of panic surge through my veins again.

CHAPTER THREE
THEN
SEPTEMBER
Five Years Ago

SCOTT STOPPED WALKING several feet before we approached the open doorway. I'm sure he sensed my tension, especially since I didn't do anything to hide my feelings. He turned around to look at me, cupping my face with his hands. His husky voice was a whisper. "Are you okay, love?"

Instead of answering right away, I looked down at my new sandals and fresh pedicure. I didn't want to make eye contact with my husband, which was completely out of character for me. I didn't think I could handle the compassion in his eyes. I usually ate up his affection but, today, I was afraid his kindness would cause me to break down. I already felt nervous and emotional. The last thing I wanted to do was walk into this parent-teacher conference misty-eyed and mascara-streaked. It was important to me to put on a brave performance. I finally met his gaze and sucked back a tear. "I'm not sure."

He opened his arms, and I fell into his embrace. As he held me, I felt all the tension evaporate from my body. Just having him near me made me feel safe and protected. He leaned down and kissed the top of my head. "Oh, my little worrywart," he joked. "Everything is going to be fine, just as I've been telling you for weeks. I can't wait to walk out of this building in a half hour and see the look of relief in your eyes."

"Me too." I gave him a small kiss. I longed for the good old days when I was as optimistic as he was. My mother-in-law's words now haunted me. Oh, how I wish I could go back in time and heed her advice about pre-schools, about play dates, about so much. I was a fool. I thought I knew better. Why didn't I realize that nothing beats experience?

When I originally told Scott about the appointment, I expected I'd be showing up solo. I was shocked, and incredibly relieved, when he told me he juggled his schedule around so he would be able to be at my side. I smiled. "All right. Let's go do this," I said with more confidence than I felt.

I entered the classroom first. "Jackie, hi." Anna Anderson, Hayley's kindergarten teacher, greeted me warmly. She was a petite dark-haired woman, who was probably ten years my senior. She had a bubbly personality and a kind demeanor. My daughter loved her.

After I introduced her to my husband, she invited us to sit down opposite her desk in two leather chairs that were clearly brought in for this occasion. Scott, who stood over six-foot-two, had wondered if he'd have to squeeze into one of the students' desks like parents did on sitcoms.

Ms. Anderson had been with the district for over ten years and had an excellent reputation, which wasn't surprising. From what Scott's mother said, all of the teachers in this school were top-notch.

Scott's parents had bought a magnificent summer home in Forest River soon after he graduated college. They fell in love with the town and its tranquil river, quaint storybook appeal, and close proximity to New York City. For years, they spent a good portion of the year here where they enjoyed shopping and dining, as well as playing golf and tennis at the country club where they were members. After they both retired a few years ago, they began to travel a lot. When they weren't jet stetting around the globe, they alternated between Forest River and their Florida beach house.

Scott's mother, Joan, was such an avid supporter of Forest River, when we first mentioned we were contemplating leaving our rented brownstone in Brooklyn to move to the suburbs, she launched into full saleswoman mode. She made it her mission to sell us on the benefits of the town. And while she did make many compelling arguments, neither one of us was one hundred percent sold on the place.

Although Scott and I knew a home in the suburbs would

probably be best for our family, it was hard for us to leave the hustle and bustle of Brooklyn. I loved that there were so many places I could walk to with Hayley. And her nursery school had such a chill and artsy vibe. My mother-in-law interpreted our "extensive research" of the area as dilly-dallying. Finally, thoroughly frustrated with our lack of action, she made us an offer we couldn't refuse. By the time we told her I was expecting her second grandchild, she had already paired up with one of her dear friends, who was a well-known local real estate agent and found, purchased, and furnished a home for us in Forest River. We could have moved right in; instead, we held off. We didn't officially make this house our home until June, about a month before Cassidy was born.

Clearly, we couldn't say no to her generous offer. At the time, Joan rationalized her actions by saying everything she and her husband possessed would eventually be inherited by Scott and me when they passed away. She explained she wanted to be able to give us generous gifts while she and Stan were alive, because they wouldn't be able to experience any joy in helping us financially after they died. And while her rationale rang true, Scott and I also realized it was a power move on her part.

I knew we were extremely fortunate. Who wouldn't want to receive such a lavish gift? Yet, I often wondered if we would have ended up selecting Forest River on our own. I do know I would definitely have decorated my house differently. My style is more transitional and modern instead of traditional and antique like Joan's. Even though I would love to redecorate, I would never dare hurt her feelings. She would be so insulted if I made major changes.

"Thank you both for coming here today," Ms. Anderson said. She looked first at me, and then my husband. "I am extremely appreciative when both parents value their children's educations enough to attend a conference together." She lifted her red glasses slightly and rubbed her nose. "Many times parents discount the importance of what happens in a kindergarten class. In this room, your daughter will learn the basics she needs to thrive in the challenging world of academia and life."

I looked around the room and marveled at how state of the art it was. This classroom looked nothing like the room in Kansas where I began my education. There were several computer stations, an interactive white board, and a karaoke machine.

Ms. Anderson reached for a folder. She licked her index finger and flipped through the pages. She removed a few sheets and handed them to me. "Hayley is talented, very artistically inclined, as you can see. I had the children attempt to draw a picture of several farm animals, and Hayley's depiction was by far the most detailed and realistic looking."

"Scott, look at this." I handed the sheet of paper to him so he could see the purple pig and green cow. Then to the teacher, I said, "I've been doing arts and crafts with Hayley for as long as she was able to hold a crayon."

"Good work! Your efforts show, Jackie." She returned her attention to the folder and pulled out yet another stack of pages. This time she handed them to Scott first. "Also, I'm delighted to share, Hayley is doing fantastic with both her letters and numbers. I'm very impressed with her word recognition, and her reading comprehension is stellar."

Pride filled Scott's eyes, which was not surprising. From the time she was two-and-a-half years old, he spent an hour with her every day reading and even teaching her how to sound out words, just as his mom did when he was a little boy. "We have a little superstar on our hands."

Sometimes he was so naïve. It amazed me how my successful hedge fund manager husband could grasp every financial situation almost instantaneously. Yet he never anticipated when someone was buttering him up to break some bad news. I knew there was a "but" barreling towards us like a freight train.

Ms. Anderson closed the folder and pushed it to the edge of her desk. Then she leaned toward us, her smile not reaching her hazel eyes. "Hayley is a superstar, Mr. Martin. All the children are special in their ways. But"—she sighed—"there is one area of concern I need to discuss with you."

I reached for Scott's hand and gave it a firm squeeze.

"I'm sure you don't need me to tell you, Hayley is an extremely shy little girl." Ms. Anderson put her elbows on her desk, steepling her fingers. "Many children are. For the most part, they grow out of it or learn how to cope. Unfortunately, I haven't been able to detect any improvement in Hayley's social skills."

I folded my arms across my chest and braced myself.

"In this classroom, I encourage the children to work together, with the goal for them to learn how to develop relationships. When forced, Hayley rises to the occasion. Fortunately, the other children seem to like her. I was hoping after enough of these mandatory interactions that Hayley would begin to become more comfortable initiating conversation or play on her own. Sadly, I haven't seen any improvement."

I wanted to shake my husband. Ever since school began earlier this month, he kept discounting my fear and observations. He told me I had let his mother make me paranoid. And while I knew Scott had a point — Joan did have a way of getting under your skin — I feared this time she was accurate in her assessment.

"But it has only been a few weeks," I said. I nervously picked at a cuticle, even though I had gone for a manicure only the previous afternoon.

Ms. Anderson shook her head and averted her eyes. "You're right, it's been *weeks*. I'm sorry. It's not her fault, but Hayley is at a definite disadvantage. I looked up her records and see Hayley didn't attend Forest River Nursery School with the other children. They have spent a couple years together and, as a result, they are quite bonded. Not by any means am I saying Hayley can't break in. I am sure, with hard work, she can acclimate herself to the school and form friendships. I don't believe in sugarcoating a situation. I want to warn you, it won't be easy for her, especially since she is so timid."

I felt the color drain from my face. My mother-in-law warned me about this! Joan must have told me a thousand times I was putting Hayley's future in jeopardy by not sending her to a nursery school with the children she'd spend her elementary years with. I thought she was ridiculous and melodramatic with her claim. Why didn't I take her warnings seriously? I should never have been so selfish and stubborn to want to stick around in Brooklyn before starting our new life in the suburbs.

The teacher must have sensed my distress because she

added in a much softer voice, "I'm not sure you have to start ringing the alarm bells just yet. Most children do grow out of their shyness over time." She opened a desk drawer and pulled out a binder, removing a couple of sheets of yellow printouts. "Here is a list of some literature that should help you help her." She then glanced from me to Scott and then back to me. "Also, if there isn't any improvement, you may want to consider bringing Hayley to speak to someone. Our school psychologist is wonderful and at your disposal, but most parents prefer something a bit more private. I have plenty of names I can provide if you are interested."

I looked at the sheets she handed me. "Thank you. I'll take your list to cross-reference. However, I have already received a list from my pediatrician." I didn't feel it was necessary to inform her that it was my mother-in-law who called the doctor to solicit the names. Scott and I already had a lengthy discussion on this subject. We decided not to pursue professional help just yet. While we felt with our help Hayley could become more confident with others, I still wanted to receive the school's recommendations. One could never be too prepared.

"Wonderful," Ms. Anderson said as relief flooded her face. "I'm so glad you weren't insulted. It does my heart good to see parents who are receptive to help."

I glanced at my husband. "Don't worry. We'll both do whatever it takes to allow Hayley to thrive and succeed." I raised my pointer finger. "I just need to clarify something. You said the other children seem to like Hayley. Is that correct?"

Ms. Anderson met my eyes. "Yes, it sure appears that way."

Then I asked the one question I truly feared the answer: "So, Hayley isn't being teased or made fun of because she's timid?" I knew too well what it was like to be picked on in school because you were different from the rest of your classmates. There was no way I was about to have my daughter follow in my footsteps.

"Oh, absolutely not. Forest River Elementary School has zero bullying tolerance."

"Yes, I know what the literature says." I tried to keep my voice calm. "I've read it so many times, I probably could recite it by memory." I paused and looked around the room. My eyes settled momentarily on the ceiling, which was painted to look like the sky on a bright summer's day. Placing my hand over my chest, I said, "I'm sorry. How do I say this? We all know children will be children. And children can be cruel and very clever. Are you absolutely sure you'd know if anyone was mistreating my daughter?"

Ms. Anderson's face fell. Then, gaining her composure, she replied, "I'm extremely confident Mrs. Martin."

The fact she addressed me by my last name, for the first time, wasn't lost on me. I sat ramrod straight and didn't utter a word. I knew anything else I said wouldn't accomplish anything.

She cleared her throat. "I guess I should have clarified. There is one child who Hayley does seem to be comfortable around. Kyle Conroy."

I squinted as I tried to envision the children in Hayley's class. "Is he the small blond boy with freckles?"

"Yes. He went to Forest River Nursery School and is an extremely popular child." Ms. Anderson crossed her arms. "He seems quite protective of your daughter for some reason. I'm sure he'd never let anyone upset her."

I leaned in and placed my elbows on Ms. Anderson's desk and silently counted to five. "Wow"—I smirked—"thank goodness. My daughter has a three-foot-tall bodyguard. Clearly, I have no reason in the world to worry."

CHAPTER FOUR
THEN

"I OWE YOU an apology," Scott said as soon as we entered our car.

"For what?" I asked as he started the engine. I wasn't going to make it easy on him. After all the years we had been together, he knew he'd need to apologize to me even though I blamed myself for the situation.

He turned to face me. "For being a jerk and not taking your worries seriously."

"You were a jerk. But I'm not mad at you," I added quickly. "Hayley's teacher is another story." I was sure she thought she'd make me feel better by telling me about my daughter's friendship with Kyle, but it brought me no relief. I feared it was only a matter of time before one or both of them would be teased for being boyfriend and girlfriend.

I reached over and squeezed his hand. I wanted him to know I was being honest. Sure, I could have reacted with anger, because he clearly deserved it. Over the past month, he had constantly brushed away every one of his mother's and my concerns about Hayley's social development. What was the point of getting into an argument with him now? It wouldn't solve anything, and more importantly, I knew he didn't mean any harm. Scott and I had two completely different childhoods. Was it any wonder we now looked at life through two very different lenses? I often mused how differently my outlook on life would have been if I had grown up with a mother like his.

Scott was calm and easy going, while I was high-strung. He tried to analyze every situation logically and rationally. I, on the other hand, let my emotions rule me. In my defense, unlike my spouse, I had to become an adult way before it was my time.

I didn't have one iota of jealousy when I compared our childhoods. On the contrary, I was extremely thankful his charmed upbringing allowed him to become the man he now was. His realistic yet optimistic outlook was one of the things I loved most about him. He had an uncanny ability to calm me down when I was anxious or angry, which seemed more often lately.

"I would be mad if I was you, Jackie."

I smirked. "I guess this proves I am the *bigger* person."

"Oh, come on, baby, don't start that nonsense again. You know I think you're perfect the way you are."

"Yeah, sure," I mumbled half under my breath.

Cassidy was almost two months old, and no matter how hard I tried, I couldn't shed the stubborn pounds I gained. It had been completely different with Hayley. One minute I was the size of an elephant and the next I was able to squeeze back into my size zero jeans. I foolishly assumed history would automatically repeat itself.

"Oh, Jackie." There was such tenderness in his eyes, and my heart swelled. I was so thankful he loved me for me and not my beach body.

"You need glasses." I teased and punched him in the arm. "Hey"—I studied his face—"why are you looking at me funny?"

"I always look at you funny," he said. This was our little joke. I usually asked him this very question several times a week when I caught him staring at me. While we bantered, the truth was he looked at me with a mix of love, adoration, and confusion, just as he did now. He leaned over and kissed me. "Look on the bright side. If you can't fit in your clothes, you have more reason to shop."

"Every cloud does have a silver lining. You better brace yourself for some major damage, my friend."

"Shop away. Seriously though, we should talk. Do you want to go grab lunch?"

"Don't you have to head back to the office?" I asked, hoping I'd jog his memory about an important meeting or fund valuation he had to review.

"Yes, I do have to get in but can squeeze a little more time before anyone will miss me too much."

"Okay, you know I can't say no to you. But we'll have to make it quick. I don't have much time. I have to get home." Even after all these years, between his runner's body and his chiseled features, he never failed to make my heart flutter.

He pulled out of the school's parking lot and started to drive toward Main Street. "Why? I thought you planned to spend the afternoon hitting the town and spending all our money."

Before we left for school, I had told Brittany, our au pair, I didn't expect to be home for hours. "Yes, I did plan to spend the afternoon shopping. Except now I changed my mind."

He stopped at a red light and narrowed his eyes at me. "I see your mind racing a million miles a minute. What are you up to?"

My eyes implored his. "I'm not mad at you, I swear. But we wasted enough time doing things your way, don't you think?"

"What I think is Hayley is fine. Nothing the teacher said in there changed my mind. I know our daughter will find her way. She's only shy. It's not the end of the world."

I wiped a tear away from my eye. "You're right. It's not. I'm worried about what comes next. What happens if she can't form friendships? What happens if she becomes the target of the mean kids because she is different?"

"That won't happen."

"How can you be so sure? I was tormented as a child in grade school. I refuse to let my daughter ever experience what I had to endure."

He didn't respond.

"I was a good sport, Scott, and I humored you. You truly believed nothing was wrong with Hayley, and I wanted to believe you were right. I went with the flow. And I hate going with the flow." I frowned.

"Don't I know it!"

I placed my hand on his thigh. "Hey, my tenacious side was what made you fall in love with me in the first place."

He took my hand and kissed it. "It sure was. Okay, fine. Whatever you need to do now, count me in. Remember, we are a team."

Before I was a stay-at-home mom, I was an event planner for

a major charity. Scott attended one of our fundraisers with a group of his co-workers. I turned on my charm full force. Not only did I manage to get a date for the following Saturday night, I also snagged a ten-thousand-dollar donation from him.

"Good, because the spit-fire you dated is back. I'm flipping this script. I am doing what I do best. I am going to take control of this situation. It will take me a little while to get all my ducks in a row, and when I do, our little girl will be just fine." I wiped a tear away from my cheek. "You wait and see."

CHAPTER FIVE
THEN

"YOU'RE NOT IN Kansas anymore," my mother-in-law, Joan, stated as a matter of fact.

Typically, the expression grated on my last nerve. The only time I didn't take offense was when my mother-in-law said it. I knew no matter how harsh her tone might be, with either her son or me, she never meant any harm. She doted on her only child since the day he was born and, as a result, I knew she had our family's best interest at heart, even if her delivery left something to be desired.

I had called her in Florida soon after I returned home from lunch with Scott. After losing a game of Candyland to Hayley and feeding Cassidy a bottle, I gave Joan the complete play-by-play of my first parent-teacher conference.

I considered myself one of the lucky ones. Unlike most of my friends from college, I had a great relationship with my mother-in-law. From the day we met, she made me feel comfortable. Often times, we didn't see eye-to-eye, and that was okay. I never felt as if I were walking on eggshells, which was refreshing. We both allowed the other to freely express their opinion. What did drive her crazy was she had a love-hate relationship with my stubborn side, which was understandable because the woman had a constitution of steel too. I also realized a long time ago that she'd resort to drastic measures if I didn't listen to her words of advice.

"Well, you can take the girl out of Kansas..." I poked my head into my den and checked on Hayley, who was sitting on the floor coloring with our au pair. I didn't want my daughter to overhear this conversation.

"Sometimes I wonder... I know I shouldn't have to spell

everything out for you. Yet sometimes I don't feel like you don't take what I say seriously, sweetie."

I grabbed a bottle of water out of my refrigerator and sat down at my kitchen table. "Probably because I don't. Sometimes I think you are nuts."

"I know!" She snorted. "I remember feeling the same way when I was your age, although Stan's mom wasn't nearly as amazing as me. Hopefully, one of these days you'll realize I am never wrong. And then, not only will you listen to me, you'll treat my sage words as gospel."

I was thankful she was across the country so she couldn't see the face I made. I cleared my throat. "You're always right?"

"Okay, fine. Maybe I make a mistake every now and again. But for the most part, I am always right. Sure, there may be one or two things I am not an expert on, but for the most part, I know what I know. I earned my black belt in suburban backstabbing and petty parental politics years ago. I won't sugar coat anything. I made my share of mistakes over the years, and I learned from each and every one. I spent years on the frontlines when Scott was growing up, and I've probably seen it all. Sure, times have changed but the end game remains the same. All I want to do is spare you some pain and heartache."

I took a sip of water. "I know. And I love you for it."

"I love you too, Jackie. But we both know love alone isn't going to get you through this. You need strength, grit, and determination, too."

"Which I've got."

"You used to. Now is the time to dust off all your skills and put them to use."

My mind had been racing since Scott and I left Hayley's classroom. "Where do I start? What should I do?"

Joan let out a deep sigh. "I'm so glad you asked. You follow my advice and you will never have to worry about our little Hayley being lonely or not accepted by her peers. She will be the most popular child in that school, and you will be the mom boss you were born to be."

"Mom boss? Come on, Joan. Aren't you a bit dramatic? All I

want is Hayley to have a happy childhood."

"There is nothing wrong in aiming for the stars. Is there, Jackie?"

I didn't reply.

"What's a matter? The cat's got your tongue?"

"We don't have a cat."

Joan snickered. "I know damn well ever since you left the prairie and headed to the East Coast, you set your sights sky high. You had an aggressive timetable and accomplished everything you wanted professionally. You busted your butt to land that dream job of yours and worked like a dog to move up the corporate ladder."

Too bad it didn't work out as I had planned. I wanted it all and had expected to continue working part-time after I had Hayley. Unfortunately, one month before I gave birth my manager was fired. Her replacement refused to consider any cut in my hours, so I resigned. I planned to find another similar position with more flexibility, but in my line of work it wasn't simple.

Joan continued, "Now, you need to work just as hard at becoming the ideal Forest River mom."

I pinched the bridge of my nose as a vision of me dressed in a fifties style outfit, pulling a meatloaf out of the oven, danced in my mind. "This all sounds very *Stepford Wives*."

"Yeah, well, welcome to the suburbs."

Before I could contemplate a reply about how she encouraged us to move to this very community, she continued. "So, this is what you need to do. First, you need to get to work and assemble your army."

"Army?" I asked as my eyes bulged. I wondered if I made the right choice in requesting her assistance. I probably would have been better off if I reached out to one of my former sorority sisters instead.

"Yes, Jackie, your army. You need to get to work and make friends with other moms in Hayley's class. Not only is it essential for you to orchestrate play dates—"

"Hayley plays with friends."

"Oh, dear, Jackie..." Joan made a tsk-tsk sound. "I'm not talking about Hayley spending time with some random children on your block who are younger than she is. She needs to spend time with the *right* children, the children who are in her grade."

"Oh," I muttered.

"And as Hayley gets to know these kids, you must get to know their mothers. It is imperative that these women become your allies. You know the old expression, united we stand."

I nodded automatically. "Yes, I do."

"Good. Put yourself out there. Volunteer your time and talents. And most importantly, you need to network! You have a wealth of tools at your disposal."

"Like what?"

"For starters, your membership to the Forest River Country Club is like a golden key."

I rubbed my head. I felt a tension headache beginning to form.

"Oh, Jackie," Joan tutted. "The club is so much more than a place to play golf and enjoy a Memorial Day clambake. Everyone who is everyone belongs to the club."

"I know," I said, understanding why Joan strongly encouraged Scott and I to turn in our application and check months before we ever moved into our new home.

"I've got it." Joan squealed. "I know the perfect person for you to join forces with."

"Who?"

My mother-in-law never failed to amaze me. Even though she spent a good chunk of the year either down south in the Sunshine State or traipsing across the globe, somehow Joan managed to keep track of all the comings and goings in this cliquey community.

"Claire Conroy."

"Claire?" I searched my memory for an image of her, drawing a blank.

"Claire Conroy has two children. No, wait. She recently had her third. She's been an extremely active member of the club for years. Unlike you, from the moment her application was accepted, she began to attend all the meetings and events at the club. I'd bet Claire knows everyone who is anyone at the school."

"Pretty impressive," I said.

"Yeah, well, I think it is more her husband's directive then hers, sadly."

"What do you mean?"

"Well, she's married to this guy who is a repugnant jerk. Keith. No, wait, Kevin. Yes, that's his name. Both Stan and I dislike him immensely. He is so obnoxious, even a blind man could see how he tries to use the club as his own personal playground, to make business connections and the like. He drags poor Claire around like arm candy. Unlike her husband, she's kind and sweet. People really seem to gravitate to her and like her. I actually served on a fundraising committee a couple of years ago with her, and she impressed me as well. I struggle to understand what she sees in her husband. I guess that old saying sometimes rings true. Love is blind."

"Have I ever met her?"

"Probably, but don't worry. I'll be more than happy to make an introduction." Joan gasped. "Oh, and do you want to know the best part?" Joan paused for emphasis. "Her oldest son, Kyle, is in Hayley's grade."

Now it was my turn to laugh as the pieces to the puzzle clicked in place. "No, Joan, that's not the best part."

"Excuse me?"

"It gets better." I chuckled. "It seems Claire's son has a little crush on our girl Hayley."

CHAPTER SIX
THEN
OCTOBER
One Week Later

To: *Forest River Elementary School Principal, Harrison Owen Williams, Jr.; Ms. Anna Anderson*
From: *Jacqueline A. Martin*
Date: *10/2 @ 7:42 AM*

Subject: *Class Mom Duties*

Good morning Principal Williams and Ms. Anderson,

I wanted to take a moment to formally thank Ms. Anderson for the attention she gave my husband and me last week. Sadly, people usually rush to complain when they are disappointed, yet they don't stop and take a few seconds to offer a compliment when they are pleased. I am not one of those people! I never hesitated to provide my honest opinion, regardless of my satisfaction level.

Frankly, Scott and I were a bit nervous about attending our first parent-teacher conference. Thankfully, Ms. Anderson made us feel comfortable, especially when she had to discuss a difficult topic. Kudos to her! Her grace was much appreciated, and her honesty about our daughter's strengths and weaknesses gave us a lot to mull over.

As I mentioned during our meeting, we are dedicated to making sure Hayley has an outstanding experience in Forest River Elementary School.

We value education and the hard work you both (and the rest of the school's staff) demonstrate every day.

I am so committed to this cause; I am willing to do whatever I can to assist in this matter. I had initially volunteered to do class mom duty. Even though school has been in session for over two months, I have not been called to serve in the classroom. I am unwilling to continue to wait. I plan to be present in Ms. Anderson's class tomorrow afternoon. I will be bringing in some treats for the children to enjoy. Don't worry. The snacks will be dairy-free, gluten-free, nut-free, kosher, and organic, so no child feels left out if they have a dietary restriction.

I understand Ms. Anderson may already have a class mom scheduled. I would never be presumptuous to expect her to cancel the other woman. I plan on just being additional support for tomorrow's educational journey.

Warm best,
Jackie

"What would you like for breakfast today?" I asked Hayley after I hit send. I prayed I didn't sound too presumptuous, especially after my snarky remark near the end of the meeting. And I hope the teacher will believe my sincerity, especially since I meant most of what I wrote.

Quicker than Hayley could scream Fruit Loops, I received an answer from Ms. Anderson.

To: Jacqueline A. Martin
From: Ms. Anna Theresa Anderson
Date: 10/2 @ 7:43 AM

Subject: Re: Class Mom Duties

Hello,

Thank you for your email. I am unable to answer your message at this time.

I am attending an essential educational seminar to better serve the children of Forest River Elementary School.

I will be returning to school tomorrow, October 3. I will answer all emails in the order they were received, tomorrow after afternoon dismissal.

Should you need immediate assistance, please contact our principal, Harrison Williams.

Regards,
Anna Anderson

I couldn't help but grin. "Guess what's going to happen tomorrow?" I asked my daughter as I filled her bowl.

"We're getting a puppy?" Hayley asked as she pushed her light brown hair off her forehead. Her sapphire-blue eyes sparkled as she held her spoon up. She didn't seem too distraught I was about to serve her granola instead of her sickeningly sweet favorite.

For over a year, my daughter had been lobbying for a puppy. She pulled out all the stops, and I suspect Joan might have given her some tips for trying to convince her parents. Hayley was so enthusiastic that Scott and I discussed getting her one for her birthday, which was still a few months away. After having the baby, I tabled the idea. The thought of training a dog, while caring for a newborn, seemed far too overwhelming even with live in help.

After an in-depth conversation with Scott's mom on the phone, I had a change of heart. What was a little extra work compared to our daughter's happiness?

Scott was shocked when I broached the subject, especially since I had originally pulled the plug on the idea. When I explained how Joan and I believed having a pet to care for and love might help Hayley develop better social skills, he couldn't say no, even though I'd bet my new Prada purse he wanted to. I had no doubt my guy was smart enough to realize, despite all my assurances, he'd end up doing all nighttime walks, especially in the winter.

I reached into the refrigerator, pulled out a carton of almond milk, and walked to the table. "Nope. Sorry, not tomorrow. But I promise there'll be a puppy in this house before Christmas," I said as I poured milk in her bowl.

"Really?"

"Yes."

"Yeah!" Screaming at the top of her lungs, she jumped out of her chair and did a jig in the center of the kitchen. When she finally settled down, she declared, "I'm going to name her Scarlett."

As she picked up her spoon and dug into her breakfast, I asked, "And what if Scarlett ends up being a boy?"

She rolled her eyes with as much sass as a teenager. "Scarlett would be a very silly name for a boy. We can't do that to a poor boy." She smacked her forehead. "The dog has to be a girl, like me and Cassidy. Daddy's the only boy allowed in this house."

"We'll see," I said, even though I knew I'd make sure we'd rescue a female pup. "Let's focus back on tomorrow. Guess who's coming to your school?"

Her tongue protruded slightly from the corner of her mouth. Then her eyes lit up. "Grandma?"

"No. Me!" I exclaimed. "And I'm going to bring a super cool snack with me."

She pumped her fist. "Cool!"

I kissed the top of her head. Then, since I seemed to be on a roll, I sat back down in front of my laptop to tackle the next item on my to do list.

To: Forest River PTA President, Pamela Peterson
From: Jacqueline A. Martin
Date: 10/2 @ 7:53 AM

Subject: PTA Participation

Hi Pamela,

Principal Williams was kind enough to pass along your contact information to me.

I am the mother of a kindergarten student. I am incredibly interested in participating in the Forest River Elementary School PTA. I am aware that the PTA board is already in place. Since my daughter and I are new to the school and the town, I am hoping you will be able to find a way for me to assist you and your team. No role is too small for me! I'll do anything and everything!

As for some background... Before I became a stay-at-home mom, I was the Fundraising Director of the Crohn's and Colitis Foundation. I have extensive experience in both event planning and soliciting funds for a great cause. Also, I have excellent organizational skills, and my written and verbal communicationare stellar. I am positive that I can make an immediate impact on your team.

Thanks so much for the consideration! I look forward to meeting you in person and discussing the various ways I can assist. Like you, I want nothing more than to help enrich the educational experience of all children at Forest River Elementary School.

Warm best,

Jackie Martin

"Wow, someone sure was hungry," I said to Hayley as soon as I hit send.

"I love cereal, Mommy!" She took after me. I had lived on the stuff when I was in college and right after graduation. I couldn't remember the last time I allowed myself to have a bowl after I decided if I were going to consume so many carbs, I'd prefer them in the form of a glass of red wine or a bowl of spaghetti.

"Go, get your shoes. We have to leave for school in a few minutes," I said as a reply from Pamela hit my inbox.

To: Jacqueline A. Martin
From: Forest River PTA President, Pamela Peterson
Date: 10/2 @ 8:00 AM

Subject: RE: PTA Participation

Hello Jackie,

Thank you for your interest in joining the Forest River PTA. As you assumed in your email, long-term PTA members currently fill ALL of the positions. Unfortunately, we don't have any space on the team to accommodate another member, regardless of qualifications.

I will retain your contact information. In the unlikely event anything changes with my team, I will consider reaching out to you. Several members will be leaving the PTA at the end of the term, as their children will be moving up into sixth grade. If you still feel a desire to participate in the PTA in June, please feel free to reach out to me again in order to obtain an application for the following school year.

Regards,
P

Pamela Peterson
Forest River PTA President

My hands started to twitch as I began to fire off a reply. Words flew from my fingers as I hastily typed. I highlighted every word I wrote. Then I hit "delete". After once sending an expletive-filled email to a well-respected, wealthy donor instead of a cheating ex, I knew better than to ever let emotions dictate an email. I closed my laptop. There was no rush for me to say or do anything right now. When I made my next move, I wanted to be prepared. The stakes were too high for me to risk making a mistake.

CHAPTER SEVEN
THEN
OCTOBER
One Week Later

"Here you go, ladies," the waiter said as he served our lunches. "Would you like some ketchup for your fries?"

"Yes, please," I said with more confidence than I felt. I must have been the only woman in Bistro Baron who didn't order a salad, with dressing on the side. God, I missed Brooklyn!

No wonder I couldn't shake the baby weight. My lunch companion, Donna Warren, was heavily pregnant, and even she had the good sense to order the arugula, fennel, and avocado salad.

"Can I steal a fry?" Donna looked at my plate as if it was a long-lost lover.

I pushed my dish closer to her. "Please do. Help yourself."

Donna reached over and grabbed a handful. "I admire you, Jackie."

I tilted my head to the side. "For my fries?"

She shook her head and then fiddled with the napkin on her lap. She let out a deep breath. "You're so confident and seem to have everything under control. I'm the complete opposite. I feel like every move I make is the wrong one these days."

I reached across the table and grabbed her hand. "Oh, Donna. I'm sorry," I said, feeling relieved. When I told Joan about my plan, she begged me to go slow. She wanted me to cultivate one relationship at a time rather than quickly cast a wide net. At her urging, I reached out to Claire Conroy first, and we enjoyed a coffee together. I'm sure part of my mother-in-law's hesitation was based on the fact she didn't have any insight on Donna or her husband. I understood where Joan was coming from, but I didn't agree. I felt it was more important for me to try and connect with people who were in a similar situation as me. I was acting only on instinct. I knew I was taking a gamble by making moves so quickly, but so far, my intuition proved to be correct; Donna seemed like a genuine, caring person, and I was willing to take the risk.

"Thanks," she muttered and popped a fry in her mouth, chewing slow enough to savor every bite.

While I was hopeful that I had chosen wisely, I wasn't yet one hundred percent convinced I could enlist Donna's help. I barely knew the woman. I had only seen her a couple of times outside the school as we waited for the kids to be dismissed. The only conversations we'd had were superficial at best. It was essential that I got to know Donna better, which was why I had invited her to lunch.

"It's funny you commented on my confidence because I honestly feel nothing of the sort. I was looking at your salad, wondering if people were going to judge me for getting a patty melt, instead of something low calorie." I frowned and put my elbow on the table, resting my head in my hand. "Is it me or do you feel like we have suddenly been transported back to high school? I feel like everyone is so judgmental and cliquey here."

Relief flooded Donna's face as she fumbled with her napkin again. "I know exactly what you mean. I was so thankful when you called and invited me to lunch. I've been struggling a lot lately. I feel like all of the other moms are surgically joined at the hip. They never make any attempt to welcome any of us newbies into their circle. It's almost like a middle school dance when you wait on the sidelines, hoping some boy will glance at you, even if he has a face full of pimples and smells like a sweaty sneaker." She glanced down at her well-endowed chest and scrunched up her face. "Fortunately, I never was left on the sidelines too long. Come to think about it, attending high school was much easier for me than this."

I snorted. "Not me. I never fit in at school when I was younger."

"What? I don't believe you."

I pushed my hair to the side of my neck. "Well, you should. I grew up dirt poor in a small, rural town in Kansas. My classmates were not kind, to say the least."

Donna didn't utter a word. Instead she put her fork down and leaned toward me as I continued.

"My parents died in a car crash when I was in first grade. They were on their way to pick me up at a friend's house when a drunk driver slammed headfirst into them. My dad died instantly from the impact. My mother managed to hang on for three days, but she never regained consciousness." I paused as my eyes filled with tears. "I was only a little older than our daughters."

"I'm so sorry," Donna whispered.

"Thanks. Both my parents were only children. My dad's parents passed before I was born. Fortunately, my mom's mom took me in and raised me. Unfortunately, my grampy passed only a couple of years later after my parents." I looked down at my designer skirt, feeling the familiar flash of guilt for all the material possessions I currently was lucky enough to have.

I pulled a face and gestured at my outfit with my right hand. "If my grandmother saw me now, she'd never recognize me. She used to make all of my clothes. She was a wonderful and strong woman. She showered me with love and attention. My teachers also all bent over backward to try and make me feel comfortable in the classroom. Too bad the other children weren't as considerate." I wiped away another tear. "I don't know why I am telling you all this."

Donna reached across the table and squeezed my hand. She said, "No, please. Go on."

"They were downright cruel to me. I was shy before I lost my parents, but after they passed, I retreated deep into myself. It was the only way I could protect myself from the scary world and my classmates' vicious taunts. It was awful. I would head off to school every morning with my stomach in knots worried how they'd try and hurt me next."

"I'm so sorry, Jackie. I can't even imagine how difficult it must have been for you. Now I feel like a fool. What is wrong with me? I'm a grown woman, and I sat here and complained that other moms don't make me feel welcome. I should be appreciative of all I have. I'm sorry."

I waved my hand. "Don't be silly. What doesn't kill you makes you stronger, isn't that the expression?"

"Yes." She smiled.

"Besides, it wasn't all bad," I said honestly. "I threw myself into my studies and I earned a full scholarship, including room and board, to NYU. I was petrified and excited at the same time. I had never even flown on a plane before I went to college. And New York was so far from everything and everyone I knew. Everyone on campus seemed so experienced and worldly. I almost chickened out, but my grandmother wouldn't hear of it. She practically dragged me across the country by my dark brown ponytail." I automatically fingered my now golden locks and wondered if there was any woman in Forest River who didn't dye their tresses blonde.

"I had been miserable at first. The other girls intimidated me. Somehow, I managed to ignore my feelings. I was desperate for a fresh start. I knew I had to project the image of the person I wanted to be, rather the insecure girl who lived inside my head. It was almost as if I took to the campus armed for battle." I sipped my iced tea as I took a mental trip down memory lane. "I worked a lot in high school to help make ends meet, and fortunately, I earned more than money. Thanks to my summer jobs at the mall, I knew how to dress the part. And I was comfortable speaking with strangers because I also waited tables," I said as a busboy filled Donna's water glass. As soon as he left our table, I added, "I pledged a sorority as soon as I could and ended securing the role of chapter president by the time I graduated."

"Wow, that is remarkable," Donna said.

"Thanks." I leaned in and hoped she'd share something about her past, but she didn't. So I continued. "It wasn't easy. And so many times, I feared I'd be found out for being a fraud."

"That's crazy," Donna said before her eyes clouded over, and I felt a rush of sympathy.

"It's crazy," Donna said again, "yet at the same time, I understand it."

"Yeah, I think we've all felt the fear at some level at some points in our life." I stared straight into her eyes and knew my instinct had been correct. Donna wasn't an easy nut to crack, which I respected. I just wished she'd share something about herself, too.

"Do you want to hear how Scott made me fall in love with him?"

"I bet it was some grand gesture."

I took another sip of iced tea. "Not even close. We had been dating for about five weeks, and he took me to this well-known swanky steak restaurant in the city." I grimaced at the memory. "I was so uncomfortable. I knew I was completely out of my element. Fancy and I sure didn't mix well together back then, unless I was running the event." I instantly regretted sharing that particular detail. I didn't want Donna to assume I was a control freak. Despite my knowing full well it was a valid assessment.

"You see, I felt much more comfortable at a greasy diner or a dive bar." I paused and looked around the room. "The truth is, I sometimes still feel a bit uneasy when we go out to certain places. Sure, I am used to it now, and constantly shop and strive to look the part. If I am being honest, I don't know if I'll ever be truly at ease."

I thought Donna would interrupt, but she remained silent, with her unblinking eyes fixed on me. She looked either riveted or a bit gassy; it was hard to tell, especially since she ate almost all my French fries.

"Scott, on the other hand, was the polar opposite. He had a charmed childhood and was used to the finer things in life. I could tell he wanted to impress me. For days leading up to the date, he kept raving about how delicious the restaurant was. His enthusiasm was contagious, and eventually, excitement replaced my nerves. Well, until I took one glance at the menu. The cost of one porterhouse could have fed my grandma and me for a week back home in Kansas. I told him all I wanted was a side salad, but he wouldn't hear of it."

I paused and took another sip of my drink. "Scott insisted I order the special, a petite filet. I tried to convince him I didn't have a big appetite, but he was persistent. I didn't want to offend him or make him think I was ungrateful. I had my choice of two sides. I selected corn and a baked potato. I will never forget the look on the waiter's face. I'd bet the guy worked at the restaurant since he graduated high school, five decades prior. I felt as if I had been scolded as the waiter said I couldn't order two starches with my meal. He made me feel like I had committed a sin against humanity. Can you imagine, back then, I thought corn was a vegetable?" Then I turned serious. "Scott saw how mortified I was."

"What did he say?" Donna asked as she pawed a few more fries off my plate.

"He met the waiter's disapproving eyes and told him, 'The lady will have whatever the lady wants.' And then, for the cherry on top of the sundae, Scott asked the waiter if he had any more issues with my meal choice."

"Ah, I love it."

"Yeah, me too." I gushed, "I felt so protected that night. I felt, for the first time in my entire life, I could finally be myself around a guy. Even though Scott shut the waiter up, that waiter's judgmental glare haunted me all evening. And in some ways, it still does."

Donna reached into her purse and pulled out a packet of tissues. "Here," she said as she handed them to me.

"Thank you," I said before I stretched slightly in my seat. "I'm sorry, Donna. I am not usually this chatty or this emotional. I swear. I'm not trying to be a Debbie Downer or anything. I guess I just felt it was important for me to show you who I am, the real me."

"Thank you," she said. "I appreciate it."

I pushed my plate away. I only had two bites of my sandwich. My appetite had vanished as soon as I spoke about my parents' passing. "Everything I've been through taught me invaluable lessons. I'm extremely skilled at reading people. I look at you, and I see a lot of myself." I placed my elbows on the table again and rested my chin against my hands. "You work hard to fit in and gain others' approval. Like I am right now, you are teetering on the edge of the Forest River maternal inner-circle, and you are desperate to be accepted. Am I right?"

Donna pushed her plate away and her eyes welled up with tears.

I dropped my voice to a whisper. "You're also worried sick about your daughter. Christie is struggling socially. And it kills you to see, doesn't it?"

When I pushed my way into being "Class Mom, Number Two" and brought treats into class last week, my heart broke when I watched Christie struggle to get out only a few simple words.

Donna was unable to hide her feelings any longer. Her tears flowed. "Yes, it does. My heart breaks every day. I hoped by enrolling her into Forest River Nursery School two years ago, she'd be on a good footing now. My efforts were worthless. Even with speech therapy, her stutter hasn't improved much. I knew when the term began, she'd have a difficult time. Yet, I never imagined the children would be so cruel to her. In kindergarten! I was a fool. I fell hook, line and sinker for the propaganda about the schools"—she made air quotes with her hands—"no bullying policy. I guess, technically, in their defense, Christie hasn't been bullied. But come on, Jackie! How is it any better to allow a child to be shunned by her classmates because she is different?" Donna buried her face in her hands and started to sob.

I swallowed down the lump that formed in my throat. I prayed I hadn't pushed her too far. Fortunately, it only took a couple of moments for her to regain her composure. When she did, I continued. "I know. Kindergarten hasn't been easy for Hayley either. But I think I know how to change everything for both our girls."

"Really?"

"Yes. But I will need your help."

CHAPTER EIGHT
THEN
OCTOBER
One Week Later

"WE WON'T BE too long," I said before I kissed the baby goodbye and handed her to Brittany. Then I turned my attention to Hayley. "Are you ready for the best day ever?" I opened the door to the back seat of my Mercedes SUV and buckled her into her car seat.

"Are we really getting a puppy today?" she asked for what felt like the thousandth time this morning.

"We are!" I checked my reflection in my rearview mirror. Then I started my engine and pulled out of my driveway.

I know we already made our decision, but I won't lie. I had second, third, and fourth thoughts at the moment. I feared I was about to bite off more than I could chew, especially after spending time in her class, I was already up to my eyeballs in project Hayley Popularity. I didn't need another full-time job. I knew a whole new level of work, responsibility, and stress was heading my way fast.

Hayley squirmed in her car seat. She could barely contain her joy. Ever since Scott and I told her the plan the night before, she has been a bundle of excitement. I don't think she slept more than fifteen seconds. I know I didn't. Fortunately, she didn't have to go to school today because they were holding the second set of parent-teacher conferences.

"And you have the very important job of picking out our family's dog."

"I do?" she asked as she squeezed her stuffed rabbit tightly against her chest.

"Yes. It's a huge responsibility, but Daddy and I trust your judgment. You are a very smart girl."

I haven't completely lost my mind. I'm far too controlling to let such an important task rest in the hands of a kindergarten student. Scott and I did narrow down the search already. Ever since we first started to discuss the idea, I had been scouring the Internet for rescue organizations. It was important to me that we saved an animal. Growing up, my grandmother encouraged me to bring stray cats and dogs into our home. Sometimes we kept the pets, but usually we found them forever homes. It broke my heart how so many cats and dogs lost their lives because of overpopulated shelters and irresponsible people.

"I'm going to warn you, Hayley. You might have a tough decision picking out the puppy. They are all so adorable and little."

Scott and I went to see the litter yesterday. I hoped my daughter would be more decisive than me because I don't think I would be able to choose. The puppies were adorable. They looked to be some mix of Bichon, poodle, Yorkie, and/or Shih Tzu and had incredible temperaments. Their mother had been surrendered to a kill shelter a few days before she gave birth. Fortunately for her, and her babies, they were all rescued and were placed in foster care. The puppies were now old enough to find homes. Scott and I took care of all the paperwork yesterday after the organization approved our adoption application.

"After we get home with the new puppy, I have another surprise for you," I said as I stopped at a red light.

"Really? Yes!" Hayley pumped her fist into the air and then bounced her bunny on her lap. "Today is the best day ever! What's the other surprise?"

I caught my daughter's reflection in my rearview mirror. "You're going to have a play date"—I paused for a second—"with Christie Warren."

The look of happiness on my daughter's face disappeared instantly. The poor child looked as devastated as if she'd found out someone else ate the piece of chocolate cake she'd been eyeing all through dinner. "What's the matter, Hayley? You don't look excited."

She folded her arms across her chest. "I don't want Christie to come over," she said with a pout.

The light turned green, and I started to drive again. I wished I had been able to keep an eye on my daughter as we spoke. I considered pulling over for a few minutes. I quickly abandoned the idea. Joan swore the best way to encourage kids to speak openly was to have the conversation in the car. That way they didn't fear having to make eye contact. "Why don't you want Christie to come over?"

"Because I don't want to," she whined.

"Not wanting to isn't a good enough reason," I said in a gentle tone.

"Fine. I don't feel good," she said softly, and she started to chew her rabbit's ear.

"You don't? What hurts you? Is your throat or your tummy bothering you?" I mustered up as much sympathy as possible for my little liar.

She pouted. "Yes," my little drama queen declared. "Everything is hurting me very, very bad."

I gave into my original impulse and ignored Joan's sage words of wisdom. I pulled over and parked my car. I unfastened my seatbelt and turned around so I could face my child. "Everything hurts? Oh no, that's horrible, sweetie. I guess we'll have to head home right now and put you into bed. I'll call Dr. Lenox, and we'll get the puppy another day."

"No," she yelled as genuine tears filled her eyes. Her bottom lip began to tremble.

"Well, if you are sick, you shouldn't be out and about. You should be at home resting."

"Fine. I'm not sick." She started to sob.

"Then why did you say you were?"

"I don't want Christie Warren to come over."

"Why? Is she mean to you?" In all the what-if scenarios I contemplated, I never considered that one possibility. I must be slipping. I knew it wouldn't be unheard of for a tortured child to become a tormenter.

She frowned and shook her head. "Nope."

I was flooded with relief. "Then, why don't you want her to come over?"

She clutched her rabbit close to her chest, choosing not to

reply. After what felt like an eternity, she finally said, "She's a weirdo. She talks funny, and no one likes her."

"Hayley Charlotte Martin, is that a nice thing to say?"

She covered her face with her rabbit.

"Put Mr. Wigglesworth down and look at me, Hayley," I said. "I'm disappointed in you. I thought you were a kind-hearted girl."

"I am!"

"A nice girl wouldn't judge someone they didn't really know so harshly. Would they?" She didn't reply, so I continued. "Christie has a problem speaking, that is true. It's something she can't help. I know she's working very hard to fix her speech. Would you call someone a weirdo because they had a cold?"

"No."

"Well, think of Christie's speech problem as a stuffy nose. She can't help the fact that she stutters just like you can't help it when you sneeze. Christie deserves the same kindness as you do, as every child does. She needs friends"—my voice began to crack—"and so do you, sweetie."

"Okay, fine," Hayley mumbled.

"Now that's my girl!" I signaled and pulled away from the curb. Guilt consumed me. Even though I knew my intentions came from a good place, I still feared I was about to make a huge mistake. Would my attempt to force a friendship between two little outcasts yield the result I prayed for, or would both children be hurt in the process?

CHAPTER NINE
THEN
OCTOBER
One Week Later

"YOU ARE THE BEST," I cooed into the phone. As soon as I closed my eyes and stretched diagonally across my bed, Scarlett jumped up and walked across my chest, immediately licking my nose. I couldn't help but laugh. Hayley sure picked a winner. This puppy was so affectionate. And smart! The foster parents did a great job training her. Even though she was still young, she barely had accidents, which was a pleasant surprise. When Hayley was home, Scarlett was her shadow, but when my daughter was at school, like now, I got all the puppy love.

"Of course I am. Tell me something I don't already know?" my mother-in-law scoffed, and I scratched Scarlett's neck. "Seriously, Jackie, I didn't do much."

"Are you kidding me?" I sat up.

"You're so sweet, but really. There is no need to gush. Save it for when I really help."

I walked to Cassidy's room to check on her. "Joan—"

"All I did was make a couple of phone calls."

Joan had spent more than half her life working as an editor for a well-known, extremely popular fashion magazine. At Stan's urging, she retired two years ago after celebrating her sixtieth birthday. It didn't matter she no longer was in the game. She maintained an extremely close relationship with all of her contacts. And if Joan called them for a favor, they didn't think twice about pitching in to help.

"It was nothing. And besides, it's the least I can do." She

exhaled. "I'm so sorry I am not going to be there to help you."

I stood over the crib and watched my baby sleep. "Why don't you come up then? It's been almost two months since we've seen you last. I'd love nothing more for you to be here with me. Cassidy has grown so much, and Hayley misses you like crazy."

It was funny. When we first moved to town, I was very apprehensive about living so close to Scott's parents. If I am honest, I know it was this fear that held me back from selecting Forest River on my own. Sure, I adored both of them and knew they'd spend time in Florida and travel. Still, I feared if we lived so close, we'd constantly be together, and I'd never be able to escape Joan's words of wisdom. I didn't want my life to turn into a bad sitcom.

My fears couldn't have been further from the truth. Scott's parents welcomed us to town. But, instead of sticking around as we got settled, they spent most of the summer abroad. Joan and Stan returned home for a quick visit, long enough to meet their new grandchild, and then dashed down to Florida in September. Joan promised they'd make some weekend trips home, but, so far, they had been completely MIA.

"I miss you all too," Joan said softly. "Of course I'd love to be there too. But you don't need me. You are a superstar."

"Need and want are two different things, Joan. Come on, let me send you a ticket."

"I'd love to, Jackie." She sighed. "Sorry, no can do. Stan and I have commitments here that we just can't cancel."

"Commitments more important than seeing your granddaughters?" I asked, pulling out the heavy artillery.

"Sorry, we just can't break away right now."

I frowned.

"I can hear your frown. Don't fret. We'll be up to Forest River soon."

"For Christmas?" I asked, allowing myself to get my hopes up, even though I knew the answer would probably be no. Scott's parents were not big on celebrating holidays. For the third year in a row, they were planning to spend Thanksgiving halfway around the world. This year's destination was Bali. And since my husband was Jewish, they never observed Christmas except to send Hayley incredible Christmas and Hanukah presents every year.

Joan didn't answer right away, and when she did her reply delighted me. "Maybe. I'm working on it."

"Really?" I grinned.

"I said maybe. Don't go basting a turkey just yet. I'll let you know as soon as I know. Don't worry, even if we don't make it then, I'll come another time. And for sure, there will be no way I will miss Hayley's birthday, especially since I know her party will be extraordinary."

Even though it was still many months away, Joan and I already had several long conversations about the upcoming bash. Joan convinced me we had to go big.

"Okay," I said in a small voice. "It's just that I miss you. We all do."

"I know, and I miss you too. That's the way it should be. I want you to welcome my visits. I never want to be around so much that you get sick of me."

"I'd never get sick of you."

"Good, because you'll be stuck with me for a very long time." I reflexively softly knocked on the wooden changing table. After experiencing so much pain and loss at such a young age, I never wanted to jinx anything by taking our good fortune for granted.

"Enough mushiness. I can't sit on the phone all day. I've got things to do. Send my love to everyone."

In her usual way, Joan hung up before I had the chance to tell her I loved her. I hated to leave the words unsaid. Even though I knew she couldn't hear me, I whimpered, "I love you," into the disconnected phone.

Then I retrieved my laptop from the top of my dresser. I sat back down on my bed and quickly scanned the drafts I had written hours ago. Old habits die hard. Just as I had done when I worked full-time, I got ready to rapid-fire my messages, so they'd bombard the recipients, maybe catch them off guard. It was a manipulative move, but it made me feel better to wield the control when I felt insecure.

To: *Forest River PTA President, Pamela Peterson*
From: *Jacqueline A. Martin*
Date: *10/25 @ 10:45 AM*

Subject: *Re: Re: PTA Participation*

Hi Pamela,

Thank you for responding to my email so quickly. Wow, you're fast! I'm sorry it took me so long to reply to you. I must admit I was at a loss for words (something that usually doesn't happen to me). And I wanted to take my time and digest your message.

I appreciate the fact that you are unable to add another parent to the PTA board. I understand there are constraints and limits to the size of the team. I must admit, I am saddened and disappointed how you immediately dismissed my general offer of aid, especially since I would be the only mother involved who has a child in kindergarten.

I keep asking myself the same question. How could one more set of helping hands hurt?

I am of the firm belief that there is no such thing as too much assistance, especially when it relates to something as important as our children's education. I am only one mother. My opinion doesn't hold any weight, I know. You are the PTA president, and I know I have to respect your opinion and decision, even if I disagree wholeheartedly.

As I mentioned in my first message, I am dedicated to ensuring my daughter, and all the children at Forest River Elementary School, have the best educational experience ever. Since I have been denied the opportunity to participate in the PTA, I have reached out directly to Principal Williams to determine ways I can assist in an unofficial capacity. We had a wonderful brainstorming meeting the other morning. The principal has been incredibly supportive and appreciative of my initiative. We have come up with a *course of action to utilize my skill set, and I am extremely excited about it!*

I hope to see you at the Mothers' Social fundraiser I am organizing: Thursday, November 21, noon, at the Forest River Country Club. It would be wonderful to finally meet you in person.

Cheers!
Jackie

To: All Forest River Elementary School Mothers
From: Forest River Elementary School Principal, Harrison Owen Williams, Jr.
Date: 10/25 @ 10:46 AM

Fwd: Mothers' Social and Fashion Show

Begin forwarded message from Jacqueline A Martin:

Hi Forest River Ladies!

My name is Jackie. I am the mother of a kindergarten student in Ms. Anderson's class, Hayley Martin. Just as my daughter is navigating her way through her first year of elementary school, I too feel as if I am in uncharted territory.

Motherhood is hard! There is so much to know, and so much we need to do each day. To survive the chaos, we need support and friendship. It saddens me how I barely know any of my daughter's classmates' moms. I know I'm not the only lady who feels this way. Many other women I've spoken to echo my sentiments. They wish they had a way to meet and get to know the other mommies better.

Well, now we can!

Thanks to the permission of our devoted principal, Harrison Williams, I am hoping you will join me in starting the holiday season off in style.

Save the date! Thursday, November 21, at noon, I will be hosting a Mothers' Social Luncheon at the Forest River Country Club with a fashion show to follow. The retailers have generously committed to donating 35% of all proceeds from fashion show purchases to the Forest River Elementary School.

Watch for your official invitation soon to follow. Please RSVP by November 15.

Cheers!
Jackie

To: Forest River PTA- ALL GROUP; Forest River Elementary School Principal, Harrison Owen Williams, Jr.; Jacqueline A. Martin
From: Forest River PTA President, Pamela Peterson
Date: 10/25 @ 10:49 AM

Subject: Re: Mothers' Social and Fashion Show

Do you believe this bitch???????

Pam

To: Forest River PTA, Forest River Elementary School Principal, Harrison Owen Williams, Jr., Jacqueline A. Martin
From: Forest River PTA President, Pamela Peterson
Date: 10/25 @ 10:50 AM

Subject: Pamela Peterson would like to recall the message Re: Mothers' Social and Fashion Show

CHAPTER TEN
THEN
NOVEMBER
The Mothers' Social

"THE GIRLS ARE having the time of their life," Donna said as she entered the Forest River Country Club's ballroom and gave me a quick hug.

I won't lie. The first twenty-five minutes or so of Hayley and Christie's forced play date had been beyond pitiful. Both children initially walked on eggshells around each other. My heart broke for Christie. She was petrified to speak. It didn't take a child developmental expert to see the poor girl was scared Hayley would burst out laughing and mock her because of her stutter.

Scarlett helped break the ice, which was a huge relief. It wasn't until I had opened the door for Donna and her daughter that I realized I had never even asked Donna if Christie had a fear of dogs or was allergic. I was so caught up in all my planning—I was mortified I let something so huge slide.

Looking back, scheduling the first play date on the afternoon we brought a new dog home was careless and stupid of me. Fortunately, Christie was just as smitten with Scarlett as Hayley, and the puppy loved all of the attention she received.

Donna and I had spent a good hour or so sitting on the floor playing with the girls. Eventually, the kids found their footing. Donna and I snuck away to the kitchen, where I brewed us a pot of herbal tea.

Over the past few weeks, we'd arranged several follow up get-togethers. Now, the girls were constantly begging to spend more time with each other. Since Christie finally seems to feel safe with

Hayley, she's trying to speak more, and often times she manages to get out a sentence or two without a stutter.

"I'm so glad," I said with a smile. "Are you sure your babysitter didn't mind having another kid to care for?"

Unlike me, and a lot of the other mothers who had live-in assistance, Donna, hired a local college student to help supplement her child's care.

"Well, if she does, she better speak up soon." She looked down at her swollen stomach. She placed her hand behind her back. My friend looked like she could pop any second. "Her workload will double shortly."

"Speaking of which, you need to get this little one out already. Otherwise our babies won't be in the same grade."

"I'm trying."

"Good," I said absently. My attention drifted back to the clubhouse ballroom once more. I had spent the last two hours at the club, clipboard in hand. I wanted to make sure every fork, plate, floral arrangement, and spotlight was in the perfect place. My hard work showed too. But even with the room looking magnificent, I still had a case of last-minute jitters I couldn't shake. Flashbacks of the time I greeted a room full of potential donors with a wad of toilet paper hanging out of my trousers bombarded me. Ever since that mortifying moment, I never could shake my fear of making a fool of myself at a big event.

I was blown away by the positive response my fashion show luncheon invitation generated. I had expected there would be interest—what suburban mom doesn't love fashion? But never in a million years did I think nearly two hundred moms would reply "yes", almost immediately. Thank goodness I had assistance. Not only did Donna agree to come to the club early to help me meet and greet attendees, so did Claire Conroy.

Everything Joan said about Claire was on the mark. The two of us hit it off at once. Hayley has also had a few play dates with Claire's son, the little boy with the crush. Hayley is far from tackling her shyness but, little-by-little, she is making social leaps and bounds. The best part is she seems quite happy, which makes me ecstatic.

"Damn, girl!" Claire called out as she entered the room and engulfed me in a hug. She said hello to Donna and then let out a slow, low whistle. "This place looks amazing! I barely recognize the grand ballroom. I feel like I've been transported to Milan during Fashion Week."

I let out a little squeal. I had instructed the caterers to set up a red carpet leading into the expansive ballroom. Waiters soon would be assembled on both sides of the entrance where they'd hold trays of champagne, red and white wine, and mocktails. About twenty tables were set up toward the back of the room. I wanted to provide space for the women to first gather and hang out, since the primary objective of this event was to encourage socialization. Then, about forty-five minutes into the event, the women would take their seats. The waiters would bring out the ladies' pre-selected lunch. Then the models would begin to walk around the room, as the master of ceremonies described the outfits.

My initial motivation for hosting this event was to meet the other moms, but I was sincere in my desire to raise money for the school. As a result, there would be approximately ten people stationed around the room with iPads and credit card machines to accept clothing orders.

My mother-in-law completely outdid herself. Besides showing off women's apparel, we'd be featuring designer belts and handbags, men's wear, as well as clothing for the kids. I wouldn't be surprised if somehow this impromptu event turned out to be this term's biggest fundraiser.

"Thanks, Claire." I squeezed her arm and let out a slow breath. "I'm so glad you like how it looks. I'm nervous."

"Why? You have everything under control," Donna replied.

"I know. I know the fashion show will go off without a hitch. I'm more nervous about meeting everyone for the first time. I had only met a few people before, and I don't want to make a bad impression." I turned to Donna: "Do I have anything in my teeth?"

"Nope."

Claire smacked her hand against her forehead. "Stop! Don't worry that pretty head of yours. You have the two things women of this town love the most, booze and fashion. Speaking of which, I'd about kill for a glass of wine right about now."

"You and me both," Donna said.

As if on cue, several waiters approached us with overflowing trays. Claire reached for a glass of white, while Donna and I selected the virgin cucumber gimlet.

Claire took a sip then squeezed my hand. "Don't worry. You have nothing to worry about. I know everyone, and I'm here to help with introductions. You'll do amazing! Everyone is going to love you, just wait and see." Donna glanced down at her shoes at this comment. I didn't have time to worry if she felt threatened by Claire's connections. I was overjoyed to have someone like Mrs. Conroy in my corner today.

When we had coffee, Claire confided that her husband, Kevin, worked as an entrepreneur in residence for a private equity fund. And as my mother-in-law warned, he used the Forest River Country Club as his second office. Claire complained he never stopped working. Initially she thought attending every event and party the club offered would be fun. Now, after years of watching him work a room, she found it draining. A couple of months ago, the firm he worked for acquired a new company, and Kevin was named CEO. Claire prayed this meant her calendar would free up so she could finally socialize simply for fun.

From the little I knew, I doubted her prayers would be answered any time soon. I hoped my intuition was wrong, for her sake. She projected the image of the perfect mom, living the ideal life, yet whenever I spent time with her, I detected an element of loneliness and sadness in her eyes.

"Oh, look," Donna said, nodding to the door as a group of ladies entered the room. "I guess it is show time."

I took a much-needed swig of my mocktail.

***

Claire had lived up to her promise. She was incredible. She took me by the arm and escorted me around the room. She introduced me to practically every woman in attendance. She made sure to include a detail or two about them or their children, so I'd have an easier time remembering their faces and their names. Not only did I already score four play dates for Hayley over the next few weeks, I also committed myself to three lunches, five quick coffees, and one book club meeting. My daughter's and my calendars were about to explode. Joan would be so proud!

Donna knocked it out of the park. She mixed and mingled easily, which was a relief. I won't lie. I was worried about how she'd fare. She was much more of a follower than a leader. I know she would have preferred to be at my side, with Claire, during the introductions. Of course, I would have loved that, but I needed someone I trusted to make sure everything was under control with the caterers and models too. From what I observed of Donna, I didn't expect any technical hiccups with the event.

Donna caught my eye from across the room and tapped on the top of her wrist. I read her cue loud and clear. I glanced at my own watch. I was shocked at how quickly the hour flew by. "We have to wrap this up," I whispered to Claire as a tall, thin blonde woman started to walk our way. "The caterers will begin serving soon, and I have to make my speech."

"Okay"— she held up her hand—"I just want you to meet one more person," she said and gestured to the approaching woman.

"Pamela?" I asked, hopeful. I had yet to meet the PTA president. It blew my mind how she didn't even bother to introduce herself to me. If I were in her position of power, I would have made it my business to arrive here extra early to try and get to know the person who was so eager to help me. I seriously wondered if she'd even bothered to show up today. After all, she had been the last person to RSVP.

Claire shook her head. "No"—gesturing to a small pink clad group of women who stood against the back wall—"that's our lovely PTA. Very welcoming, don't you think?"

I studied the group. I remembered when they entered the ballroom. They all made a beeline to the back where they stood with their arms folded across their chests and scowls on their face. Several women approached them and spent a few seconds making small talk, but I didn't notice any of the PTA members make any attempt to move from their spots or mingle with the rest of the crowd.

"Which one is Pam?" I asked, even though I suspected the miserable looking mother in the center was our fearless leader.

"Pam's the one in the pale pink." And in case I had any doubts, Claire added with a slight tilt of her head, "The one with the resting bitch face."

I smiled automatically as I locked eyes with the most miserable looking woman in the room. "Should I go introduce myself?"

"No," Claire said as the tall blonde reached our sides. "Mia, you're here," Claire exclaimed cheerfully. She gave the woman an air kiss on both of her cheeks. "I didn't think you'd make it."

"I know"—the woman placed her hand across her chest and smirked—"I wasn't sure either, but I decided at the last minute to cancel Jacques. I figured I could work on my abs with him any day, but there would only be one mommy mixer this entire school year." She turned to me and not so subtly checked out what I was wearing. She seemed to approve of my Chanel suit. "Are you the famous Jackie Martin?"

"I am. But not famous." I held out my hand to shake hers.

"Mia Montgomery." She flashed me a toothy grin, showing off the whitest teeth I had ever seen. I couldn't help but wonder how many cosmetic procedures this bone-thin, big-busted woman had undergone over the years. I wouldn't be surprised if she single-handedly funded a doctor's dream home in the Hamptons. Don't get me wrong, she was beautiful, but she looked more plastic than perfect. "My youngest, Melissa, is in Ms. Anderson's kindergarten class with your daughter." Mia had a nasal voice, which made every word she uttered sound as if she were whining.

I didn't have to do a mental inventory of the kids in the class to know who her kid was. Her child stood out in my mind from my stint as the class mom. Melissa was an adorable little girl who had a big personality. All the girls in the class gravitated toward her. In turn, she seemed to love being center stage. She was the exact type of kid I wanted Hayley to socialize with, regardless of what kind of impression her mom made on me. "I know her," I said. "I met her when I volunteered."

"Of course you did," Mia said. Before I could say anything further, she added, "Well, since the girls are in the same class, we should definitely try to get them together."

"I'm sure Hayley would love a play date with Melissa."

"Wonderful." Mia clapped her hands. "How about Wednesday?"

"Wednesday would work," I said automatically, without even mentally reviewing my calendar. I feared I had already committed Hayley for that afternoon. In a split second, I made the decision that I'd reschedule any other plans. I knew a play date with Melissa would be important for Hayley's social success.

"Excellent." Mia smiled widely. "So, can you be a plum and pick them up after school and bring them to your house? Melissa will need a snack, of course." She held up her hand—"If you don't mind, please make sure it's low carb and low sugar. Plain cut up carrots, and celery sticks would be perfect. Please, no dressing or hummus. There is no need for the extra calories now, is there?" She didn't even allow me a chance to answer. "It's so essential we train the girls at a young age. We don't want them developing any bad habits now, do we?"

I ignored her question. "Of course, I'll give her a snack."

She squeezed my arm. "You're the best! As soon as I saw you, I knew you'd be the type of person I could count on." Mia flung her long blonde mane over her shoulder. She exhaled deeply and clutched her forehead. "You are a godsend. Seriously, you saved my life! I was so stressed out, I had to pop a Xanax on my way into the club. I have a crucial physician appointment on Wednesday."

My mind automatically began to assume the worst about her possible health care crisis when Mia not so subtly tilted her head toward Aimee Roberts and winked. Aimee was a first-grade mom I met earlier. According to Claire, Aimee was married to a well-known cosmetic surgeon, who was impossible to schedule an appointment with.

"Yeah, so my live-in help up and quit a couple of weeks ago. I've been trying to make do with a part-time babysitter while I search for a replacement." She placed both hands over her face. "It's a horror! Literally ten minutes ago, she texted me she needed two days off next week. Can you believe it? She claimed she has a final or something, and she has to study. I was about to start scrambling, but you saved my life." Looking around the room, she whispered, "I can tell you and I are two very different people."

"Excuse me?" I asked. Then, worried I might have come across too judgmental, I added in a softer voice, "What do you mean?"

"You strike me as a high performer," Mia said as she studied me and then gestured around the room. "Yeah. I bet you are a classic overachiever. Just look at what you pulled off in such record-breaking time. Me, on the other hand...my motto is to do the bare minimum whenever possible. I never understood the need to overburden myself. Like in school, I bet you did all the extra credit assignments, right?"

I took a sip of my drink. "I sure did."

"I knew it!" Mia exclaimed. "Not me. I almost flunked out of college. But in the end, what difference did it make? We both married well, and now we live practically identical lives. I know Melissa will love spending time at your house. You are just the kind of friend I need."

CHAPTER ELEVEN
THEN
NOVEMBER
Later That Night

"ARE YOU OKAY?" Scott tossed his keys and laptop bag on the coffee table and leaned down to kiss me. I stirred slightly and managed to maneuver myself into a somewhat seated position. I must have dozed off. I was wrapped up like a burrito in a blanket on the sofa while Hayley colored on the den floor, Scarlett asleep at her side.

"Mmhmm." I stretched. While I didn't know what time it was, I knew it was late. I fed my daughter dinner a couple of hours ago. And since tomorrow was a school day, Hayley should have been fast asleep by now, like her baby sister. But to her delight, I told Brittany I'd tuck her in this evening but hadn't made one move to try and shepherd her into bed. I yawned. "I'm just exhausted. But I know what would make me feel better."

He leaned down and kissed me.

"Yuck!" Hayley covered her face with her hands. The dog yapped, echoing her disgust, which encouraged both of us to continue the kiss.

He sat down next to me. "And so you should be exhausted! You kicked butt today, just like I knew you would."

"I wish you could have been there. It was amazing. I still can't believe I managed to raise over ten thousand dollars for the school with this silly little event your mom and I concocted only a couple of weeks ago."

"I'm not surprised. Look how you swindled me out of my money the night we met."

I sat up and pulled my knees up to my chin. "Getting money

out of you was a piece of cake. You were putty in my hands, my friend." I nuzzled his neck. "I probably could have taken more from you, but I took pity on you because you were so cute. The moms of Forest River? What a different story. Oh, my god!" I ran fingers through my hair. "You're talking about a whole new animal. Those ladies are all a bunch of nut jobs."

He chuckled.

I started to count off on my fingers: "First, you have the aging beauty queens who think their plastic surgeons can work miracles and restore them to their glory days. Then there are the gym rats that must spend their entire day dashing between Pilates, hot yoga, and kickboxing classes. Also, there is a whole cluster of moms who would be more comfortable feeding their prodigies a dash of arsenic than a gram of sugar. And don't even get me started on all of the want-to-be social media influencers. By the way, apparently, I must set up an Instagram account for Scarlett immediately. My head is still spinning, and I left the club hours ago."

"You're exaggerating, right?" He patted his thighs, and I placed my feet on his legs. He began to massage my toes gently. I felt so loved and safe. He had a very special way about him; I was a fortunate wife.

"I wish." I rolled my eyes. "Also, I am going to need a scorecard to keep track of which moms are in fights. Thank goodness I didn't have assigned seating, because if I did, there would have probably been bloodshed. Oh, Scott. Your mom tried to warn me how being a suburban mom would bring drama, but I didn't want to believe her. I thought for sure she exaggerated every single story she told me. After this afternoon, I'm worried she might have downplayed the absurdity." I placed my hand on my forehead. "Am I making a mistake by trying to ingratiate myself with these lunatics for Hayley's social wellbeing?"

"Definitely." He sighed. "But I know you too well. There is no way you'd be able to sit idly by without trying to make a situation better for someone you love. So, while I think you're nuts for going to all this trouble, I don't think you'd be able to play this situation any other way."

"I know. You're right. I pray I will be able to maintain my sanity. Please promise I won't turn into one of these crazy characters."

"Oh, Jackie." He stopped massaging my feet and gave me the funny face he was famous for.

"What?"

He shook his head and stared at his lap. "Scott…"

"Okay, fine. I'm sorry, but I think we both know you will never be the same after today."

I sighed. "What are you saying?"

He leaned over and kissed me. "I love you, but I know you better than you probably know yourself. You will go overboard. With you, there is no middle ground. You are an all or nothing kind of girl, which is one of things I love most about you. Your determination is fierce, and you are going to put all your energy into mastering the minutiae of Forest River Elementary School."

I looked deeply into his eyes. "Yeah, you're right. Does that scare you?"

"If for one second I thought you'd end up being one of the characters you described, maybe. I doubt that will happen. You'll get out of control, and you'll do things you probably never would imagine. I also think you are going to enjoy every second. I think this will be good for you. You have never admitted it, but I know the truth. Once you stopped working to stay home with Hayley, you've been bored."

I shuffled in my seat. "Scott, I'm so lucky. We have the perfect life. I could never ask for more."

"Yes, everything is great, but you still have a right to desire some more stimulation. I honestly think this project is just what you needed. It will give you some more purpose."

I knew he was right. I missed feeling accomplished, and I craved the thrill of contributing to a good cause. "How did I ever get lucky enough to snag a man like you?"

His eyes shined. "You're not too shabby yourself, Mrs. Martin." He patted my legs. "You're exhausted. You need a good night's sleep. Once you get a little rest, you'll probably push all your fears aside and kick yourself that you waited this long to take over the town."

"Maybe."

"Seriously, go. Take a bath. I'll put Hayley to bed."

Hayley turned around and faced her father and put her hand on her hips. "I have to warn you, Daddy. I'm going to need at least three bedtime stories to be able to even think about falling asleep. Dealing with Mommy tonight was very stressful for me."

I took that as my cue to jump off the couch. Two stories were usually his limit, and I didn't want to risk him changing his mind when my tub was calling my name. I leaned down and kissed the top of my daughter's head. "Sweet dreams, baby girl." Then I grabbed my cell phone off the table. I figured I might as well check my emails while I soaked. As soon as I unlocked my phone, I quickly realized I'd have plenty of bath time entertainment. In only a couple of short hours, my phone had blown up.

CHAPTER TWELVE
THEN

To: Jacqueline A. Martin
From: Mia Montgomery
Date: 11/21 @ 6:19 PM

Subject: Re: Subject: Mothers' Social and Fashion Show

Hi Jackie!

It was great to meet you today! I had such a blast at the fashion show/luncheon. I can't wait to model all my purchases for my husband tonight. He's going to be putty in my hands, especially when he sees me in the red lace teddy...

Melissa was so excited when I told her she's going to spend Wednesday afternoon at your house next week with Bailey. She mentioned Bailey didn't take ballet. I'm sure you had a reason for not enrolling her, but I think you should reconsider! All the Forest River girls adore ballet class; it is almost a rite of passage for them. You wouldn't want Bailey to miss out now, would you?

I know it is late in the season to sign her up, but I know Miss Lydia exceptionally well. I was one of her prized pupils when I was the girls' age, and my baby sister, Kara, followed in my footsteps. Did I mention I grew up in Forest River? So, all it would take would be one call from me and Bailey will be welcomed into the class with open arms and a grand pirouette.

Let me know,

Mia

PS – Classes are Tuesdays and Thursday at 3:00 PM and last for forty-five minutes. I assume you'll be able to join the carpool rotation if I help you get Bailey into the class.

To: Mia Montgomery
From: Jacqueline A. Martin
Date: 11/21 @ 9:35 PM

Subject: Re: Re: Subject: Mothers' Social and Fashion Show

Hi Mia!

Yeah! I'm glad you enjoyed your afternoon! The mini skirt you snagged was my favorite. I have no doubt your husband will be delighted to see you model all of your purchases! I know you'll look fabulous! All your time with Jacques sure pays off!

Claire didn't tell me you grew up in town. It must be so wonderful to be able to raise your children in a place you know so well. I must say I'm jealous. I grew up very far from here...

I'd love to take you up on your offer. I'm sure Hayley and her friend Christie would love to learn ballet. I'm sure, given your relationship with Ms. Lydia, you can arrange for both girls to participate.

And I'll be able to participate in the carpool. You know how us overachievers roll... LOL... Seriously though, I have plenty of available time, and I'd love to help! Honestly, I don't mind doing every drop-off if that works for you.

XO,
Jackie

To: *Jacqueline A. Martin*
From: *Forest River Elementary School Principal, Harrison Owen Williams, Jr.*
Cc: *Pamela Peterson, Forest River PTA President*
Date: *11/21@ 6:45 PM*

Subject: *Kudos*

Dear *Jackie,*

Wow! When you approached me about hosting a moms' social/fashion show fundraiser, I was apprehensive. You are a new member of our Forest River parental family, and our interaction has been limited thus far. My first inclination was to say no.

Many people consider me a pessimist. When I make a decision, I tend to identify all the worst-case scenarios first, as I am responsible for shaping hundreds of young minds every year. You made a strong case for your cause, refusing to take no for an answer. Ultimately, my public backing of your event boiled down to one key fact: you hosted the event off school premises and conducted it as your own party (with the school being the beneficiary of the fundraising efforts). The decision to allow you to proceed was mine alone. I didn't consult with Pamela or the PTA board since it wasn't an official school event.

Needless to say, I was anticipating something to go awry. Instead, I was amazed by your efforts! I'm still in awe you managed to raise over ten thousand dollars in only one afternoon. You sure have the Midas touch!

Sadly, our fundraising efforts as of late have not been as successful. Previously, the annual penny auction came close to generating similar numbers. However, the last few years, we have not been able to approach five grand.

I know Pamela will second my sentiments. On behalf of the entire school's faculty, PTA, and student body, thank you for your stellar accomplishment.

The money you raised will enhance the educational experience of our children. I look forward to working with you on many more projects, and I am sure our PTA president will echo my sentiments because, at Forest River Elementary School, our main priority is our children!

Sincerely,
Harrison

Harrison Owen Williams, Jr.
Principal, Forest River Elementary School

To: Forest River Elementary School Principal, Harrison Owen Williams, Jacqueline A. Martin
Cc: Forest River Elementary School PTA
From: Forest River PTA President, Pamela Peterson
Date: 11/21 @ 7:05 PM

Harry,

How dare you take it upon yourself to speak for me? Before you quote me, I deserve the decency of a conversation, don't I?

Yes, I agree it was very impressive this woman managed to raise such a large amount of money for the school in one day. But by no means do I feel like she is a superstar! My team and I have an excellent track record, yet I don't see you holding a ticker-tape parade for us! I hope you don't rush to purchase any blue ribbons.

I'm sorry. I don't believe she has any special talents or skillsets. Today's results were a FLUKE, plain and simple. She had a lucky break, made possible by outside help. You realize she pulled strings and called in favors from well-connected family members and the like.

You know full well, the Forest River PTA doesn't believe doing things willy-nilly. Each and every single one of our events and fundraising efforts are extremely well thought out, and properly planned. Furthermore, they generate fine results, which we are all tremendously proud of. I find it extremely disappointing and hurtful you'd tell a STRANGER otherwise.

If you have any criticism for my team, or me, I hope you would speak to us directly, instead of broadcasting your beliefs to random mothers.

Thanks for understanding,

Pamela

To: Forest River Elementary School Principal, Harrison Owen Williams, Jacqueline A. Martin
Cc: Forest River Elementary School PTA
From: Forest River PTA President, Pamela Peterson
Date: 11/21 @ 7:08 PM

Subject: Pamela Peterson would like to recall the message Re: Kudos

---

To: Jacqueline A. Martin
From: Forest River PTA President, Pamela Peterson
Date: 11/21 @ 7:59 PM

Subject: Re: Kudos

Jackie,

As usual, Principal Williams was very kind. The man is the ultimate gentleman. He has a way with words, which is very important considering his position in our town. He is practically a politician! And we all know how far we can trust a politician...

Today's event was special. The amount of money raised was shocking. I am sure you are proud of your work.

As I mentioned before, the PTA is adequately staffed. We don't need further assistance. In fact, I'd greatly appreciate you not overstep any more boundaries. I'm sure you mean well, but please don't interfere with the mission of the Forest River PTA by conducting any more "special events".

Thanks in advance for understanding,

Pamela

PS—I know you were in your glory and were quite the busy bee today. I must say I'm disappointed you never bothered to seek me out and introduce yourself to me or the other PTA members. Considering we are the group you are desperately trying to worm your way into, I find your actions rather rude. I'm sorry, poor manners don't belong at Forest River Elementary School, especially in a position of power.

CHAPTER THIRTEEN
THEN
DECEMBER
Two Weeks Later

"EVERYONE IS STILL raving about your luncheon," my mother-in-law announced as soon as I answered the phone.

"Well, hello to you too," I joked quietly as I walked out of the nursery where Cassidy was fast asleep in her crib.

"Oh, sorry. Hi, Jackie. Ugh, you know I hate wasting time with pleasantries," she added even though she knew I was a stickler for formalities. Joan was famous for starting a conversation in her head and finishing it out loud with someone else. You had to be on your toes with Joan. Her mind worked incredibly fast, and she was usually onto her next thought before she finished her first.

"You're still getting calls?" I asked as satisfaction filled my heart. Over two weeks had passed since I hosted the event. I, too, received a lot of positive feedback, but as people began to get busy preparing for the holidays, conversations moved onto other things. The principal informed me the other day that the money I raised was going to be used to enhance the art department's digital photography and graphic arts program.

I opened the refrigerator and studied the bleak shelves. Nothing struck my fancy, so I made an executive decision to order in Chinese tonight.

She ignored my question. I'd bet she deemed the answer obvious and moved on. "How is Hayley faring with ballet?"

"So far, so good, I think. She seems to be enjoying the experience."

I had taken Mia up on her offer to arrange a place for my daughter in class. At first, she was hesitant to call in two favors and score a spot for Christie, too, but I made Mia an offer she couldn't refuse. I assured her that between Donna and me, she'd never need worry about doing a pickup or delivery run ever again. Donna had given birth to Julia a few days later. I ended up doing double driving duty, but I didn't mind at all.

"You think?" Joan asked. I could hear the frown in her voice.

I struggled with how to reply to my mother-in-law. Instead of rushing and saying the wrong thing, I remained quiet, which was most likely what she wanted.

After a second or two, when she was satisfied with my silence, she said, "I'm sorry, Jackie. I am very disappointed in your laissez-faire attitude. I truly thought you were paying attention to what I've been saying. Now I fear my words of advice have fallen upon deaf ears."

"I've been listening to everything you've told me, Joan." I plopped down at my kitchen table and opened up a fashion magazine Brittany had saved for me. I absently thumbed through the pages.

"You say so, but I don't think so." She let out a deep sigh. "No offense, Jackie, but you can't afford to assume anything anymore. I hope you don't mind me saying you sat on the sidelines far too long this year before you stepped in and took action. You allowed the chips to fall where they may. It didn't work out too well for you now, did it?"

I bit my lip so hard, I tasted blood. "No, I guess not."

"But you've been a star trying to turn the ship around. You can't just throw a successful fundraiser and think that things are magically going to change overnight. You need to keep your eye on the prize."

"And what is the prize again?" I asked as I closed the magazine. Where was Joan going with this?

"Your daughter's happiness."

"Hayley is happy," I said as Scarlett wandered into the room and gently scratched my legs. "She's been having regular play dates with the children I mentioned, you know, Christie, Melissa, and Kyle too. Also, we have some other play dates scheduled for next week."

"That's great," Joan said before she sighed deeply again.

"You're off to a good start. But you can't rest on your laurels, sweetheart. You need to keep plowing forward. Hayley must be exposed to more children in a social setting, especially since she is so shy and quiet. You don't want her only to be comfortable with a select few."

"Why not? Isn't she better off having a few dear friends than having a lot of casual acquaintances?"

Joan moaned. "Oh, god. Have I not taught you anything? Jackie, please, she's a child. She's five years old, not thirty-five. She doesn't have the capacity to form deep-seated long-lasting relationships yet. Children's friendships are fluid. There is a high degree of ebbs and flows. At her age, nothing is permanent. She can be best friends with a child today, and then tomorrow"—I heard her snap her fingers—"they can have nothing to do with each other."

"But they all get along fine." Sure, the other moms and I had to break up several disagreements over the past few weeks, but once the children mastered the concept of sharing, I was sure they'd be fine.

"Yes, for now, I'm sure everything seems rosy. Open your eyes, Jackie. It's not only about the children playing nice. You have to worry about the other women too."

"Yes, but—"

"What happens tomorrow if you, heaven forbid, say something to one of the mothers and they take offense?"

I opened my mouth to speak, but she didn't give me the chance.

"I'll tell you what happens. Hayley's invitations for play dates will dry up, like that!" Joan snapped her fingers once more for emphasis. "And even if you behave perfectly and watch everything you say and do, *maybe* you'll find a way to miraculously remain on everyone's good side. I hate to burst your bubble, but the chances of you being able to pull something like that off in a town like Forest River will be slim to none."

"If this town is so bad, why did you insist we move here?"

"It's not this town, Jackie. They are all the same. I hate to break this to you, but the suburbs are ruthless when you have children. And before you say it, cities are no better. When you are dealing with a woman's quest for her child to succeed academically and socially, you need to be prepared for the unexpected. You may think you are doing everything perfectly, yet it will be impossible not to slip. Things happen all the time that are beyond our control."

"Like what?" I rubbed my forehead, hoping to ease the tension headache that was quickly forming.

"Oh, Jackie. Children get sick. What happens if one of these select few friends of Hayley's gets the chickenpox and has to be out of school for a few weeks? Hayley will once again be alone and isolated. Also, parents are transferred all the time. My friend Ester had to move twice when her daughter was young. They both had to start from square one each time Samantha started a new school. A move doesn't only hurt the child who has to relocate. It affects the ones that are left behind, you know. Where would Hayley be if one of the terrific trio moved across the country?"

I frowned. "Not in such a great spot, I guess."

"My point exactly."

"So, what should I do?" I would never admit it to her, but I rummaged through the junk drawer for a notepad and a pen. I expected Joan to rattle off instructions. Instead she surprised me.

"Jackie, unfortunately, there isn't a magic formula I can just give you. You need to be creative and smart. You need to approach this obstacle the same way you did when you worked full time. What was that expression you loved to tout?"

"Proper planning prevents poor performance?"

"Yes, that's the one!" Joan exclaimed. "Before you planned an event, you surveyed every situation from a hundred angles before you acted. Well, you need to start doing the same thing now."

"That was different, Joan. That was work."

"This is work too, Jackie. Motherhood is the most important job of your life. Oh," Joan exclaimed, "I so was wrapped up in all the parental politics, it almost slipped my mind. Sadly, Stan and I won't be able to make it home for Christmas."

"What?" I sat back down at the island. "Why?"

Last night I voiced my concerns to Scott about his parents and their peculiar behavior. I couldn't understand why they were avoiding Forest River and us. He assured me I was blowing everything out of proportion. He pointed to numerous times in the past where they had acted the exact same way.

"I'm sorry."

"I know! We can come down to you guys instead if you prefer. I can book flights right now, and we can spend the holidays together in Miami. It would be amazing."

"Yes, it would be wonderful. And you are so sweet, Jackie." Her voice hitched slightly, but then she quickly cleared her throat. "I'm sorry. It just isn't going to work for us, either way. Don't worry. We'll be together soon enough. There is no way I'm going to miss Hayley's party, which I know will be incredible especially after everything we spoke about today."

"Oh, Joan. We all really had our hearts set on seeing you this month."

"I know. Just think how much more excited you'll be to see me when we come. Oh, and before I forget. I did some snooping like you asked. Wait until I tell you what I learned."

CHAPTER FOURTEEN
THEN
DECEMBER
One Week Later

"MAYBE YOU WOULD like to join us for dinner one night?" I casually asked as I folded paper napkins into triangles and laid them out along the snack table.

The school was hosting its annual Snack with Santa event. The children were excited about having Old St. Nick show up in their classrooms. Ms. Anderson had hyped up the event all week, and Hayley was barely able to contain her enthusiasm this morning. I, too, couldn't wait for today. I was dying to witness our PTA in action. However, their lackluster attempt at a holiday party felt disgraceful to me.

The PTA gave strict orders to every teacher to only select a handful of parents to bring in assigned snacks. I had been all set to bring my famous red velvet cupcakes, and then I was told I couldn't contribute any cookies or cake. The concept seemed crazy to me. I even complained to the principal, but my comments fell on deaf ears. Now, I realized why the lazy leaders were so adamant about portion controls. The less snacks they had for the children meant less set-up and clean-up for the PTA. The cliquey group didn't want any "outsiders" assisting in the set up either, but I didn't let that stop me. I practically elbowed my way to the table to help with the paper goods.

On the bright side, they made sure to include one bland-looking nut and gluten free option for the children with allergies. As a whole, the selection for everyone else was abysmal. Don't get me started on the rest of the party. How difficult would it be to drape some streamers around the room or bring in a bunch of balloons? And the gifts! When the PTA president brought in the presents for "Santa", I snuck a quick peek at the cartons. It looked like a sleepy third grader wrapped the gifts. There was no care for the presentation. I didn't hold out much hope that the contents inside boring paper would be anything that would bring a smile to a child's face. In fact, it wouldn't shock me if the PTA had taken the easy way out and handed every student a Forest River calendar.

Initially, I feared I would be guilty of overstepping boundaries again. Mercifully, instead of listening to my head, I trusted my gut. I was so thankful Donna and I decided to take matters into our own hands and purchased additional presents for the children in Ms. Anderson's class. Donna volunteered last week in class, and she managed to find out every kid's favorite color and animal. We were able to design a personalized sweatshirt for all of them.

"Excuse me?" Pamela Peterson, the perpetually perturbed PTA president sniped as she stared at me with pure disdain. "What did you say?"

"Maybe you would like to join us for dinner one night?" Then, I shrugged and added, "I don't know. I feel like we have gotten off on the wrong foot. I would love to see that change. So I was thinking, it would be nice if we could get together outside of school."

The day after the Mothers' Social I had even sent her a beautiful bouquet of flowers. In my accompanying note, I apologized for not speaking to her at the event. I made sure not to mention how she and her friends made a beeline out of the club before dessert was served.

"Oh, I don't think so," she said in a dismissive tone.

Her cavalier response made me rethink my initiation of goodwill towards her and I smacked my head lightly. "I'm so sorry. I forgot your husband is away." The color vanished from her face. She grabbed the edge of the table as if to steady herself. Her eyes blinked quickly.

"What?" Pamela asked as her eyes bulged.

A sly smile was my only reply.

My mother-in-law had asked around and found out that

President Pamela, a part-time pharmaceutical rep, had kept her maiden name after she married, as many professionals do. Then, a year before her oldest son entered Forest River Elementary School, she hired an attorney to legally change her children's last names to her own, erasing all traces of their father's surname. Sure, this action was innocent enough on the surface. But it raised Joan's suspicions, as it did mine. Taking the tidbit of information, I did some digging and ferreted out the truth. I learned that around the same time the name-change papers were filed, Pamela's husband, a podiatrist, had been indicted for Medicare fraud. Shockingly, she somehow managed to keep his incarceration under wraps.

"Oh, you little..." Spittle began to form at the edge of Pamela's mouth, but then she quickly regained her composure. "I don't know what you think you know, but you are quite misinformed. My husband and I separated years ago, long before my boys entered school, very amicably by the way. He now lives in Virginia near his family."

"Of course he does." I glanced at my watch, and the words just flew out of my mouth. "Maybe in twelve to eighteen months, he'll move closer to home."

At my reference to his next parole hearing, steam practically came out of her ears, but she remained silent. She had more self-control than I gave her credit. Worried about onlookers, and regretting I went too far, I plastered a grin so wide I felt like my cheeks might crack. "But about dinner," I added breezily, "we can make it a threesome. My Scott won't mind. He loves getting together and spending time with my friends."

"I hate to break this to you, we are not friends, Jackie."

"Well—"

"Oh, don't play all sweet and innocent with me. I know your type. You think you can just waltz into this school and have people falling at your feet, worshiping your"—she made air quotes with her fingers—"skill set and talents. Please. You just are another spoiled brat of a woman who has spent her life being doted on, first by her parents and then by her spouse." She flicked her strawberry blonde hair over her shoulder.

I fought the urge not to laugh or set the record straight. I knew it was best I remained quiet. It wouldn't have mattered what I said or did. She'd made her mind up about me before she even knew my name. At least now, I knew why she disliked me from the get-go. But I also felt a little guilty that I played dirty. Clearly the woman was hurting. I needed to work on keeping my temper in check.

She continued. "I have news for you, sweetheart. I, and everyone else, can see right through your saccharine smile and phony attempts to contribute to the school. You are not the first woman to try to make a name for herself, and you won't be the last. But like the others, you'll realize we actually work hard, and the glamor will quickly fade. I get it. You want to relive your head cheerleader heydays, but Forest River Elementary School is not the place to try and recapture your glory days."

"Alrighty then. I guess there is nothing left for me to say." I placed the last napkin down on the table and turned to walk away.

Pamela grabbed my arm. "And one more thing, if I so much as hear you whisper your farfetched story about my ex-husband, you'll need to reach out to a real estate agent because living in Forest River will become a living nightmare for you. Have I made myself clear?"

"Crystal. Don't worry. I know a great real estate agent. Maybe I should give *you* her contact information. You seem so worried, for someone who has nothing to hide. Maybe her number will come in handy," I said as I shrugged off her arm. My heart hammered so fast that I actually saw stars. What a horrible human being! I almost felt sorry for her, but then she had the audacity to threaten me!

"What's wrong, Jackie?" Donna asked as soon as I found her. I didn't think we had spent enough time together for her to be able to decipher my game face, but she did. "Did Pamela blow you off again?"

"Something like that." I let out a slow, deep breath. "That woman is miserable. I have never met anyone like her. She has a chip on her shoulder the size of a boulder."

Donna squeezed my arm. "Don't let her get to you. Some people are just impossible. She's one of them. I don't understand why you are so determined to participate in the PTA when it's apparent you are not wanted."

I glanced in Pamela's direction. "I know. Rationally, I know I should just table the idea of breaking into the group. If I felt like the PTA had our children's best interest at heart, maybe I could let it go. The more I see them in action, the more disappointed I am with their performance. They don't care about the kids. They only care about themselves." I pointed around the room. "Just look at this event. It is so lame. My mother-in-law's friend Marie's children grew up in town. Marie raved how Snack with Santa had been the highlight of the term for the children. I want our daughters to have that kind of experience. I want them to look back on their childhoods and remember how lovely everything was."

"But you are working too hard."

I knew Donna was trying to comfort me, and I appreciated it. But I didn't want to be placated. I wanted results.

"I know. It doesn't make any sense why we have to fight for the opportunity to help the students."

Donna arched an eyebrow.

"I know no matter what I say or do, Pamela will find fault, but I am not going to stop trying"—I winked—"and neither are you."

She smirked.

"Together, we will be unstoppable. We can make Forest River Elementary School great again. What do you say?"

CHAPTER FIFTEEN
THEN

"LET'S TAKE A group picture," I exclaimed to Donna right after the kindergartners opened their presents. Our gifts were so well received that about half the class were already wearing the sweatshirts.

"Great idea," she said as she helped Ms. Anderson arrange the kids.

"Jackie!" Claire called out from across the room. I waved and then walked to where she was holding court with two other ladies. I gave her a quick hug. After making introductions, she said, "You and Donna did such a wonderful thing today." She gestured to the other women. "We were just saying how thoughtful it was for you guys to go this extra step for the class."

"My Emma loves anything with her name on it," said the woman rocking her natural brown locks. Trisha Dickens didn't look the part of a Forest River mom. She didn't have the prerequisite blonde hair! In fact, she had a bright purple streak on the right side of her head. It was refreshing to meet someone who wasn't consumed with the social norms of this town. She reminded me of my Brooklyn tribe. I couldn't help but take an immediate liking to her. I made a mental note to make sure to invite Emma over for a play date.

"All the children do," said Aimee Roberts, the perfectly toned plastic surgeon's wife said. Then she pointed to a little boy with a monkey on his blue sweatshirt and added, "I bet Chad will have to be pulled out of his shirt tonight and beg to wear it again tomorrow, and the next day."

"You both are so kind. Thank you, but it was really nothing."

Claire waved her right hand. "Oh, don't be so modest. You

and Donna put way more thought into the presents than the PTA did."

Aimee held up the beige Forest River Elementary School piggy bank for emphasis and pulled a puss. "What? Your kid wasn't begging Santa for one of these?"

I couldn't help but chuckle. "I guess you do have a point, Aimee."

Claire said, "Seriously, next time you plan on doing something like this, let me know. I'd love to participate."

"Me too," Aimee said.

"Don't forget about me," Trisha chimed in.

I was impressed; Claire sounded quite sincere and the others equally excited. I had learned from past experience that most people were all talk and no action. I hoped Claire and the others would be the exception.

***

"You still look sad," said Donna, studying my face. We had left school about twenty minutes before, and we now sat at a corner booth at Jax Coffee Shoppe. This was the first time we had gone out together since she had her baby, who was home with a sitter.

I opened up my phone and looked at the picture of Donna and I with the class. Ms. Anderson insisted we be included in the group picture. It was a great shot, but Donna was right, it wasn't enough to lift my somber mood.

"I would have thought the delight on the kids' faces when they opened the sweatshirts would have erased the pain caused by Pamela's petty comments."

I forced a smile. "The kids did lift my spirits." I stirred some honey into my green tea. "I'm not upset about Pamela. I learned the hard way: you can't be angry with a crazy person."

"True"—Donna blew on her cup—"but you don't seem like yourself this afternoon."

I picked out a blueberry from my muffin and popped it into my mouth. "You're right. I'm a little down."

She reached across the table and grabbed my hands. "Want to talk about it?"

I said, "It's nothing, really. I guess, I'm just disappointed."

While I felt comfortable enough with her to let my guard down, I still was a bit hesitant to open up completely.

"Why? What happened?"

I looked around the cozy café, which was practically full. It appeared Donna and I were not the only moms who craved a hot beverage after the extravaganza at the elementary school.

"Christmas is right around the corner, and my in-laws didn't officially commit, but I believed they'd be in town for the holidays, and I got my hopes up. Scott's mom told me they aren't going to be able to make it, and it won't work for them if we go to Florida."

"Why not?"

"I don't know." Looking up, I said, "Would you believe it? I didn't even ask. I didn't want to know what they had planned that was more important than spending time with their son and grandchildren."

"And you." Donna leaned in. "I thought you said you were all so close. Didn't you even tell me they were responsible for you moving to Forest River because they had a home here?"

I picked at the top of my muffin and took a small bite. "Yes. I love Scott's parents. I was worried we'd be spending too much time together when we moved here. But man, was I wrong. I wonder if they regret having us so close to them. Maybe that is why they keep avoiding coming home."

"Oh, I can't imagine they'd feel that way."

"Me neither," I answered automatically, despite all the hours of sleep I lost mulling over the possibility. "I talk to Joan, Scott's mom, on the phone all the time. She doesn't seem upset or angry with us at all. It's just weird. I wonder if something is wrong. Maybe they are hiding something. On the bright side, she swears up and down that she'll be here for Hayley's birthday." I exhaled deeply. "I know I'm probably overreacting. Thanksgiving and Christmas were never important to the Martins. I don't know why I expected this year to be different."

"Because the heart wants what the heart wants. The holidays must be a hard time for you."

I closed my eyes. "Yep. They sure are. I dreaded Christmas growing up. All of my classmates would come back to school after the break sharing stories of amazing presents and great times with their families. Sure, my grandmother tried to make things special, but it wasn't the same. I couldn't wait to grow up and be part of huge family celebrations. Then I married another only child. Scott's family's idea of a holiday tradition was seeing a different part of the world. Despite my efforts to plan a perfect Hallmark affair, his parents preferred to jet set around the globe. After a few years, I gave up trying to change them. I rolled with the punches. Scott and I went on some amazing holiday trips ourselves. Once Hayley came along, I didn't want to celebrate Christmas out of a suitcase. For the past few years, if his parents were abroad, we spent the holidays with friends. I turned down all the invitations we received this year from our old friends in Brooklyn because I was foolish enough to get my hopes up. And while I know we'd be more than welcome to join them, I'm embarrassed to make last minute calls."

Donna's eyes sparkled. "You don't have to make any calls. You'll celebrate with us!"

"Oh, Donna. You are too kind, but I don't want to impose."

Her eyes bulged. "Impose? Don't insult me like that, Jackie. You are my friend. We may not have known each other that long, but you've been so wonderful to Christie and me this year. Thomas and I would be so honored if you joined us."

I fought back my tears. "Are you sure?"

"Absolutely. It will be a bit crazy at our place, though, I have to warn you. My dad and sister will be flying in from Chicago. He's a character and will probably flirt with you the entire time."

"He sounds charming."

"He has his moments. Also, my sister and Thomas's brother probably will get into a battle—or seven. They fight like cats and dogs and never see eye to eye on anything. I have an ongoing bet with Thomas that one day they'll hook up, if they haven't already."

My mouth hung open, but in a good way.

"Oh, and Thomas's sister, well, she's a pill. She never has a kind word to say about anything or anyone. With her, it is complaint after complaint. Fortunately, her husband is a doll."

I closed my eyes and visualized the picture she painted. "We'd love to join. It sounds crazy and amazing. Are you sure hosting all of us won't be too much trouble for you, especially with the new baby?"

"No. You'll all be exactly what we need to make the holiday complete." She reached across the table and grabbed my hands once more. "Jackie, you never have to worry about being alone on a holiday again. You will always have a place at my table."

I stood up and hugged her. I whispered into her ear, "Thank you. I am so lucky to have you."

CHAPTER SIXTEEN
THEN
DECEMBER
The Day After Snack With Santa

To: Jacqueline A. Martin
From: Forest River PTA President, Pamela Peterson
Date: 12/20 @ 12:45 AM
Subject: Actions

Hello Jackie,

I had hoped you wouldn't force me to write another email of this nature, especially after our conversation yesterday. Regretfully, after your blatant disregard for authority, I feel like I don't have any choice but to confront your transgression head-on. Over twenty-four hours have passed, yet my team and I are still in shock at the audacity you and Donna Warren exhibited yesterday at the PTA-SPONSORED Snack with Santa extravaganza.

Jackie, you have once again stepped out of line. The school has a PTA in place for a reason. Each and every member of the team has known talents and a proven track record. The PTA has clearly defined goals in place. We don't take any matters related to the school lightly. We carefully consider every action we take and don't take from a multitude of angles.

While I believe your heart is probably in the right place, your insistence to push has caused extensive problems. I had hoped you would have learned your lesson after your last stunt with the Mothers' Social. Instead, you continue to go rogue. This can't continue. Your actions yesterday caused turmoil to our children, their parents, and our educators since every child in the school did not receive an extra extravagant gift. I kindly ask you to cease and desist all attempts to ingratiate yourself in the school's events immediately, before any more innocent children and their families are offended.

As I have mentioned, there will be a few available PTA spots for the next school year. Initially, I thought you could possibly fill one. Honestly, the likelihood of you being elected to a role now has dwindled dramatically in a very short period of time. As I am sure you can imagine, there are a lot of parents who would like to be part of our elite team. Any of these candidates, I feel, would be far better suited to carry out the vision and mission of the Forest River PTA without all the grandstanding. Of course, after my youngest graduates the year after next, my say will no longer matter. Then, maybe you'll get the opportunity you are lusting after.

Regards,
Pamela Peterson
Forest River PTA President

CHAPTER SEVENTEEN
THEN
DECEMBER 31st

"Happy New Year!" I practically sang as I opened my front door. Christie dashed inside the house, eager to find Hayley.

Donna placed the car seat on the floor and wrapped her arms around me. After she gave me a hug, her husband, Thomas, handed me a bottle of champagne.

"Thanks so much," I said as I gestured for them to come in. Donna gave the baby to her husband and immediately bent down and picked up Christie's discarded coat from the floor.

"Scott"—I stood up on my tippy toes and kissed him—"can you do me a favor and take Thomas and Julia to the nursery? Introduce him to Brittany?"

Celebrating Christmas with their clan was not what I had expected when I accepted the invitation. Sure, Donna warned me there might be drama, but she completely downplayed the craziness of the cast of characters who were going to be in attendance.

When she said her sister and Thomas's brother got into a disagreement, I expected them to banter about politics, since it was an election year. Instead, every time the man, or anyone else for that matter, opened their mouth to speak, Donna's sister readied herself to pounce. At one point, she got so heated over a joke Thomas's brother-in-law made about his wife putting on makeup to go to the mailbox, I was afraid she would hurl a spoonful of mashed potatoes across the table at him. I had never met such a narcissistic person in my life. She had an opinion about everything, and if anyone had differing beliefs, watch out! I was so worried about possibly causing an altercation, I barely uttered two words to her. Unfortunately, the few words I uttered were the wrong ones.

I complimented Donna on her turkey and asked if it was organic. When her sister found out that it was, she spent the next fifteen minutes rattling on how splurging on organic food was not fiscally responsible considering there wasn't enough data to prove the long-term benefits.

I don't know how Donna was able to survive having such a hothead in her house for three days, especially since they had to be in close quarters. Donna's home was pristine but also very compact, especially for Forest River standards. I can't even imagine how many fights her sister initiated. The woman needed massive anger management, and fast! Thank goodness Donna didn't have her sister's toxic personality.

I doubted I'd rush to celebrate Christmas with the Warrens' again, because of the tension her sister brought. But all of us did have an enjoyable evening, especially Hayley. More importantly, being with Donna's dysfunctional family taught me a valuable lesson. I realized that sometimes you reach a point when you understand no matter how much you try, there are some things you can't control. Sometimes you needed to follow your heart. I decided that night I was going to stop trying to make my childhood dreams my adult reality. Instead of waiting for old fantasies to come true, I would focus on creating new traditions for my family, which was why I invited Donna's family over to celebrate New Year's Eve with us, even before we left her house. And then, as usual one thing led to another.

"Wow," Donna muttered as she stopped dead in her tracks by the doorway to my great room. Her eyes widened.

My heart glowed at her reaction. "It looks amazing, doesn't it?"

We had moved most of the furniture out of the large room and set up several small high-top tables and chairs throughout the space. The walls were draped with white fabric and decorated with thousands of tiny, sparkling lights. I cordoned off a portion of the room to create a dance floor. There wasn't enough time to hire a DJ, so Scott created a playlist. We rented a bar and hired a local mixologist to create cocktails. About fifteen couples were milling about, and more guests were still due to arrive. In about fifteen minutes, the caterers would begin to pass around hor's d 'oeuvres. A buffet was also set up in the kitchen for later in the evening.

"Yeah, I guess it does," Donna said with no enthusiasm as she wrinkled her forehead. With a sweeping gesture, she added, "I just wasn't expecting something like this."

"You know me, I love to throw a party."

"I know." Her shoulders slumped. "I'm sorry... It's, well...I guess what I am trying to say is you never told me you were holding a party. When you mentioned New Year's Eve at Christmas, the invitation seemed so impromptu. I guess I assumed tonight was going to be just us."

My heart sank. I had been so focused on planning the perfect event, I never mentioned the party to her. If I were in her shoes, I probably would have assumed the same thing. "I'm sorry. I should have told you."

"Yeah, you should have" — she looked me up and down — "I love your dress. Is it new?"

It was, but I didn't want to make things more awkward. "Oh, no. It's been hanging out in my closet forever. I found it tucked away the other day."

"Well, you look beautiful, as usual." She looked down at her sweater dress. "Thank goodness I decided to change my outfit at the last minute. Otherwise I may not have passed the dress code. I almost came in yoga pants."

"You would have still looked beautiful." My heart continued to tighten. I realized I had made a major mistake. I would never intend to hurt her. She had to realize that, didn't she?

She didn't say anything, so I filled the silence.

"I figured I'd have another couple or two come over. I didn't intend to have so many people, but you know how things go."

"I guess." She glanced at the crowd once more. "I didn't think you even knew this many people."

"I really don't." I glanced around the room. "There were a bunch of women I ended up texting and emailing with after the fashion show. I reached out to them. With so many families out of town and the short notice, I never imagined I'd have such a large turnout. I guess a lot of people wanted to celebrate the New Year and still be with their kids." My voice raised a few octaves. "Christie will have a blast! I hired a few sitters, a face painter, a storyteller, and a puppet master to entertain the older kids. And Brittany, obviously, will look after Julia and Cassidy upstairs."

"It sounds lovely, really," Donna said tightly.

"Yes, it's going to be epic." I reached for her hand and started to walk toward the others. "You're going to have the best time, I promise."

"Okay." She exhaled deeply. "Is Claire here?" It probably was my imagination, but I felt Donna tense up every time I said Claire's name. Part of me wondered if she was jealous of her or even my relationship with her.

"No, unfortunately, she's spending New Year's with some of Kevin's colleagues. Don't worry"—I gestured to Aimee Roberts and Trisha Dickens—"I'm sure you'll recognize most of the people, but if not, I'll introduce you."

"Great. I can't wait," she replied with more than a speck of sarcasm, and Joan's multiple warnings about how easily it was to land on someone's bad side came back to haunt me. What was I in store for next?

CHAPTER EIGHTEEN
THEN
JANUARY
One Week Later

"**WELL DONE, JACKIE,** well done," Joan said with a chuckle as soon as I answered the phone.

"Whatever do you mean?" I asked even though I knew full well why she was calling. I yawned as I glanced at my bedside clock. I was shocked to see it was after seven. Joan usually never called so early on a Sunday morning. While her son loved to get up at the crack of dawn and go for a five-mile run, she knew I usually tried to sleep in, at least to six-thirty, on the weekend. Typically, we never heard from her until after lunchtime.

"Oh, no," Joan said. "Did I wake you up, dear?"

"No," I lied as I rubbed my eyes. "I've been up for a while."

"Good, me too."

"Do you and Stan have a big day planned?" I asked as if on autopilot. I already knew the answer. My in-laws must be the busiest retirees in the world. They were constantly on the run. In fact, for the last few days, Joan was virtually impossible to track down. Sure, we had a couple of quick text message exchanges, but I was only able to get her on the phone once. Our conversation only lasted for a few seconds before she claimed she had to run.

"You know us, constantly on the run." Her voice sounded strange. I struggled to decide if she was being sincere, sarcastic, or was coming down with something.

"What are you guys up to today?" I stretched and got out of bed.

"A little this and that, but enough about us. I want to chat about you. My phone has been ringing off the hook for days!" she said dramatically. "Or better yet, I should say all year long."

I glanced out the window and smiled as I watched Scott kick a soccer ball around the backyard with Hayley. I was so lucky. He was an incredible husband and father. "Yeah, the party was amazing, if I say so myself. I wish you could have been here."

"Me too. Promise me you'll host another party next year, and I will move heaven and earth to be in attendance."

"Deal!" I said, letting my excitement show. Then I turned serious; the disappointment of her Christmas cancelation still stung. "You better not back out on us and accept a better proposition. I know how quickly your social calendar fills up."

As expected, she ignored my comment. "So, are you considering making this an annual event?" Before I could reply that I was, she added, "I certainly hope you do, Jackie. You know, being proactive and consistent, it is crucial for your image and Hayley's social success.

"My friend Elaine is an excellent baker, truly top-notch. When her girls were in grade school, she began to make exquisite holiday cookies. People went berserk for them. Initially, she gave them out to her children's entire class. Soon she started to become more selective with her distribution. No mother, and certainly no child, wanted to miss out on receiving a box of her baked goods. Do you follow what I am saying?"

I took a deep breath and entered my walk-in closet. If I could live in this space, I would in a heartbeat. Although I wasn't a fan of how Joan decorated my home, she outdid herself here. She stuck Scott with the original walk-in closet, which fit his needs fine. But my mother-in-law dreamed big for my wardrobe and me. She had hired a contractor to break through the wall of a small bedroom, which was adjacent to our room. Then she had the space customized to fit my present and future clothes and shoe needs. She also installed a dressing table that had designated spaces for my makeup and hair products. And to add a little pizazz, a crystal chandelier hung in the center of the room. When Scott first saw the closet, he asked where the cash register would be placed. Yes, she designed it to look much like a retail-clothing store. It was truly heaven.

"Your friend manipulated other mothers by making cookies?" I asked as I flipped through my dresses to figure out what I would wear later when Scott and I went out to dinner. I grabbed a plush terrycloth bathrobe and put it on.

"No!" Joan scolded as I walked to the baby's room. "Elaine didn't manipulate anyone. She had something that others wanted badly. Sometimes she simply had to be selective. You know, there are only so many hours in the day. Elaine couldn't help how the other women reacted to the thought of getting the shaft. She tried her best to keep everyone happy, but how many gingerbread men can one woman make?"

"So, it is all about perception, huh?" I leaned down and rubbed my hand along my sleeping baby's back. It amazed me how different two kids could be. When Hayley was a baby, she refused to nap. I was so sleep deprived that I was barely able to function. I think the first time she managed to sleep through the night was only days before she began nursery school. I expected Cassidy would follow in her footsteps, which was why I agreed to have live-in help for the first nine months. I can't believe how much this baby sleeps. She is so good and quiet.

"I say to Scott all the time, he married a smart woman."

I sat down in the rocking chair in the nursery. "I guess now I know why you've been jockeying for me to invite the full grade to Hayley's birthday party."

"Well, it will be her first birthday party in elementary school. You don't *want* to make any kid feel left out. You know things will be very different next year. You won't have full-time help when your au pair leaves. Cassidy will be a toddler. You remember how challenging that stage is, don't you?"

"Yes."

"Cassidy will be getting herself into all sorts of predicaments. You'll have two kids to run after. There is a very good chance you won't be able to entertain such a large group again, right?"

"Right?" I agreed even though the word came out as a question.

"I know what you are thinking, Jackie. You love to throw

events and parties. I don't doubt for a second every parent and child will be praying you don't have to make any unfortunate cuts."

I snorted. "You are constantly five steps ahead of every situation."

"I've had to be. How else do you think I was able to accomplish all I did, personally and professionally? Jackie, you need to start thinking the same way. Did you follow my advice and find out if any of your new friends have any interesting connections?"

"What do you think? I don't follow your sage words of advice to a tee?

"Yeah, right."

"Well, it turns out, Claire Conroy's kid sister is a literary agent. She was able to get us an assortment of autographed paperbacks. We're going to do another unofficial fundraiser for the kindergarten class. I already received the principal's blessing, and the event is in the works."

"Excellent!" I heard the sound of Joan clapping her hands. "Speaking of Harrison Williams. I've had a niggling suspicion about him for quite a while. I put a few feelers out there, just to see if I was on the right track. I don't know why I ever doubt myself," she said, laughing. "I should be a detective. I found out the most interesting tidbit about him yesterday."

"Really?"

"Oh, yes." Joan paused, building my anticipating. "Jackie, you are going to love what I learned. With this information, the sky will be the limit for you if you play your cards right."

CHAPTER NINETEEN
THEN
JANUARY
Two Weeks Later

IT MIGHT HAVE been my imagination, but I felt like Donna had been increasingly distant during the last few weeks. I first noticed the change right after my spontaneous New Year's Eve party. I knew I was wrong to have not told her what I had planned but I did apologize numerous times. It worried me she was offended so easily.

I am not trying to say I was without blame. I realized I made a mistake and I acknowledged my actions, immediately. Let's face it. None of us are perfect, despite our efforts. We all make errors, but when someone shows remorse for a minor slip up, a friend should be able to move on, shouldn't they?

I hoped I didn't rub salt in her wounds by partnering with Claire to host the book sale, but Claire was the one who had the connections. Still, I couldn't shake the feeling that Donna was jealous of my friendship with Claire. I knew my nervousness was most likely a result of Joan's constant warnings and criticisms. I wished I didn't allow my mother-in-law's cautionary tales to get under my skin so easily. But so far, she had been on the money, her hand on the pulse of this town.

Joan uncovered that our esteemed principal had close family ties to a PTA member. My mother-in-law insisted it was imperative I meet this other woman. Unfortunately, she wasn't able to orchestrate the meeting from Florida, but Claire came to the rescue and put us in touch. We met over lunch at Bistro Baron, where the meeting didn't go at all how I anticipated.

I planned to call Joan with all the details as soon as I

returned home. But before I could kick off the shoes that made my toes numb, my cell phone rang. I assumed it was my impatient mother-in-law. Instead, I saw it was Donna. I was so happy to see her number, I answered on the second ring. My joy turned to panic when she screamed my name before I even had a chance to say hello.

Oh no. Joan had warned me a fall out from New Year's Eve might be inevitable if she wasn't able to get past her apparent jealousy. I braced myself for battle as images of Donna's sister's rage flashed in my mind. I didn't expect Donna to have blown her top, but as Joan pointed out this morning, I didn't really know her very well.

"What's wrong?"

"I don't know. It's Christie," she shrieked, hysterical.

"What?" My heart raced.

"I need you. We're in the ambulance now. Please, meet me at the hospital. Now. Please."

"I'm on my way," I immediately replied, even though she had already disconnected the call. I swallowed the bile that rose in my throat. "I've got to go," I called out to my nanny as I ran out of my house.

I still had another two hours before pickup time, but I didn't want to take a chance. I called Claire as I drove.

"Hey Jackie. What's going on?"

Usually, such an innocent question, but at this moment, it felt so poignant. I had no idea what was going on or what I would find when I reached the hospital. All I knew was it couldn't be good if an ambulance was involved.

"There's been an emergency. I don't know what is going on with Christie, but I am meeting Donna at the hospital now." I tried to keep my voice steady. "I'm sorry. I really can't chat now. I'll let you know when I know anything. Could you pick up Hayley and bring her home with you?"

"Of course," she answered. "Let me know if there is anything else I can do."

"Thanks so much. I'll tell Scott. I'll call you later. I've got to go. Bye." I disconnected the call as I pulled into the emergency room parking lot.

I ran in the building and surveyed the reception area. I didn't see Donna. I dashed to the front desk and said to one of the nurses, "Hi, I'm looking for Christie Warren. Her mother, Donna, asked me to come."

"Are you Jackie?" a gray-haired woman asked.

"Yes."

She stood up. "Come with me."

No matter how tough you think you are, nothing guts you more than seeing a child lying on a hospital bed. Christie, a child who tended to be hyperactive, looked so weak. Her face was white as the sheet that covered her tiny body. Donna didn't look much better than her daughter. As soon as she saw me enter the cubicle, relief filled her eyes.

Donna gave me the biggest hug, filled with so much raw emotion, and we both broke down in tears. Then she gestured for me to sit in the chair she had vacated. I peeked in the car seat where her infant slept, and Donna perched herself on her eldest daughter's bed.

As she gently caressed Christie's leg above the blanket, she faced me and said, "Thank you so much for coming so quickly. Thomas is traveling. He's in Texas for business. Jackie, I was so scared. I knew I couldn't be here alone."

"Oh, sweetie. I'm sorry. What happened? Is Christie okay?"

"She is now. Thank god." She reached for Christie's hand.

"I can't even imagine how difficult this is for you. But you're not alone. I'm here, and I'll stay as long as you need me. Tell me. What happened?"

I let out a deep breath as Donna began to fill me in.

"She wasn't feeling well this morning. She was complaining about her stomach hurting. She didn't have a fever, and I feared she was making up the ailment. But I let her stay home. It wouldn't be the first time, especially since today was show-and-tell. Usually Ms. Anderson gives her a free pass, and lets her skip participating because of her stutter. But thanks to her therapy, and her friendship with Hayley, her speech is improving, greatly. I told Christie last night she probably would have to begin speaking up in class one of these days."

I shook my head but didn't interrupt.

"So, as the day progressed, I didn't need a pediatrician's diagnosis to know my theory was accurate. She was fine. She was a bundle of energy and refused to stay in bed. She played all day and had quite the appetite." Donna and I both glanced over at Christie, who blushed slightly when she realized her mom caught her in a lie. It was such a welcome sight to see some color return to her cheeks.

Donna continued. "Not only did she polish away her lunch, she wanted a snack an hour later." A tear rolled down Donna's cheek. "I made her celery sticks with peanut butter."

"Okay," I said. Hayley and I loved this snack too.

Donna buried her face in her hands. "I am the worst mother in the world, Jackie."

I stood up and put my arms around her. "Don't say that, Donna. You are an amazing mom."

She freed herself from my embrace, and I sat back down.

"No, I am not." Her voice cracked. "I ignored all the signs. Christie often appeared itchy after she ate peanut butter. I never paid much attention. I figured I was being paranoid because she never complained once. I should have been smarter. Instead, all I did was keep feeding it to her."

I shook my head and closed my eyes. I didn't need my friend to elaborate any further about what occurred today. "Oh, Donna. No. Don't blame yourself."

"Who else should I blame?" She spat. "I'm her mother. I should have protected her."

"Donna"—I reached for her hands—"listen to me, and listen to me good. You are not doing yourself or your daughter any favors by playing Monday morning quarterback. You had no idea she would ever have such a severe allergic reaction. If you did, you would have acted differently. You can't go back in time and change anything. All we can do in life is keep plowing forward."

She wiped away a tear. "I know, you're right. But it's hard. I feel so guilty."

"I know. I would too if I were in your shoes. It is a natural reaction. And I am not saying you shouldn't allow yourself the time and space to process your emotions. You both went through a very dramatic experience. You need time. Just please don't beat yourself up unnecessarily."

"Thank you. You are such a good friend. I'm lucky to have you."

"The luck runs both ways. We both need each other, and we both should lean on each other. Right now, your only focus should be on caring for your daughter. I'm not going anywhere now. I'll drive you all home, and after you're situated, I'll tend to the rest."

CHAPTER TWENTY
THEN
JANUARY
The Next Day

To: Forest River Elementary School Principal, Harrison Owen Williams, Jr.
Cc: Ms. Anna Anderson
From: Jacqueline A. Martin

Date: 01/19 @ 10:45 AM
Subject: Making Forest River Elementary a safer place for all

Good morning Principal Williams,

As I am sure you are aware by now, one of your kindergarten students in Ms. Anderson's class was rushed to the emergency room yesterday from her home in anaphylactic shock. Thank goodness, the child is now doing well and resting comfortably at home. She plans to return to school tomorrow.

This child's severe allergic reaction was a result of ingesting peanut butter. Up until this horrific moment, her allergy was unknown. Given the fact that nut allergies are affecting more and more children each year, I fear other unsuspecting children are in the same vulnerable position.

No child should have to experience what this little girl went through!

No food should cause a mother to fear for her child's life!

I met with Ms. Anderson this morning and expressed my concerns. As usual, she was terrific. She assured me that she would reach out to all parents and inform them that beginning tomorrow, her classroom would become a nut-free zone. And while her efforts are enormously appreciated, I fear they are not enough.

I expressed my concerns to her, and she directed me to you.

Principal Williams, on behalf of all parents and students of Forest River Elementary School, I implore you to declare the building, and all of its property, a nut-free zone. Don't allow any child to risk being put harm's way.

Thank you for your compassion and dedication to your students and their families.

Warm best,
Jackie

To: Jacqueline A. Martin
Cc: Forest River PTA President, Pamela Peterson; Ms. Anna Anderson
From: Forest River Elementary School Principal, Harrison Owen Williams, Jr.

Subject: RE: Making Forest River Elementary a safer place for all

Date: 01/19 @ 11:15 AM
Greetings and salutations Jackie,

Bravo, bravo! Once again, I must applaud you for your initiative and empathy for our students. Thank you for bringing this most serious matter to the foreground.

I was made aware of yesterday's situation. As you can expect my heart goes out to my students and their families in all times of challenge and crisis. I echo your sentiments about being extremely thankful that this little girl is on the mend.

Jackie, you bring up a fascinating concept, one that I have considered for quite some time. Recently, across the nation, there has been a massive movement to make elementary education facilities nut-free for the very reasons you mentioned. There is nothing that fills me with more pride than seeing Forest River Elementary School on the cutting edge. And I believe a move in the direction you request would benefit our students.

I am sure you can appreciate that much thought and careful research must occur before we can implement true change on an all-campus level. As a result, I will form a committee to research the pros and cons of such an action plan. It would be an honor if you took the lead role.

Thank you in advance,
Harry

Harrison Owen Williams, Jr.
Principal, Forest River Elementary School

I raised my fist high into the air and yelled, "Yes!" My outburst was loud enough to wake my dog from her sound sleep. I had no doubt Principal Williams would take the situation seriously. And never in my wildest dreams did I imagine he'd form a committee and place me in charge. This was precisely the opportunity I needed to prove I could be of assistance to the school in a meaningful way. I had no doubt that Pamela was probably beside herself. Oh well! I didn't have one second to worry about her feelings. I had to get to work. I took a sip of my iced coffee and began typing.

To: Forest River Elementary School Principal, Harrison Owen Williams, Jr.
Cc: Forest River PTA President, Pamela Peterson; Ms. Anna Anderson
From: Jacqueline A. Martin

Subject: RE: RE: Making Forest River Elementary a safer place for all

Date: 01/19 @ 11:21 AM
Hi Principal Williams,

Thank you so much for taking my concerns so seriously. The speed at which you replied was remarkable. The students of Forest River are fortunate to have a man like you at the helm.

It would be my pleasure and honor to lead this task force. I look forward to working with you and the team to serve the parents and students.

Warm best,
Jackie

As soon as I hit send, my computer beeped alerting me to a new email.

To: Forest River PTA- ALL GROUP; Jacqueline A. Martin; Harrison Owen Williams, Jr., Ms. Anna Anderson
From: Pamela Peterson
Date: 1/19 @ 11:21 AM

Subject: RE RE: Making Forest River Elementary a safer place for all

WTF?!?!?!!?!?

My head is about to explode!

What the hell is happening in this town, ladies??????

Who the hell does Jackie Martin think she is anyway??????? This is NOT ACCEPTABLE!!! Her meddling must stop!

And what the F is wrong with Harry???? He wants this piece of work to head up a committee???? Speaking of heads, what "head" is he thinking with anyway??????

We can't have parents go rogue!

I won't stand for this. We can't stand for this!

We must strategize ASAP. Meeting details will follow.

Pam

To: Forest River PTA- ALL GROUP; Jacqueline A. Martin; Harrison Owen Williams, Jr., Ms. Anna Anderson
From: Pamela Peterson
Date: 1/19 @ 11:22 AM

Subject: Pamela Peterson would like to recall the message Re: Re: Making Forest River Elementary a safer place for all

---

I cracked up. Was poor Pamela bright enough to realize even if she recalled a message, all the recipients still were able to read her original note? The woman needed to learn how to rein in her rage. This was at least the third time her emotions caused her to have an email snafu. She must be dying right now! It would have been bad enough if she only copied me in error, but she sent her note to the principal too.

I reached for my phone to call Donna. Before I could begin dialing, it rang. I answered without checking the caller ID.

"Who the hell do you think you are?" A woman screeched into the phone. She didn't need to state her name; the animosity in her voice gave her identity away.

"Pamela, is that you?" I tried to steady my breathing. Contrary to popular belief, I wasn't a fan of confrontation.

"Don't play all sweet and innocent with me, missy. You

know exactly what I am calling about, so don't pretend otherwise. How many times have I warned you to stay out of the school's business?"

"With all due respect, Pamela, you may be the president of the PTA, but you don't control the school or me."

She let out a low laugh. "Oh, that is what you think? First time kindergarten moms are so naïve. You keep thinking that way, and let me know at the end of the term how that works out for you."

I silently counted to five and then said, "You know what, Pam, I am a parent, and I have every right to express my concerns to the principal. And if the principal wants me to lead a committee, that is what I will do, regardless of what you want or think."

"What I think? Well, here is what I know. You are wasting your precious time. I'm the one with the power here, not you. If your plan is to push me off to the side and make changes to this school without the PTA, good luck. You are even more fool-headed than I thought you were."

"Let me get this straight. Are you trying to say you plan to fight me on this important and potentially life-threatening issue, because you are afraid I will steal your political thunder?"

"You need to learn your place in this town."

"And you need to think twice about your attitude and actions. I'm sure you won't appreciate me going to the press and informing them how the PTA president is opposed to instituting a safety precaution."

"You won't dare."

"Don't push me."

I closed my eyes and rubbed the bridge of my nose. I couldn't comprehend how a mother could be so self-absorbed, so callous. As my blood boiled, I let out a low whistle. "Wow. I realized right away you were an extremely insecure woman, Pamela, but I never expected you to stoop so low. What kind of person feeds their ego at the expense of innocent children? I'm trying to save lives here, and you are worried that I didn't ask your permission." I made a tsk-tsk sound. "You should be ashamed of yourself."

"Oh, please, get off your high horse already. Don't threaten me. The game is over."

"Oh no, Pammy, this is no game. You're right. I may only be a first-time, naïve kindergarten mom, but you have no idea what I am capable of, but you will. Just wait and see."

CHAPTER TWENTY-ONE
THEN
JANUARY
One Week Later

"WELCOME!" I EXCLAIMED as I opened my front door to a very bronzed Mia Montgomery and her equally tan daughter, Melissa. I knew they had spent the holidays basking on a beach in Barbados, but that was almost a month ago. Their golden glow should have been a distant memory by now. I had no doubt Mia was vain enough to subject her body to the harmful rays of a tanning bed, but would a mother supplement her daughter's tan artificially too? Nothing surprised me anymore.

I had expected Mia and her daughter to arrive at my house over fifteen minutes earlier. All of my other guests managed to show up on time. And unfortunately, because Mia was tardy, again, they all had to sit idly by, making chitchat, as we waited for her to waltz in and make her grand entrance.

I took a deep breath. I knew I was overreacting. The other ladies seemed quite content just to hang out and nibble on appetizers. I had more than a couple of pet peeves, and nothing irritated me more than people who were perpetually late. I found it so offensive when others acted as if their time was more valuable than everyone else's. I prayed I didn't make a mistake by inviting Mia. But I didn't have much choice. I was a firm believer in strength in numbers. And fortunately for me, Mia did owe me a couple of favors.

"Hi, Jackie," Mia said in her nasal voice. Then she gave me a double-cheek air kiss. If she sensed any of my frustration, she didn't show it. She pushed her oversized Gucci sunglasses on top of her head and gave my hallway an obvious once over. Subtlety was not one of her strong suits, and maybe it was my insecurity, but I felt so judged by her. My décor didn't reflect my style at all. Instead, it looked as if a seventy-year-old woman designed the room…

It was pretty sad. I had entertained her daughter practically every week since we first met at the Moms' Social, yet Mia never once stepped foot inside my home. Unlike the other moms, she never swung by a bit earlier to chat over a cup of tea. Without fail, she had pressing plans, which consistently ran late on the afternoons Melissa came over. By the time she'd show up to collect her daughter, I would be getting ready to feed Hayley her dinner. I would have loved to have Melissa stay, but Mia repeatedly turned down the invitation—she likely worried the meal would be too caloric. Instead, Mia would text me from the driveway, and I'd usher the little girl outside.

"Thanks for inviting us today." Mia grinned. "Melissa adores spending time with your Bailey."

I opened my mouth to speak, but before I could form words, the little girl rolled her eyes and said, "Mommy, oh man! How many times do I have to remind you? Her name is Hayley. Hay-Ley." She turned to me and smacked her hand across her forehead. "I don't understand her problem. It's really easy to remember, you know."

I placed my hand on the little girl's shoulder and squeezed her gently. She was adorable.

Mia scrunched her face. "Hayley. Right." Then she threw her hands up. "I'll try and remember, but it's hard, you know. I can't help it if you and Seth have so many friends. I need a scorecard to keep everyone's names straight, all the time. I'm sure no one minds if I make a minor mistake every now and again, right, Jackie?"

Through gritted teeth, I said, "Right." Then I turned my attention to Melissa. "Hayley is down in the basement with the other kids. You know the way, sweetie?"

"Yup." In one fluid movement, she flung off her jacket, kicked off her shoes, and zipped down my hallway. Her mother didn't make any attempt to pick up her daughter's discarded apparel, which didn't surprise me in the slightest. A part of me wanted to leave the coat where it a landed. But I knew Scarlett was actively teething, and I didn't want to take a chance that my pooch would mistake Melissa's belongings for a new chew toy, especially the brand-new Dolce & Gabbana leopard print sneakers. I bent down and picked everything up. "I'll take your coat too, Mia."

"Thanks." Then with a look of panic, she added, "Be careful, please. It's Russian sable, you know."

I inwardly cringed and wondered how anyone would want to walk around in a dead animal. I tried to not let my revulsion show as I gently placed the garment in my closet. "Everyone is already here. Let's go into the den."

Claire and my new friend, Stacey Williams, were deep in conversation. Trisha threw her head back in glee at something Aimee said. Donna sat off to the side where she played with the cheese and crackers on her plate.

"Mia's here," I announced.

All the women stood. Mia rushed over to Claire and gave her a friendly kiss on both cheeks.

Mia's smile threatened to overtake her face when she spotted Stacey. "Oh. I didn't think you knew Jackie," she said before she gave Stacey a double-cheek kiss too. Both of them had sons in the third grade, and according to Claire, the boys were close friends.

Stacey and Claire had known each other for years since their husbands played golf together at the club. Claire had been instrumental in helping me form a relationship with Stacey. We didn't know each other long, but Stacey and I connected easily. We have spent quite a bit of time together and on the phone since our first meeting.

Mia only afforded Donna, the only woman present who wasn't a member of the Forest River Country Club, with a tight nod instead of an air kiss as she gave the other two kindergarten mothers. It surprised me how cold Mia behaved to her. I would have thought since Donna drove Melissa home from the last four ballet classes, Mia would have tendered a warmer reception. Fortunately, if Donna was offended, she didn't let it show. I feared Mia would end up being one of the people who'd baffle me no matter how long I knew her.

"I hope I didn't keep you all waiting," Mia said. "Jacques was riding me hard today. He took one look at my abs and practically lost his mind, not that I could blame him. Vacation was rough on me. The food at the resort was too good. I even had dessert."

I knew I was super sensitive, since I still hadn't shed the baby weight from Cassidy, but I found her comment cruel. I was about to make a snide remark but Claire, who also struggled to lose the pounds she gained when she carried Chloe, said, "Seriously, skinny Minnie? No one wants to hear your belly aching. I haven't been able to squeeze into my old jeans in months." She leaned over and reached for a bottle of white wine, which I had on my coffee table. She poured a generous glass and handed it to Mia. "Drink this. It will make you feel better."

"Thanks." Mia took a sip and she let out a slight moan. Then she turned to me. "Nice! This afternoon is really starting to look up."

Everyone laughed and launched into yet another wave of chitter-chatter. I glanced at my watch, shocked to see how much time had passed. I needed to get this meeting back on track, so I picked up a chopstick from the sushi tray I ordered and clicked it against my glass of white wine. As I stood in the center of the room, I said, "Ladies"—I cleared my throat—"ladies, can I get your attention, please?"

Eventually, everyone turned to face me.

"I'm so glad everyone was able to come over this afternoon, especially on such short notice. This is a very exciting time for me"— I coughed nervously—"I mean it is a very exciting time for all of us. Or at least, I hope you all will agree."

I took a sip of wine. "Before we begin, I have to stress one thing. Everything that is said today must remain in this room." I paused and looked each woman in the eye. "What we are going to discuss here today can't be shared with any other person, except your spouses, of course. If anyone is unable or unwilling to maintain this level of confidentiality, don't worry. I will not be upset, and I won't judge. I will only request that you remove yourself from this meeting."

Mia, my last-minute invitee, looked puzzled, so I called her out. "Will you be able to keep this quiet?"

She flipped her hair back and batted her eyes. Then she added, "Well, I certainly don't have time or energy to waste by spreading gossip around town."

"Good. So everyone can keep secrets. Spectacular." Taking people at their word wasn't something that came naturally to me. Talk was cheap, but actions were golden. Now was the time to put these women to the test.

CHAPTER TWENTY-TWO
THEN

"STACEY, WOULD YOU like to begin?"

She took a sip of liquid courage. "Sure."

I sat down on the love seat next to Donna and gave her knee a gentle squeeze, and my friend offered me a warm smile in return.

As did practically all the moms in town, Stacey had long, chemically treated blonde hair, which was a shade darker than mine. She also had the most perfect biceps. Before I met Stacey and Mia, I considered myself physically fit, but their physics could put a supermodel to shame. I felt so self-conscious around them. I knew I had to get my act together soon. And while I didn't want to become obsessed with my body and working out, I knew it was time to reach out to one of their personal trainers—just maybe not Jacques.

Stacey took another sip of white wine as she gathered her thoughts. "Everyone at school knows me as Franklin's wife, Jonathan and Kimmy's mom, and a member of Pamela Peterson's PTA posse. I've been keeping a pretty major secret under wraps for years." She dramatically turned to the left and then the right so she could face each woman. She then smiled widely. "Most people think it's a coincidence I share the same surname as our acclaimed principal. Williams is a fairly common name, right? Well, Harry"—she blushed slightly—"or Harrison, as most of you know him, is Franklin's older brother."

"What?" Claire exclaimed as she startled in her seat, spilling a little wine on my couch. She automatically reached for a napkin to wipe up the liquid. She whispered, "Sorry." She stared at Stacey, seemingly in shock.

The other four women looked equally surprised. I didn't

think Donna, Aimee, or Trisha would have known about this relationship, but I had thought that Claire or Mia might have had some inside scoop or suspicion. Mia's son was friends with Stacey's boy, and Claire appeared to have so many connections in town thanks to her husband's obsessive networking. Unless Claire had the secret talents of an Academy Award-winning actress, she never suspected a thing.

"No way." Mia leaned in. Her nasal voice sounded even more pronounced from the shock. "How did I never know this? Girl, you are so lucky. I'm sure you never have to worry about your kids getting less than perfect grades. Tell me, does Uncle Harry get you advanced copies of the state exams?"

Stacey shook her head. "If only." Then she turned serious. "Listen, my son has not received any special treatment, and neither will Kimmy when she enters elementary school. Jonathan earned every grade he received on his own, just like everyone else."

Mia arched an eyebrow.

Stacey sighed, and her cheeks colored. "Fine. Yes, of course, he has tutors, too."

Her embarrassment was for the kindergarten moms' benefit since there was no need yet for us to break out the heavy educational artillery. It was common knowledge, once children entered first grade, it was customary in Forest River to supplement their educational experiences with private tutors in practically every subject. Parents in this town were obsessed with making sure their offspring obtained perfect grades right from the beginning of their academic careers. Upon the first inclination their prodigies might not receive a stellar report card, they hired help so their child would excel in everything they attempted.

I found this practice completely ridiculous. It went against my moral code. I thought it was essential for a person's emotional well-being to have a realistic expectation of their self-worth. Still, I wasn't foolish to kid myself into thinking I'd follow my moral high ground. I knew this time next year I too would have a parade of people prancing in and out of my home, aiding Hayley in her schoolwork. In fact, at Joan's urging, I had already interviewed and hired a tutor for next term. I knew there would be no way I would ever risk my daughter falling behind her classmates. Groupthink was such a dangerous thing.

"We know everyone has tutors," Mia said. Her tone was so exaggerated that it exasperated her natural whine. Mia tilted her head to the side and glared at Stacey. "Are you going to sit here and say your principal brother-in-law has never helped his nephew out?"

Stacey closed her eyes for a quick second and then rubbed the back of her neck. She let out her breath in a huff. "Yes, that is exactly what I am saying. God"—she turned and faced me—"Jackie, I'm sorry. Clearly, this was a mistake."

I got to my feet and walked over to where she sat. I put my hands on her shoulder, squeezed gently in a gesture of support. "No, it wasn't."

I then turned my attention to Mia. "Stacey has kept her relationship with the principal silent for years because she feared people would jump to the wrong conclusions like you just did. Honestly, Mia, you should be ashamed of yourself." I shook my head. "Of all the people in this room, you know the various players the best, don't you?"

Mia pouted and avoided making eye contact with me. "I guess so," she mumbled.

"You certainly do, and you should know by now that both Principal Williams and Stacey have extremely high ethics. I'd bet there have been times over the years Stacey could have called for preferential treatment, but she didn't, did she?" Mia remained silent, so I continued. "Despite his genetics, Jonathan never received any preferential treatment. In fact, he faced the same ramifications as his fellow pranksters, isn't that right, Mia?"

Mia's face turned crimson, as the other ladies sat riveted by the show before them. It didn't take more than a few seconds for her to realize Stacey had filled me in on the incident involving her son, Seth, Stacey's son, Jonathan, and another boy at the end of last term. Dared by another child, the three troublemakers painted a mustache, beard, and glasses on a statue in the hallway during lunch. They were caught and suspended.

Mia backpedaled. "No. You're right. Seth and Jonathan have been friends for years, and I've never once seen Jon receive any special privileges." She cleared her throat. "I'm sorry, Stacey."

"It's okay," Stacey said.

I glanced at my watch. The time had flown by, and we hadn't accomplished anything. Trying to keep to an agenda with seven mothers together in one room was like attempting to herd kittens. I raised my hands into the air. "Now that we settled the speculation, let's get down to why I called everyone here today, shall we?"

"Okay," the moms said in unison.

"By now, you should all be aware of the fact I am involved in a crusade at school. I'm trying to make it a safer place for many of the children."

"You mean the nut ban?" Aimee asked.

"Yes," Donna said softly before I could reply.

Trisha faced Donna. "You are so lucky to have such a good friend who is willing to fight so hard for you and your daughter."

"Yes, I guess so," Donna replied with a smile that didn't quite reach her eyes.

I swallowed down the lump that formed in my throat. Was it possible Donna didn't appreciate all the attention my hard work for this cause had already brought? Sure, she asked me to reach out to Ms. Anderson, initially, but I never warned Donna that I intended to escalate the matter to the whole school campus, because that was never my intention. As usual, I got caught up in the moment, and one thing led to another. Besides, I figured she'd be relieved her daughter would be able to experience her elementary school years in a safer environment once I achieved my goal.

I tried to get back on track once more. "As you may know, Principal Williams created a special committee to consider this important issue, and he placed me in charge."

Mia said, "Sounds like a dream come true for someone like you."

Someone like me? I decided to let her comment slide. "I met with the other members last week. We had an excellent discussion. I was shocked to learn not only was the PTA president not present, the principal only picked one PTA member to serve on this important committee."

"Are you both sure he didn't invite them?" Claire glanced at Stacey and rolled her eyes at me. "Maybe Pam declined his offer. Didn't you tell me she read you the riot act, *again*, for putting your nose in her business? It wouldn't be far-fetched for Pam to flat out refuse to share center stage with you. Maybe her loyal followers boycotted the committee in an act of solidarity?"

I was champing at the bit to reply, but before I could, Aimee asked, "Um, who was the PTA member that was present?"

Donna bolted up in her seat and asked what Claire clearly realized at once, "You?"—pointing to Stacey.

"Yep," Stacey said.

"Well, this is rich," Mia said as she folded her arms across her chest. "Stacey, spill. What are you and Jackie—and your brother-in-law—cooking up?"

"What are you talking about?" I asked.

Mia ran her hand over the rim of her wine glass as if she was deep in thought. "No offense, but you are a bit much to handle." She took a sip. "You entered the elementary school scene, like five minutes ago. Most moms just roll with the punches, but not you. You've become a woman on a mission, trying to make a name for yourself. I'm sure you've driven everyone in power crazy in the process."

"Mia, why must you be so mean?" Donna jumped to my defense. "Jackie is doing critical work. Safety should come first."

"I'm not being mean. I'm just being honest. I'm just voicing what all the other moms surely are thinking. I have no doubt every action our friend Jackie has made was based only on noble intentions, isn't that right, Jackie?"

I watched as the color drained from Donna's face. My jaw tensed as I said, "Yes, it is. I care a lot about the kids of this town."

"We know you do," Mia said.

"Enough." Stacey stood up. "Why do you love to stir the pot? What is wrong with you?" She jabbed her index finger in Mia's direction. "You are a guest in Jackie's home. It would be nice if you showed her an ounce of respect."

"What did I do?" Mia raised her palms. "What did I say?"

Stacey clenched and unclenched her hands, and her nostrils

flared. "You're right, Mia. Jackie is different than most new moms. She isn't content to sit on the sidelines and let things happen around her. She wants to take an active role in her children's education. Her attitude should be commended, not mocked. Keeping the status quo has been the goal of the current PTA for years. For the most part, it has served our children well enough. Times are changing, and my brother-in-law realizes his school can't move forward if some parents insist on holding it back. He is desperate for some fresh ideas."

"No principal would ever admit something like that to a PTA mom," Mia mumbled half under her breath.

Stacey shook her head. "You're right. No principal would, but a man would confide in his sister-in-law, especially after she opened up the conversation and complained how frustrated she was."

"Oh." Mia pinched the bridge of her nose. "Sorry."

"You should be," Stacey fired back.

I took the opportunity to once again get back on track. "And speaking of fresh ideas"—I practically sung—"brings me back to why I invited you all here today in the first place..."

CHAPTER TWENTY-THREE
THEN

I WAITED UNTIL all eyes were on me. "As Mia so eloquently alluded, I am not the type of person to sit idly by and let the chips fall where they may." I smiled at the woman. "In fact, when Mia and I first met, she asked me if I was a classic overachiever. I can't help it. I like to be a success, and I've never been afraid of a little hard work. I research everything thoroughly." I winked at Stacey, even though she knew my mother-in-law tipped me off about her family dynamics. "I also don't hesitate to take action when needed. Like everyone, I want to be liked by others, but I am smart enough to realize that's an impossible goal. I can't please everyone. I know, by really no fault of my own, I have already made an enemy in Pamela, and by extension, most of the PTA. I'm not happy about it, but it is what it is. I can't move back and change anything. I can only move forward."

"Oh, my god!" Trisha practically jumped out of her seat. "Are you trying to tell us you two have concocted a plan to overthrow the PTA?"

"Probably," Mia said half under her breath. Then speaking more clearly, she added, "I can see the revolutionary war now."

"Oh, goodness, no." Stacey sat back down. "We'd never do something so crazy."

"So then what are you getting at then?" Aimee asked.

Donna chimed in, "Why are we all here?"

I continued with my script. "Stacey and I invited you all here today because you all have something in common."

Mia glanced around the room and pulled a face when her eyes settled on Donna. Fortunately, Donna, whose unblinking eyes stared at mine, didn't seem to notice Mia's glare.

"We all have a child in kindergarten. Like it or not, we will all be together for at least another five more years." I flashed what I hoped was a killer watt smile. "Each one of us has a vested interest in making Forest River Elementary School the best place for our children."

"Yes, we do," Claire said.

"Yeah, okay." Mia pointed at Donna. "Like Dina asked, why are we all here?"

"It's Donna," I said, interrupting Mia.

"Pardon?"

"Her name is Donna."

"Oh, right. Look, I cancelled an appointment with Jacques to come. Now I am regretting the decision. Do you have a point for this gathering?"

"Yes, there is a point for this meeting," I said. "As individuals, none of us can accomplish much. If we band together, we can make a difference. We can try to give a voice to all of the other parents who also aren't happy with the status quo."

"And how do you plan on doing this?" Aimee asked.

"Baby steps." I stood up and retrieved several manila folders I had tucked away in my wall unit and handed them out to the women.

"There are a lot of words here," Mia complained as she flipped through the pages. I should have expected she'd need cliff-notes.

"The first set of documents is a petition to declare Forest River a nut-free zone. Stacey and I have prepared it as an insurance policy. The committee is pretty much in agreement that the school needs to move in this direction. Having the added voices of other mothers will help make the decision a slam dunk for Principal Williams."

"So, you want us to get signatures?" Trisha asked.

"Yes, as many as possible," Stacey said.

"Seems easy enough," Aimee added as Donna and Claire echoed their agreement.

"For you, maybe," Mia griped. "I don't have free time to spend working for Forest River Elementary School. I have tons of commitments, and I really can't spare a second. Sorry."

"This shouldn't take much time, Mia. No one is asking you to go door-to-door to canvas signatures. But during your busy day, I bet you come in contact with so many other moms. I'm sure when Donna or I am driving across town to drop off or pick up Melissa from ballet, you can manage to ask one of the moms in the next manicure chair or stair climber to scribble her signature on a piece of paper as a favor, can't you?"

"I guess so." Her mouth formed an *O*, and she waved her finger. "The dry cleaner we use is right next to the studio"—she looked me directly—"if you and your friend would be able to pick up my cleaning when you get Melissa, I probably could figure a way to handle this task for you."

I swallowed down my annoyance. "I'm forever going there with Scott's shirts, too. It would be no problem for me to pick up a few more pieces of laundry, when I go, Mia."

"Sweet! Okay, continue." Mia took a sip of wine and waved the folder like a fan. "What else is in this folder, anyway?"

Keeping with the agenda I memorized, I explained. "The other day I stumbled upon this great group on Facebook called Forest River Moms and Dads Group. I submitted a request to join and ended up messaging with the administrator. She was a lovely lady. She told me she created the group about five years ago when her youngest daughter entered middle school. Her goal was for the group to help parents connect. She wanted to offer a safe haven for residents to communicate about issues they felt were important to the community."

As I expected, every one of the women had reached for their phones and started to click away. I'd bet two pairs of Manolo Blahniks that they all were searching for the page even though I included a printout of it in the folder. As they scrolled, I continued. "Unfortunately, while the membership is high, close to seven hundred people, the activity on the group is quite low. The bulk of the posts center around restaurants and retail establishments instead of issues that plague our community."

"What a waste," Claire replied.

"I know," I said.

"I, for one, disagree," Mia said. "Keeping up-to-date with all available food options is important, especially when the restaurants deliver. I'd do anything not to have to cook a meal again. Am I right?"

"Absolutely," Aimee said.

"I love to cook," Donna said. My mouth watered as I remembered the delicious lobster mac and cheese she served on Christmas. Scott and I had eaten in renowned restaurants all over the globe. Yet I had never tasted a better lobster dish.

Mia pulled a face again. "No wonder you two are bosom buddies, Dina."

Donna looked crestfallen.

It wasn't easy, but I chose to let Mia's remark slide and tried to stay on task. "Can we get back on track, ladies?"

"Yes, please," Trisha said as she glanced at her gold watch.

"So, I was thinking, if we all join the group, and invite people we know to join the group too, we can start to change the tone of the page by posting topics that really pertain to the parents of the town, like issues at school, fundraising events, recommendations for birthday parties and pediatricians. The founder was not only on board with this idea, she adored the concept."

"She was?" Donna asked. I didn't blame her for being surprised. The parents of Forest River were a prickly bunch.

"Yep, it would be what she had envisioned but wasn't able to accomplish."

"Are you going to take it over from her?" Mia asked.

I shook my head. "Absolutely not."

"Really? You're not dying to get control and rebrand it as your own?"

"No, Mia, I'm not. Contrary to what you and Pamela Peterson probably believe, I am not the type of person who needs to take control of everything. I am quite content being an active participant."

"Yeah, okay," Mia replied, unconvinced.

Claire came to my rescue. "So you want us to recruit people to the page and then drum up conversations?"

"Yes," Stacey and I said in unison.

"Sounds easy enough," Tricia added.

Mia exhaled deeply. "Have you forgotten, ladies? I must have said a thousand ways from Sunday, I don't have any desire to devote any of my limited personal time to anything involving school activities. Count me out of this little ploy."

I counted silently to five before answering. "Mia, you made your concerns crystal clear. Stacey and I understand your involvement will be minimal, but we still need your help."

She looked pained as she asked, "Help to do what?"

"Mia," Stacey said, "after everything we discussed, I am sure you realize, based on my current position with the PTA, I can't risk Pamela finding out I am involved in this experiment. I need to stay under the radar. We all know there is strength in numbers, and you are so well known in the community and the school. I'll do the work, but we want you to be part of the public face."

"It's a win-win." Then, before I could stop the words, I asked, "Why would you say no, Mia? Sure, you might not have too much to gain, but I am sure you realize what you stand to lose, don't you?"

A faint line creased her forehead as she likely contemplated having to drive her daughter all over town.

Joan would slaughter me if she knew I threw out a veiled threat to the mother of the most popular girl in Hayley's class. I knew better than to let my temper get the best of me. And now, I knew all my hard work and Hayley's friendship with Mia's daughter Melissa hinged on how Mia would react.

CHAPTER TWENTY-FOUR
THEN

FIFTEEN MINUTES after the meeting broke up, Donna was the only woman who remained at my house. Stacey seemed somewhat reluctant to leave my place. She made it clear she had hoped to rehash the meeting in gory detail, but I needed a break. I never expected the gathering to have lasted as long as it did. The event drained me. I desperately craved some downtime. I assured Stacey I would call her tonight after I put Hayley to bed, which seemed to satisfy her.

"How can you stand that woman?" Donna asked as she helped me put the leftover food into Tupperware containers.

"Mia?" I asked automatically.

"Yeah." She pulled a face. "She's a horrible human being."

"I don't know if I'd go that far, *Dina*," I joked, but Donna didn't look amused. I pulled my hair into a messy bun on the top of my head. Then I twisted my neck from side-to-side as I tried to ease the built-up tension. "She's definitely a lot to handle. I honestly think she is harmless, though."

"You do?"

"Yeah. I think she's too self-centered and lazy to do any real damage to anyone."

"I don't know. We spend half of our lives running around town doing her errands. I'm not sure we get much of a return on our investment." Donna opened my refrigerator and moved a few items around to make space for the leftover hummus and vegetables. "Maybe you're right, but I don't trust her as far as I could throw her."

I popped a pretzel stick in my mouth and offered the bag to Donna. Then I said, "Considering she doesn't have an ounce of fat on her fit little frame, you probably could toss her pretty far."

Donna snorted. "What is the deal with her and her personal trainer anyway? Do you think they have something going on? I mean, really! I don't think I ever heard her mention her husband, yet every other word out of her mouth has something to do with Jacques."

I roared. "I know! She is totally obsessed with the guy. I doubt there is funny business going on, though. I think she is petrified that if she eases up on her training schedule in the slightest, she may slide back to her old ways."

"Old ways?" Donna asked.

I retrieved my phone from the charger. I scrolled to the picture I had found and saved a few weeks ago. "Look." I handed the device to Donna.

She enlarged the image with her fingers, and her eyes grew wide. Donna gasped. "No way! Don't tell me that's Mia?"

"Yep! This shot was taken soon after she graduated college and returned home to Forest River. Instead of the freshman fifteen, it looks like our girl came home with the graduate fifty-five, or something." I took a deep breath. "Clearly, it wasn't a healthy weight for her, but I do think she looked much better with a little meat on her bones than she does now."

"I do, too," Donna agreed, frowning slightly. "She definitely looked much happier." Donna reached for another pretzel rod. Before she took a bite, she asked, "Did Mia give you this picture?"

I shook my head and rolled my eyes. "What do you think? She'd probably die if she knew I had this."

"Probably." Donna pulled out a stool and sat down at the island. I joined her. "How did you get this anyway?"

"I have my ways." I smirked.

"Seriously, Jackie. How do you seem to know all the dirt about everyone in this town?" I had confided in Donna what I learned about Pamela Peterson's incarcerated spouse on Christmas day. I didn't intend to tell her; it just slipped out. Sharing the secret with her had been freeing though; I felt confident she'd maintain my confidence.

"Fine." I rubbed the back of my neck. "I get a lot of my

information from my mother-in-law. She's been an active member of the community for many years and has a lot of connections. Joan was the one who figured out Stacey was related to the principal."

"Okay, makes sense. But what about the rest?"

"I can't tell you all my secrets," I said in mock outrage.

She crossed her arms. "Oh, yes, you can, and you will."

"Fine." I exhaled deeply and continued. "I have a natural curiosity about what makes people tick. I love to figure out what motivates people, and what shapes them into who they are, or better said, who they pretend to be. Let's face it, so many people wear a mask and hide their true feelings."

"Very true."

"Well, thanks to the Internet, there is a wealth of information out there about every one of us. Most people just look at the cursory information and move on, but not me. I have an insatiable thirst for details, and when I am interested in someone or something, I invest the time and dig deep. I go all the way down the rabbit's hole, and it's amazing what you can find if you invest the proper time."

Donna's eyes darted downward. As she avoided eye contact, my mind raced as I tried to explain properly.

"Don't misunderstand me. I'm not a stalker by any means. I like to consider what I research. When I worked, it was essential for me to know as much as possible about potential donors. The better I tailored the events to their tastes, the more money I raised for the charity. It was a win-win for all. I honestly never thought I'd have to dust off my investigative skills after I stopped working, but navigating all the drama and petty politics with the parents of Forest River has proven to be tricky business."

"Well, you sure have that right." Donna put her elbows on the counter and rested her head in her hands. "Sometimes, when I think about what I hear and see, I have to ask myself if this is real life."

"I know what you mean."

Donna looked me up and down. "When we first had lunch, I didn't know what to make of you. I was very apprehensive, to say the least, but you are not what I expected you to be."

"Is that a good thing?" I asked with a nervous laugh. I hoped

I didn't scare Donna off. I knew I could be intense.

She reached for my hands and relief flooded me. "Yes. It is a very good thing. Somehow, I felt instantly comfortable with you, which hasn't happened since I moved here. Like Mia, you are a lot to handle, too, but you are more real than I would ever have imagined. I wish the other moms were more like you."

"Thank you. You are so sweet. So we are okay?" I finally found the nerve to ask the question that had been on my mind since New Year's Eve.

"Why wouldn't we be?"

"I don't know." I paused for a second as I searched for the right words. I found it so strange how two people could see a situation so differently. "It felt as if you pulled away from me. You've been distant lately. And you were so quiet during the meeting. You barely said two words the entire time. I was petrified I had offended you by not briefing you before the meeting."

Her face expressionless, she said, "I won't lie. I would have loved to have had some inside scoop about what you were cooking up, before I came here today, especially the part about the petition, since it relates to my daughter and her health."

"I know that now." I picked imaginary lint off of my pants. "I'm sorry. I realize I should have spoken to you first and asked your permission. I got carried away. I had hoped to make it a loving surprise for you."

"Thanks. And while your enthusiasm is a bit much sometimes, I do appreciate your efforts. I'd rather you be on my side than not, and I'm sure your heart is in the right place."

"It is," I answered quickly, even though I wondered at her assessment.

"And I'm realistic, too, Jackie. I understand you can't tell me everything in advance all the time. I would love it if you could, but I understand you have a lot of balls in the air. I'm just glad to be part of the journey with you. I know, thanks to your help, Christie is in a much better place. My little one is thriving with her new friendships, just as Hayley seems to be, and it makes me very happy. I won't lie, though. I'm not completely comfortable with the other women."

"You're not?" I asked, surprised. Except for Mia, they all

seemed warm, inviting, and genuine to me, especially Claire.

"No, I'm not." Donna pulled her blonde hair into a low ponytail.

"Why?"

She picked up her water bottle and put it down before she took a sip. "It's hard for me to explain. I know it is probably my insecurities running rampant." She looked around my kitchen, and her eyes lingered on my double SubZero refrigerator. "I feel like everyone is so materialistic and judgmental."

"Really? Sure, Mia can be a complete snob, but the others are very down to earth."

"Who knows? Maybe I am reading too much into everything." She paused for a second. "Like you, I didn't grow up in an environment like Forest River. Thomas's dad preached how the best move in real estate was to buy the worst house in a great neighborhood. We followed his advice to the tee. Most of the homes we looked at were way outside our price range, but we kept looking and found a wonderful place to settle. Don't misunderstand me. We are very comfortable and can hold our own. And I know there will always be differences. I don't have live-in help. Our home is modest in comparison to others in town. I don't ever anticipate a day I am going to decide to throw money down the drain to dress my children in designer clothes they will grow out of in fifteen seconds flat. I can't picture us packing up our kids practically every school break to traipse all over the globe like most of the other families. And while we have a blast as your guests, I don't see Thomas and I joining the club anytime soon. We are just not those people."

"I know, which is why I think I gravitated to you in the first place," I answered honestly. "I think we have similar values. I love spending time with you and your family. You guys are so real. It is so refreshing."

"Thank you." Donna offered me a small, sad smile. "I appreciate it. You're different than the others, though."

I leaned in. "I am not so sure. You have just spent more time with me and were able to see the real me. You need to have an open mind with the other ladies."

"I guess you are right. I don't know why I even brought it

up. I shouldn't be so judgmental. Maybe I am being protective of you."

I sat up ramrod straight as my heart beat fast and asked, "Protective of me?"

She looked a bit nervous. "Yeah. Only a few short months ago, it seemed like no one knew your name. The other mothers barely gave you the time of day. Then you threw a fundraiser and hosted a party. And like that"—she snapped her fingers—"you are the new *it girl*. All of a sudden everyone wants to be your best friend. How do you know if they are sincere?"

"How do you know if anyone is?" I asked, raising my brows in question. I prayed she was sincere. Joan had warned me not to get too close to anyone, and I chose to ignore her advice when it came to Donna. I opened up a lot to her. I trusted her, which was why I worried when she didn't act like herself.

"I guess you're right. It's just that I don't want to see you get hurt."

"You're so sweet, Donna." I placed my hand over my heart. "I appreciate your concern, but don't worry about me. I'm a big girl. I can take care of myself perfectly fine. I've done so for years."

"I know." She closed her eyes briefly. When she opened them, I saw they were filled with tears. "You don't have to continue to fly solo, you know? You have a great husband, and you have me in your corner. I don't want you to ever feel like you are alone. I'll never let you down."

"Oh, Donna. You are the *best* friend," I said as I reached for her hands.

"That's because you are my best friend, Jackie. You are the person I know I can call in a pinch. I know I can count on you being there for me because you've proved it time and time again. I am so thankful you came into my life."

Her words were like a balm to my soul. But old habits were hard to break. Just as the words got caught in my throat and prevented me from reciprocating the sentiment the first time Scott had told me he loved me, I couldn't tell her what I was sure she wanted to hear, that she was my best friend too. Instead, I just replied simply, "Thanks."

She looked as dejected as Scott did back then, and I felt guilty. Opening my heart and trusting others didn't come easy to me. I swallowed down my fears and added, "I'm so thankful you are in my life too." I knew I had to try and change my ways. The reward of her friendship was far greater than the risk of getting hurt. I prayed I chose my closest friend wisely, but only time would tell.

CHAPTER TWENTY-FIVE
THEN
FEBRUARY
A Month Later

To: Forest River Elementary School Parents

From: Forest River Elementary School Principal, Harrison Owen Williams, Jr.

Date: 02/28 @ 12:45 PM

Subject: Fwd.: Parents' Spring Fling

Begin forwarded message from Jacqueline A. Martin:

Hello Parents!

Yes!

You read it right! I'm delighted to announce Forest River Elementary School will be hosting its First Annual Parents' Spring Fling on Friday, May 27, at 7:00 PM on the south field. The rain date will be May 28.

For years, there has been a sense of disconnect in our community... While we all have so much in common with each other, we tend to only associate with our neighbors or our children's friends' parents. Many people have confided to Principal Williams that they wished there were more opportunities for moms and dads to mix and mingle with each other. Well, our principal listened!

This year a special committee was formed to transform your desire into reality. We are going to start small, but if the feedback is as positive as the team and I feel it will be, next year, the sky's the limit!

So mark your calendars.... Prepare to celebrate the end of the term.... And register early! This is an event not to miss. And the best part...

All proceeds from the Spring Fling will be used solely to enrich our children's educational experience. The success of the event's raffles and auction depends on generous contributions from the community. If you have anything to donate—fun experiences, gift cards, products, or services from local businesses—please note on the online registration form. Click HERE.

Looking ahead,

Jacqueline A. Martin, Donna Warren, Claire Conroy, and Mia Montgomery - The Parents' Spring Fling Committee Chairwomen

---

"You are brilliant!" Stacey screamed into the phone as I plopped down on the couch in my living room to feed Cassidy a bottle. Squeals could be heard from older children downstairs in the basement. There was nothing I loved more than having a full house and hearing the sound of my daughter having a blast with her friends.

"I don't know if I'd go so far as all that." I tried to sound humble, but I knew every word of her praise was well warranted. Only about a month had passed since Stacey and I held our first meeting with the kindergarten moms. In that short period of time, we had generated stellar results. It was clear the other moms in our community were hungry for knowledge. The outpouring of participation in our endeavors blew us both away.

First, our petition worked perfectly! I'm proud, thanks to the efforts we made, our little elementary school now was the first in the area to be declared an entirely nut free facility. At Joan's suggestion, I had contacted the region's local newspaper. They wrote a beautiful story about our plight, which they featured in print and online.

Speaking of online, the ladies also managed to generate so much traffic to the Forest River Moms and Dads Facebook page! Practically overnight, the site became a morning must-read for every mother in town.

Even Mia managed to get into the swing of things when she asked the group where she could find some new exercise classes in the area. The feedback was phenomenal. Mia now supplements her training time with Jacques by catching the waves at a nearby indoor surfing facility. She's also begun underwater cycling, which sounds like so much fun that I just registered for class too. I wouldn't have thought it would be possible, but each day she looks even more toned than before.

Trust me, I know. Not only am I now fetching her dry-cleaning and daughter on most afternoons, she also begged me to take over her spot in the morning carpool. By my last estimate, I put close to fifty miles a day on my car without ever leaving town. Sure, driving in circles daily is grueling, but it paled in comparison to the joy in my heart. Watching Hayley thrive by spending more time with other children makes the mileage worthwhile.

"Oh, stop being so modest," Stacey scolded. "I know you're putting on an act."

"Yeah, you know me too well." I stroked Cassidy's cheek. Then I turned serious. "I think I'm obsessed. I can't stop clicking refresh on the Parents' Spring Fling's registration page. I know I only sent out the email a few hours ago, but the response has been outstanding."

"I know. I'm doing the same exact thing. I can't believe how many people have offered donations. This is going to be tremendous. We are going to make a killing for the school." As we promised Mia at the original meeting, we only needed her to be a face for our work. In all communications, Mia would be named as part of the committee, but behind the scenes, Stacey is handling the work.

"Yes, and the money will be put to good use, which will benefit our children." I cringed slightly. "It will be a welcome relief not having to worry about any funny business."

Stacey was silent for a second. A week or so ago, Stacey shared some troubling news with Donna and me about how the PTA planned on spending their surplus funds. We both found their plan quite unsettling, and I knew we wouldn't be the only ones.

In the past, they probably would have been able to make the purchase without any interference. Those days were now history. When the time came there was no way I would sit idly by. I planned on making my feelings known, big time.

I felt bad I brought up the unpleasantness. I knew Stacey wasn't in support of the action, either, but I asked the nagging question anyway: "Do you think it was a mistake to have sent out the invitation so early? I had a much smaller RSVP window when Scott and I tied the knot."

Stacey groaned. "Well, three months is a long lead time."

My heart fluttered.

"True. However, we are planning a brand-new event, and we need parental participation in order to succeed, so I think the timing is perfect. In the future, when this becomes an annual activity that everyone eagerly awaits, we can send out the invitations closer to the date."

"Makes sense, I guess."

"Oh, don't be a worry wart, Jackie," she scolded. "Honestly, I think the timing was perfect. People are still reeling from how disappointing last weekend's penny auction had been."

I burped the baby. Joan told me in the past, this was the premier fundraising event at the school. She said her friends told her the excitement in the room was electric, because all the parents ended up in awe over the amazing items that were up for auction. I couldn't wait to experience the event. I warned Scott I would most likely do major damage to our credit card.

Instead of the room being electrified, it was a real snoozer, literally. My spouse and several other fathers actually nodded off to sleep. I felt so guilty that there was not one single item I had a remote interest in bidding on, I ended up scribbling a check payable to the school which I handed to Principal Williams before a group of us left to grab a bite.

I sighed. "Yeah, it was pretty horrible. At least Franklin

didn't let out a snore that could wake the dead like Scott did."

Stacey laughed again. "True. It was pretty funny, though. Seriously, I was embarrassed to be associated with the event. I knew it wasn't going to hold a candle to years past, but I didn't realize it would be as badly received as it was." The posts on the Forest River Moms and Dads Facebook page were vicious.

"Well, at least now you will be secretly redeeming yourself," I tried to joke. "Have you spoken to Pamela since the parents' formal invitation went out? How is she handling everything, anyway?"

"She called me twice already." She paused for a second. "How do you think she's handling things?"

"Does she suspect your involvement at all?"

"Oh, no." Stacey snorted. "She's clueless. Oh, Jackie, you should hear her. Man, the woman's temper is running thin. She's not happy about how you are rallying the troops. She rightly feels the tide's changing."

"I'm sure. And so far, we've just been having some fun. We haven't acted on the big issue yet." I don't know why I found it so hard not to speak my mind, even when I knew my comments wouldn't be welcome.

Fortunately, Stacey didn't seem to mind. She jumped in. "I know. Speaking of the money, we really need to coordinate our—" Scarlett started to bark as my doorbell chimed.

"Shoot. Sorry. I've got to run," I said as I stood up and started to walk toward the front of my house. "Someone's at my door. I'm sure it's Kevin to pick up his kids."

"Okay, call me later and let me know how Claire and the baby are doing."

"Will do," I said as I placed Cassidy in her bassinet. As I passed the door to the basement, I called out, "Kyle, Sarah! I think your dad is here!" Their infant sister had to have hernia surgery this afternoon, and I knew both children were worried about her.

With Scarlett at my feet, I threw open the door without even looking out the window. Instead of finding Claire's spouse on the other side of my door, I found two unfamiliar older women. "Oh, hello," I said in surprise. I expected them to try to convince me to join their church or sell me some useless gadget I'd feel forced to add to my fully stocked junk drawer.

The younger of the two ladies thrust out her hand. "Jackie? Hello! I'm Maureen Cavanaugh, Claire's mom."

"Hi!" I said brightly, surprised to meet Claire's family.

Kyle and Sarah darted out of the house, with Hayley trailing behind. Kyle gave his grandmother a high five as his younger sister flung herself into the older woman's arms and yelled, "Gigi! Yeah!"

"So nice to put a face to a name." Claire's mother smiled widely. "My daughter has told us so much about you. You've been such a wonderful friend to her. Thank you." The other woman loudly cleared her throat and Maureen lightly smacked her hand against her forehead. "Where are my manners? Sorry, Jackie. This is my mother, Catherine Ryan."

Catherine pushed her magenta half-moon glasses further up on her nose and dramatically craned her neck up and down. She didn't make any attempt to hide the fact she was checking me out from head to toe. Apparently, I passed muster because she thrust out a liver spotted hand and squawked, "Nice to meet ya!" Then she winked at me and added, "You can call me Gigi. Everyone else does."

"Thanks, Gigi." I gestured inside my house. "Do you want to come in for a moment?" I felt extremely uneasy releasing Claire's kids to these women. Sure, it was clear the children loved them, but I had expected their father to come get them as planned. As I tried to figure out how to handle this delicate situation, my cell phone buzzed. "Excuse me," I said as I glanced at the device. Relief washed over me when I saw the message was Claire advising me of the change of plans.

"Thank you. You're sweet, but we really must get going." She glanced at her wrist. "It's getting late. I want to settle the kids down with my mom before dinnertime so I can head back to the hospital to be with Claire."

"How is Chloe?" I asked.

"She's a real trouper. She's tough like her momma," Maureen said. "She should be coming home tonight."

Gigi practically drowned out her daughter's voice when she screamed at the top of her lungs: "Get a move on you two, will ya?

Stop monkeying around! You've got pizza to eat! I, for one, am starving." The older woman rolled her eyes at me. "My daughter thinks she's the food police. She watches my carb intake like a hawk. It takes a baby to need an operation for this one to allow an old woman the simple pleasure of eating a piece of pizza. Don't get old, dear."

Maureen rubbed her temple as Gigi helped Sarah zip up her coat.

"I'll try," I answered as a wave of jealousy flooded over me. Claire was so fortunate to have such a lovely mother and grandmother at her age. I missed my family so badly. Fortunately, my in-laws would be arriving in town tomorrow for Hayley's birthday, assuming they don't cancel their trip again. "It was so nice to meet both of you. I was expecting Kevin to collect the kids, but this was such a pleasant surprise. I'm guessing he stayed at the hospital to be with Claire and the baby?"

Maureen opened her mouth to speak, but her mother interjected. "You don't know the man too well now, do you, dear?"

I shrugged. "Um—"

Gigi grimaced and howled. "At the hospital, my foot! He stuck around long enough for the surgeon to snip-snip and do his business. Good thing there were no complications! I don't want to think how he would have behaved if something went wrong. For all I know, he might not have stuck around. Seriously, I don't know what is wrong with that fool. He needs to get his priorities in order, pronto, I say."

Claire's mother looked mortified at her mother's outburst. "That's enough, Mom." She rubbed her eyes. "I'm so sorry, Jackie."

"Don't apologize for me, missy," Gigi scolded as indignation filled her eyes. "I've earned the right to speak my mind a long time ago. And I will speak the truth whenever I feel fit."

I didn't know what to say, or do, so I plastered on a phony smile.

"Please"—Maureen's voice dropped to a whisper as her eyes implored mine—"Don't tell Claire what my mother said. She'd be so embarrassed."

"I won't say a word."

As soon as the ladies walked away, I ushered my daughter back inside the house. I kissed the top of her head, cherishing the smell of her strawberry shampoo. "Time for you to do your homework, sweetie. Brittany is waiting for you." Being the obedient girl she was, she headed into the kitchen to handle tonight's assignments; Scarlett trailed behind. Then the doorbell rang again.

"Did someone forget something?" I asked automatically without seeing who was standing there.

When I realized who was at my door, I felt the color drain out of my face. Something was terribly wrong.

CHAPTER TWENTY-SIX
THEN

I OPENED MY MOUTH to speak, but I struggled to find my voice. My throat felt as if I had run across the Sahara Desert, twice. I managed to choke out one word. The result sounded more like a question than a statement. "Joan?"

She didn't pause. She stepped inside the hallway and wrapped me in her arms. "You look amazing, darling. I am so happy to see you finally. It's been way too long, and I've missed you so much."

My arms hung awkwardly at my sides. I was petrified to hug her back. She looked so frail. I worried if I used any bit of force, I'd break her in two. I carefully and gently placed my arms around her, and tears filled my eyes. She rubbed her hand along the back of my head. "I know," she mumbled into my hair, "it's okay, honey. Everything is okay."

We stood frozen in the spot for what felt like a mini lifetime. When I felt strong enough, I broke the embrace. "Oh, Joan. I'm sorry. Come inside. Sit down. Can I get you anything to eat or drink?"

"No, I'm fine," she answered as she walked toward the living room and peeked in Cassidy's bassinet. "Wow"—she ran a finger under her eye—"she got so big. I missed so much."

"Do you want to hold her?"

"Oh yes, but she's sleeping so peacefully. I don't want to wake her." Joan sat down on the couch. She adjusted the multicolored Hermes scarf, which covered her head, which I had no doubt was bald. She then patted the cushion next to her. "Come, sit down with me, Jackie. I've given you a shock."

I did as I was told, and she reached for my hands.

"Why didn't you say anything to us, Joan?" I knew Scott had

been kept in the dark too. There would have been no way my husband ever would have been able to keep a secret like this from me.

She let out a long breath. "I didn't want to worry you or Scottie. You both are such sensitive children."

I opened my mouth to speak, but she didn't give me a chance.

"Come on, Jackie. You know you both would have spent the last few months being worried sick." She hesitated. "And for what? It wasn't like either one of you could have done anything to help me, anyway."

"That's not true!" I frowned. "We could have been with you and supported you. We would have tried to make the situation easier for you."

"No," she said firmly. "You both would have just fussed and fretted. You would have driven Stanley and me crazy. Instead, you managed to make the situation easier for me without even knowing."

I raised an eyebrow. "How?"

She leaned in slightly, and our shoulders now touched. "You distracted me, darling. Every time I had a treatment scheduled, I called you. Instead of thinking about what I would be soon facing, I would focus my thoughts on you, the children, and everything else that was happening in Forest River. It was a godsend."

"It was superficial nonsense." I pouted. Then I added, "I knew something was wrong—I should've trusted my gut."

"I'm not surprised you suspected something was wrong." She smirked. "You are very intuitive, you know."

My breath hitched in my throat. "So I've been told once or twice. Did you see Scott yet?"

Uncharacteristically, I hadn't spoken to my husband all day. I left him a message or two, but he had only texted me saying he was swamped and was in back-to-back meetings all day.

She shook her head. "Not yet. I wanted to speak with you first." Then as the grandfather clock struck seven, she added, "I was hoping I'd speak with him tonight after we had a chance to catch up."

"He should be home in a half hour or forty-five minutes, at

the latest."

"Perfect! That will give us plenty of time."

The events of the past few months played in my mind's eye like a bad movie. "So now I guess I know why you've been avoiding Forest River like the plague. To think, I even imagined you didn't love us anymore."

Joan looked down at her lap and smoothed out her black linen slacks. "I'm sorry. I felt horrible lying all the time to you and Scottie about all the exciting places Stan and I were going. I just felt it was easier for all of us this way." She placed her left hand over her the right side of her chest. "Everything had happened so fast. Stan and I were only down south a few weeks before I felt a lump in the shower."

"Mommy!" Hayley called as she stormed into the room with Scarlett trailing behind. "Where are you? And what are you doing? We've been waiting!"

Brittany stood in the doorway and mouthed "sorry" to me when she realized I wasn't alone.

"Hayley, girl!" Joan called out as she rose from her seat and squatted down on the carpet.

My daughter's face lit up like a Christmas tree as she flew into her grandmother's open arms. "Nana!" If she noticed any difference in my mother-in-law's appearance, she didn't show it. As usual, I was in awe with her optimism and innocence.

Joan smothered her grandchild with kisses. "I missed you so much, sweet girl. You grew so much! Are you as tall as your daddy yet?"

"No, silly." Hayley smacked her forehead. "Maybe by tomorrow, I will be. It's my birthday, you know!"

"I know," Joan cooed. "And wait until you see what Poppy and I got you for the big day. I think you're going to be very, very happy!"

Hayley started to dance in place "Yeah!" She pumped her fist into the air. "I can't wait! What did you get me?"

"I can't tell you now. It's not your birthday yet. You have to wait until tomorrow."

Hayley frowned and brushed a stray strand of light brown

hair away from her face. "That's not fair. Tomorrow is like forever away. I missed you so much, Nana." Scarlett started to sniff my mother-in-law's pants. Hayley pointed at the pup. "That's Scarlett. She's so much fun! Not like Cassidy. She's boring! She's such a baby! The only thing she does is sleep and poop. She never plays! Can you stay for dinner? Mommy's ordering Thai tonight. I learned how to use chopsticks, the real kind, not the baby kind. I want you to see me use them. You'll be so proud!"

Joan's eyes widened when Hayley finally came up for air. "Wow, I'm impressed. Maybe you can teach Poppy how to use them. The man is so old, and he still manages to get more food on his lap than in his mouth when he tries to eat with chopsticks."

Hayley burst into laughter as Joan's eyes glistened with tears. She gave Hayley another hug. "I missed you so much. I'd love to stay for dinner if your mom doesn't mind."

"Mind? I'd love nothing more." My mind whirled. "Is Thai okay for you? Will it be too spicy? We can get anything you like. Do you want me to order chicken soup or something light instead?"

Joan threw back her head and chuckled. "And you wonder why I didn't reach out to you when I received my diagnosis? Look at how you are fussing over me." Hayley didn't understand, but it didn't stop her from laughing as she watched her grandmother scold me. "Thai is perfect. I'll text Stan and have him come by to join us."

"Excellent," I said while Joan took her phone out of her purse and fired off her message.

"Are you coming to my birthday party on Saturday?" Hayley asked.

"Of course. Poppy and I can't wait."

"Me neither!" Hayley pumped her fists. "It's going to be so cool! There's going to be a petting zoo, a bouncy house, a face painter, a clown, and an ice cream truck just for me!"

"Oh, and don't forget the magician," I added.

Hayley smacked her forehead. "Oopsy."

"Good job," Joan mouthed to me. She had been instrumental in the planning. Also, tomorrow afternoon's scheduled trip to the American Girl Doll Place in the city with five of Hayley's closest friends was Joan's idea.

I knew my daughter could chat with her grandmother for hours, I was desperate for some alone time with her first. I cleared my throat. "Um, did you finish your homework?"

"No." She pouted.

"Well, what are you doing still standing here then? Finish your homework while Nana and I talk. Then you can hang out with her until bedtime, okay?"

"Okay," she said. She started to walk back to the kitchen but stopped three times along the way to check over her shoulder as if to make sure Joan was still sitting there.

"So, I see you didn't change a thing in this house," Joan remarked as she craned her neck and gave the room a once over.

"Why would I?"

"Well, you've lived here for months, and I fear it is completely not your style."

I felt my cheeks redden. If Scott mentioned something to his mother, I'd kill him.

"It's okay"—she raised her hand—"I know I came on too strong and overstepped every single boundary. You were very kind at the time. You never uttered a word, but I'm not blind. I was able to see your frustration in your eyes, which I selfishly chose to ignore. I didn't completely see it then, but I've had a lot of time to meditate and reflect over the last few months. I know I acted like a bulldozer in a china store. I pushed and pushed so I'd get my way. I should have kept my big mouth shut, and pocketbook closed. You and Scottie deserved the opportunity to decide where to settle on your own, and I stole it from you. I should never have forced this home, its furnishings and decorations, and especially this town on you. I'm sorry."

I covered my mouth with my hand. I would never have expected to hear words like those come out of Joan's mouth. "Wow"—I exhaled deeply—"I appreciate you saying all this, Joan. I won't lie, at the time it was unsettling and overwhelming. As you said, it's been over ten months, and I know you acted out of love, like you constantly do. And we're all extremely happy."

"Are you really?" Her ice-blue eyes pierced mine.

I paused. It was strange. For months, Joan and I spent hours on the phone strategizing and discussing my next move so I could get a leg up in this parental power struggle. We had been laser-focused on the prize, which was my daughter's acceptance and popularity. I followed the rules and played the game well. My efforts have paid off. It hasn't been easy. It appears like Hayley and I are in the position I had hoped we'd be. I'm competitive by nature, and I love to win. I knew I let the adrenaline and excitement propel me forward each day. I acted without even thinking most days. But now that the question hung in the air, looking at my mother-in-law looking so frail, I had to ask myself: Was this the life I truly wanted for my children and me?

CHAPTER TWENTY-SEVEN
THEN
The Next Day

"JACKIE!" I HEARD a door open, and then Ms. Anderson called out my name in her upbeat voice. "Wait a second."

I yawned and turned around in slow motion. I rubbed my aching forehead. I felt ancient. I remember the days when I would be able to stay up practically all night and then dash off to work, feeling energized by adrenaline. This morning I felt as if I had been plowed over by a freight train. I blinked a couple of times and rotated my neck in a slow circle toward Hayley's kindergarten teacher. "Is something wrong?" I asked, slightly irritated. I had just spent the last half hour celebrating Hayley's birthday with her classmates. And while I enjoyed the experience immensely, I had so much I needed to accomplish today. I barely had a second to spare. I started to walk back down the corridor to where she stood.

The morning had passed at warp speed. Not surprising, after Joan's visit the day before, I found it impossible to calm my racing mind. I don't even remember what time I crawled into bed. Scott took the news about his mother's health in stride. He asked her all the right questions about her test results and treatments. He was focused on her positive prognosis, rather than wild what-if scenarios like me. I should have been the one to comfort him, but instead, he calmed me down as I cried against his chest.

When my tears finally ran dry, I convinced him to get some rest. The poor man was asleep before his head hit the pillow. I knew sleep would elude me, so I took to my computer. I spent hours researching everything from cancer statistics to real estate trends and prices, and other local school districts. Eventually, the words on my screen began to blur, and I joined my husband in bed.

I was exhausted, but I barely slept. By the time I finally drifted off, it was practically morning. I never even stirred when the alarm sounded. Even though Scott was probably running on fumes too, he didn't make any attempt to wake me. Instead, he silently slipped out of bed.

An hour later, I finally came to. When I glanced at the clock, I launched into complete panic mode. I had previously planned to have an extra early start since my to-do list was jam-packed. I cursed my stupidity. I was so angry I had allowed myself to fall behind schedule before the day had even begun.

Fortunately, Scott was a champ, as usual. With Brittany's help, he did everything to keep the morning flowing smoothly, which managed to ease some of my stress. I was lucky. Scott was incredible. He had Hayley's morning routine completely under control. As a special birthday treat, probably for himself too, he made her his special banana pecan pancakes for breakfast. He not only helped her get dressed in the pink dress she had selected two weeks ago for the big day, he also styled her hair in two French braids, her all-time favorite style. He was probably the only man in Forest River who could expertly plait hair, and I was so proud of him. I had taught him years ago how to do it—just in case something happened to me. I remembered how frustrated and sad I felt as a child when my grandmother was unable to style my hair as my mother had done. It was crazy how often the littlest things haunted me the most.

Then, to our daughter's delight, Scott handled this morning's carpool duties, so I could enjoy a leisurely shower before starting my day.

My first stop had been a bakery, about twenty minutes away from Forest River. This place was famous for its designer cupcakes, and I had ordered the most adorable puppy-inspired treats. As I hoped, Hayley and her classmates had been delighted. I couldn't wait to share photos online later. And even though I knew the majority of the moms wouldn't touch a decadent treat, I already placed an order with them for the Spring Fling.

"Nothing is wrong, Jackie." Ms. Anderson flattened down

her skirt. "I only have a second." She glanced back at her classroom's door. Even though every class had a capable teacher's assistant, I knew from experience, Ms. Anderson hated to leave the students unless absolutely necessary.

"Okay. What's up?"

"I didn't get a chance to chat with you in there"—she pointed behind her—"I wanted to speak with you about the spring concert, which is right around the corner."

The show was scheduled for the end of May. According to Stacey, this event was supposed to showcase the students' musical abilities; instead, it managed to shine a spotlight on the parents' entitlement and selfish behavior.

The school had a strict four-ticket limit. The administration didn't care if you had one child performing or six. It also didn't matter to the powers that be if the children came from a large blended family. Four tickets were all any family could obtain. Period. End of story. Ironically, in their infinite wisdom, they didn't set any rules to prevent parents who needed less than four tickets from selling them to the highest bidder. Stacey told me last year, the mother of a second grader, who had a trombone solo, actually shelled out three thousand dollars to get three extra seats for her siblings.

And just when it sounded like things couldn't get any worse, to add more tension to the trying situation, the ticket seats were issued on a first come, first served basis. No parent wanted to risk having to watch their prodigy perform from the back of the auditorium. As a result, at the crack of dawn, the moms would line up in groups on the morning the tickets were made available to jockey for premier seats. The competition was so fierce, Stacey confided, on more than one occasion, she witnessed mothers become physical. It was nuts.

"What about the concert?" I asked. I knew Hayley's class would be singing two songs, one on their own and the other with the other kindergarten class.

Ms. Anderson's face shined, and she placed her hand over her heart. "Hayley is gifted with a beautiful singing voice."

"Thank you. She loves music. She's been singing for

probably as long as she's been speaking."

"Well, whatever you've done with her has worked. It is very unusual, but I have asked Principal Williams if I could work a solo into one of our songs."

My heartbeat's pace increased as she continued.

"Usually, he prefers to have the kindergarteners and first graders perform as a cohesive unit. But after he sat in on yesterday's song hour and heard Hayley's lovely voice, he was moved. He agreed to make an exception if you gave your blessing."

I hesitated. "I don't know. Having her take center stage seems a bit much, especially considering her shyness."

"I know." Ms. Anderson reached for my arm. "Oh, Hayley has come so far in such a short period. Your work with her, and the other mothers, has certainly paid off."

I willed the tears that formed in my eyes not to fall. Yesterday, this would have been everything I had hoped for. This morning, after a night of soul searching, I was concerned I had done my daughter more harm than good. I had been laser-focused on making sure her classmates accepted her. I constantly pushed her outside her comfort zone. I was petrified I had set unrealistic expectations on her. I didn't want to scar her for life. I felt so uneasy. "I guess, she's come a long way."

"You guess? A long way?" Ms. Anderson covered her mouth with her hand. "Jackie, she's almost like a new child. I remember how afraid you were when you thought she might be ostracized. Now, she's probably the most liked child in the class. She's a true star."

"You're so sweet," I said. "I'm proud of her too. I'm just not sure. Don't you think giving her a solo is too much? Singing in front of all those people will be so intimidating."

"Maybe." She bit her bottom lip. "Or maybe it will be a defining moment, teaching her she can do anything she wants. You don't have to answer me now. Take your time deciding. Discuss the opportunity with your husband. Please remember one key fact: I asked the children if anyone would want to sing by themselves at the show, and Hayley was the first child to raise her hand and *screamed* 'yes'."

I lingered in the hallway for a few moments after Ms. Anderson returned to her students, debating what we should do. I was no closer to making a decision when Donna called out my name.

I gave her a quick hug, careful not to smush Julia who she carried on a sling across her chest. "What are you doing here?"

She frowned. "I just had a meeting with the principal. He wants to terminate Christie's speech therapy."

"That's wonderful!" I exclaimed automatically. Christie still had a slight stutter, which usually sprang to the surface when she was upset or tired, but for the most part, she had made remarkable progress over the past few months.

Donna didn't look thrilled. "No, it's not." She exhaled deeply. "She still has a long road to go. I bring her to private speech lessons twice a week, but the extra attention she receives at school helps keep her on track. I worry if they cut this benefit, she'll regress. I know I can just increase her private therapy, but then she'll probably have to drop out of ballet. There aren't enough afternoons in the week for her to do everything, especially since it is almost soccer season."

"I didn't think of that. Sorry. Do you want me to speak to Harry? I probably can't do much, but it is worth a shot. I do have a meeting scheduled with him next week."

"No. Don't bother. I'll handle it."

"It's no bother, really. It would be my pleasure to help Christie." I raised a finger. "In fact, I know exactly what I will say to him." I stroked the top of the baby's head.

"But —"

"There's no need to thank me." I waved my hand—"it is my pleasure."

Donna studied me. "Are you okay? You don't look yourself. You look wiped out."

"I'm a little tired." I downplayed my exhaustion.

"A little?" She squinted at me. "Is anything wrong? You must have so much to do for the trip to American Girl Doll Place and tomorrow's party. Can I do anything to help?"

I wanted to collapse into her arms and cry. I wanted to share how devastated I felt when I learned my mother-in-law was so sick and chose to keep her illness a secret. I wanted to tell her I was up half the night researching breast cancer survival rates and the other half trolling through Zillow, wondering if there would be a better place to raise my children. I wanted to ask her if I had been a good mother or a selfish woman, pulling out all the stops in my attempt to get Hayley accepted by the other children. I wanted to scream I needed help.

Instead, I replied, "Thanks, but I have everything under control." I wished I had been strong enough to show her my vulnerable side.

CHAPTER TWENTY-EIGHT
THEN
MARCH
Two Days Later

To: Jacqueline A. Martin
From: Claire Conroy
Date: 03/2 @ 8:25 PM

Subject: Hayley's Birthday Party

Hey Jackie!

I'm so sorry I missed the party! I would have loved to have been helping out at your house instead of being stuck at home caring for a recuperating baby. But Chloe is doing amazing, so I can't complain!

Wow, girl! I heard it was quite the event, and not just from the other mommies!

Normally, getting Kyle to share one simple detail about his day is as difficult as pulling teeth. But not today! My boy kept rambling on about how much fun he had. In fact, he said multiple times that today was the best day of his life!

Thank you for making him so happy. The past few days have been a bit rough for him. My mom and I have I've tried to cheer him, but you know how it is with... Unfortunately, Kevin hasn't been much help. He just landed a big, new client and has been working around the clock...

Hayley's party was just what Kyle needed. You rock, my friend!

Lunch next week, maybe?

Claire

To: Jacqueline A. Martin
From: Mia Montgomery
Date: 03/2 @ 8:34 PM

Subject: Stuff

J,

Melissa had a blast at Bailey's b'day party 2day. U sure know how 2 throw a party!

Can you do me a solid???????

When U pick up Bailey and Melissa from ballet on Monday, can U also swing by Tony the Tailors & then the dry cleaners for me too???? The hubs has so much stuff at both places... UGH! He's killing me.... He thinks I'm made of time....

Don't' worry - I'll call ahead so you don't have to get any tickets from me...

TX a mill!

M

To: Jacqueline A. Martin
From: Lucy Alexander
Date: 03/2 @ 8:37 PM

Subject: Major Snafu

Hi Jacqueline,

Please accept my deepest apologies.

There was a massive mistake in the gift Kayla brought to Hayley's birthday party today. When my daughter received the invitation to the party, I was a bit taken back. After all, she isn't in Ms. Anderson's class. As far as I knew, our girls never interacted once this whole school year. When I saw Hayley was having a "house party," I wrongly assumed the event would be small and low key. I guess I automatically pictured a party like they used to have in the '70s or something. As a result, the gift Kayla brought was just a mere token of appreciation for being included. The trinket was nowhere in line with what Hayley's party warranted. I have since picked up a proper birthday gift for your lovely daughter. I hope it is okay if Kayla and I drop it off tomorrow afternoon? I can swing by your place anytime that works for you. Also, Kayla would love it if Hayley would come over to play next week.

Mortified and apologetic,
Lucy

To: Jacqueline A. Martin
From: Karen Anne Fitzgerald-Collins-Watterson-Riley
Date: 03/2 @ 9:12 PM

Subject: Fit To Be Tied

Good evening Jackie,

I hope you don't take this note the wrong way. I definitely don't want to be viewed as a complainer or appear ungrateful. I'm smart enough to assume your heart was in the right place when you planned today's event. Too bad the execution left a lot to be desired in my humble opinion. I am extremely upset about what occurred today at Hayley's party, and I felt I owed it to you, to be honest. If you don't know the truth, how else can you learn and improve?

My daughter, Jocelyn Anne, loves nothing more than playing in a bouncy house. She was so excited when she learned Hayley would have one at her party that she immediately made me RSVP.

I expected Jocelyn Anne to be on cloud nine when she and her nanny returned from your house. Instead, I can't even begin to tell you how devastated my little angel was when she was banned from reentering the bouncy house a second time.

Jocelyn Anne is a very discriminating child. She doesn't care for animals of any sort, especially farm animals. Needless to say, she had zero interest in the petting zoo or the pony rides. Also, like me, Jocelyn Anne finds magicians juvenile. They bore her silly. How many times can they try to pull off the same trick as something original? And don't get me started on Jocelyn Anne's feelings about clowns? You do know the children are in kindergarten and not nursery school, don't you???

Again, the one and only part of the day Jocelyn Anne found remotely enjoyable was the bouncy house. Yet your dictatorship ways prevented her from partaking in her favorite pastime twice? You should really be ashamed of yourself for ruining my poor Jocelyn Anne's afternoon.

Sincerely,
Karen Anne Fitzgerald-Collins-Watterson-Riley

I nuzzled up to my husband on the couch and kissed the side of his neck. All of the last few days' worries drifted away after this magical day. I held up my cell phone and waived it. "I got my first bad review. I feel like I've finally arrived."

"Oh, you little devil. My mother will be so proud," he joked, and he put his iPad down on the table. "Too bad she left before you had a chance to read your reviews." I made a mental note to forward her a few emails in the morning for kicks. She'd definitely enjoy the read.

"I know, but your dad was itching to go home." I placed my phone face down next to his device. "The way Stan was yawning and carrying on about being tired after dinner. You'd think he was the one who just finished chemo."

"I was shocked he stayed as long as he did," Scott said. "I expected him to leave halfway through the party. I told Mom yesterday I'd drive her home if he wanted to leave early."

Joan and Stan arrived at our house about an hour before the guests and entertainers. Stan made a beeline for the den to watch television and Joan made herself indispensable. She helped me with all the last-minute touches. Scott and my worries about her being frail or feeling weak vanished as we watched her race around, mingling with the mothers, playing with the children, and caring for Cassidy.

After the crowd cleared out, Hayley opened her presents while Joan sat on the floor next to her. Then to my daughter's delight, we ordered sushi from her favorite place, and her grandparents stayed for dinner. While we ate, we discussed the upcoming recital. Hayley showed us how excited she was to have a solo by serenading us with several numbers until she literally couldn't keep her eyes open one second longer. She practically fell asleep face first in a plate of edamame.

Jocelyn Anne may have had a bust of a day, but Hayley Martin, like her friend, Kyle, and her grandmother, had the time of her life, and that was all that truly mattered to me. Today was a day I'd never forget, and fortunately it wasn't over yet.

"Come on, you." I kissed my husband's neck again. I stood up and gave him a backwards glance. "Don't you think it's time for bed?"

CHAPTER TWENTY-NINE
THEN
MARCH
Three Weeks Later

"I CAN'T BELIEVE you are having another one of these gatherings," Mia said as soon as I opened my front door. I opened my mouth to speak, but before I could, she graced me with a double air kiss. Wow! Look at me go! I moved up in her world.

"Like, didn't we just have the first meeting, like, five seconds ago?" She shimmed out of her floor-length Chanel tweed coat. If it were anyone else, I would have been shocked she chose to wear something so warm since the temperatures were unseasonably high for the end of March. I now knew Mia well enough to realize that the coat must have been either a gift or a new purchase, which she wanted to show off.

"Hi, Jackie!" Melissa squealed as she flung off her shoes and sprinted down the hallway toward the basement in search of Hayley and the other children.

"Hey, sweetie," I replied, even though I'd bet the little girl didn't hear a word. Then to her mom, I added, "It's been almost four months since the group met last." I struggled to keep my voice on an even keel. I was annoyed she once again was tardy. I'd bet my designer shoe and handbag collection she never dared to keep her precious Jacques waiting one second. I made an executive decision that the next time I held a group meeting, I'd make sure to invite her fifteen minutes earlier than the others.

"Four months?" She looked as perplexed as if she was trying to figure out the square root of pi. "Really?" She puckered her collagen-plumped lips. "Huh. Wow, it feels like much less time has

passed." Then she studied her freshly manicured nails. "What do I
know? It's so hard for me to keep track of everything. You know
how I have so much going on every day. And if life wasn't already
overwhelming, bikini season is right around the corner." She sighed
dramatically. "Oh, Jackie. If you only knew how hard Jacques was
riding me, you'd die. The man doesn't give me one moment of rest."

"I'm sure it's been rough," I replied. Thankfully, I managed
to shed a few stubborn pounds, but I still doubted I'd feel
comfortable enough in my skin this year to prance around at the club
in any of my two-piece suits. Although a high waisted one might
work, I realized as I started to walk toward my den. "Come on, let's
go. The others are all here, so we don't want to keep them waiting."

"Okey-dokey," she said as she trailed behind me.

"Mia's here, finally," I announced with more than a hint of
sarcasm in my voice when I entered the den. The ladies all stood up
to greet her. As she did last time, Mia attempted to make a grand
entrance, dramatically kissing everyone's cheeks. Finally, sensing my
annoyance, Claire, my angel, lured her to the couch with an
overflowing glass of Chardonnay.

"Where is your little friend?" Mia asked me right after she
took her first swallow of wine.

"Do you mean Donna?" I asked, even though she was the
only woman missing today that was present at our first meeting.

"Yeah, that one," Mia said before she took another swig of
wine. "She's usually, like, your shadow. I'm surprised she's not
sitting on the edge of your sofa, gearing up to hang on your every
word like a loyal puppy dog."

"Mia," Claire warned, raising her brows.

"What?" Mia asked. She placed her glass on the wood table.
She didn't even bother to use one of the coasters or cocktail napkins I
had artfully arranged. Trisha must have seen me cringe because she
placed a napkin under the glass. Mia didn't seem to notice the action
because she was too busy eyeballing Claire. "Why are you so testy?
All I asked was where she was?"

Trisha and Aimee stared at their laps. Stacey jumped in.
"Sometimes, I swear you need a muzzle, Mia."

Mia let out a slow, deep breath. "Shoot me for speaking my

mind. Wow, why so sensitive? Is it everyone's time of the month or something?" Mia covered her mouth when she realized she was the only one who found her joke amusing. "Sorry, I just wanted to lighten up the mood here. I'll try and behave. Seriously, where is Dina anyway?"

I cleared my throat. "Donna."

"Dina, Donna." She waved her hands as if she were swatting away a fly.

"Donna is home. The girls are getting over a stomach bug, and she didn't want them to spread any germs to the other children."

Mia dramatically wiped imaginary sweat from the top of her brow with the back of her hand. "Phew. Good move, Dina! The last thing I need right now is to have Melissa get sick all over my house. I just had new carpeting installed in our den. Who wants to see a picture?" She pulled her phone out of her Prada purse and passed it around.

"Beautiful, Mia," I said. Her room was so much more my style than my own house.

"Thanks." She put her phone back in her handbag. "So I'm confused. I get why the kids are home but why isn't Dina here today? Doesn't she have a nanny to stay with them?"

"No. She doesn't," I stated as a matter of fact.

"Oh, my god," Mia exclaimed. "How quaint! Does she think we have been magically transported back to 1985 or something?" She traced the rim of her glass with her finger. "Wow! In this day and age, in a town like Forest River, what woman in her right mind doesn't have hired help, at least during the first few months? I can't even imagine what her life must be like."

"I think it is sweet," Claire said.

"Sure, you do, honey." Mia winked. "That's why you're here, looking like a million bucks, sipping Chardonnay with us while your nanny is burping Chloe and folding Kevin's tighty-whities at your house."

I folded my arms across my chest. "I think Donna's approach to motherhood is great. Let's face facts. The first few months are the most critical period of a baby's life. I admire her for choosing not to have help."

I hoped my righteous indignation was convincing. As far as I was aware, no one else knew the truth. Months ago, Donna arranged for an au pair to come and live with the Warrens' for the first three months of the baby's life. Then, without so much as a discussion, about a week before she delivered, Thomas cancelled the contract. She was shocked and hurt, and initially expressed her frustration and outrage to me. As quickly as she showed me her true feelings, she clammed up. Then, not only did she cover up her feelings, she pretended she was pleased with her husband's change of plans. She begged me to keep her secret, which I have done, and will continue to do. With the exception of her sister flying in from Chicago to stay with her to help for the first week and a half, she's been on her own. I've tried to be as supportive as possible, including covering all carpool duties and having Christie come over to the house a few days a week.

"Of course, you'd defend your friend. But come on. You have the amazing Brittany at your disposal. It's a good thing I love you, Jackie, because otherwise I would have stolen her away months ago." Mia absently twirled a lock of hair around her index finger. "I'm sure your friend thinks she's noble going it alone. But in reality, look at all she's allowed to fall by the wayside in the process. You know full well she has been incapable of keeping up with her day-to-day duties. She hasn't handled one ballet pick up or drop off in two weeks! Now if that isn't selfish, I don't know what is."

I opened my mouth to speak but Stacey interrupted. "Ladies, can we please get on track? I don't know about you all, but I have a lot of stuff I need to take care of this evening, and I don't want to spend all afternoon arguing over another mother's choices."

Trisha waved her hand. "I'll second that."

"Me too," Aimee added as she placed some mini carrots and a dollop of hummus on a plate.

"Fine," Mia said with a pout. "Tough crowd. I was just trying to make conversation. Mercury must be in retrograde or something."

"Or something." Stacey laughed. "Now let's try and focus our attention on our hostess, shall we? Jackie has called us here today to discuss something important. Let's hear what she has to say."

I took a quick sip of white wine. "Stacey and I have done a

bit of investigating, and we've discovered something very unsettling."

All the ladies, including Mia, perked up. "I'm sure you've all heard the rumors by now that the PTA board has been working diligently planning to purchase an enormous LED marquee which they want to install in front of the school's main entrance on Forest River Road."

"Yes," the women all said in unison.

As quickly as Mia's attention had come, it vanished. She yawned and pulled out her phone and started to scroll. "Ugh, old news. Boring! I thought this meeting was going to be about the Spring Fling. Parties are fun. Please remind me why I'm here?"

"The free wine?" Claire said as she topped off Mia's glass.

"Oh, yeah. This is very good by the way." She snapped a picture of the label with her phone before she took a sip.

I reached over for the hot pink folders I had placed earlier on the table and distributed them to each woman.

Claire, Trisha, and Aimee eagerly flipped through the pages. Mia's face fell. "There are a lot of words here. Can you summarize for me? Please?"

I caught Stacey's eye. "Sure," I said. "Mia nailed it. This subject should have been put to sleep a lifetime ago. Talk about erecting a marquee outside the school has gone on for years, almost eighteen years to be exact."

"Really?" Aimee asked.

"Yes. Looking back, when the notion first was discussed, the sign would have been a valuable tool for our community. After all, back then, we barely had any technology at our disposal to alert parents of the comings and goings at our school."

"True"—Trisha nibbled on a fingernail—"but in today's day and age, what is the real point for the sign? Between emails, text messages, Facebook groups, Instagram, Twitter, and WhatsApp, we are bombarded with information. Why do we need a huge, expensive LED sign also?"

"Exactly," Stacey said. "The usefulness of this type of equipment diminished year after year."

Aimee raised her hand. "If this has been in the works for so many years, why wasn't the project ever completed? And why are we moving forward now?"

"Excellent questions, Aimee." I was glad most of the woman seemed engaged. "In your packets, you will find the copies of the competitive bids the PTA received."

Claire let out a slow, low whistle. "Holy cow! I think my parents' first starter house cost less money."

"I know! And remember, this is just the estimated cost of the project," I added. "If you've ever done construction at your home, you know you must have a buffer of money available for the unexpected incidentals that inevitably pop up."

"Does the PTA even have this much cash available?" Trisha asked.

"Yes," Stacey jumped in. "They do because they've hoarded the funds and spent the bare minimum on the children." She took a sip of wine. "Do I need to remind you about the lame presents they handed out during the holidays?"

"No." Aimee shook her head. "Chad broke that cheap bank fifteen seconds after he brought it home."

"This is ridiculous." Claire crossed her arms. "I could think of about a thousand better uses for this money."

"Me too," I said. "I am equally outraged. The thought of all of this hard-earned money going down the drain for a vanity project infuriates me. Pamela and the current PTA—" Stacey cleared her throat loudly. "Sorry. Pamela and *most* of the current PTA have designed the sign so it will feature all of their names. They want *their legacy* to live on."

"Legacy? Talk about ego"—and Mia burst out laughing.

Trisha said, "We can't sit idly by and let them do this."

"You tell us what you need us to do, and we'll handle it," Claire chimed in.

I turned my attention to the one silent woman and said, "I'm so happy to see everyone so on board and enthusiastic to help."

Mia frowned. "I miss the good old days when I had friends who were satisfied with the simple pleasures in life like going for a manicure and pedicure, instead of crusading. Fine. I guess I can do a little something, too. You are such a menace, Jackie. Do you ever *not* get your way?"

"Rarely." I smirked. "But when the stakes are high, I never back down." And to myself I thought, "One day, my tenacity will be her   saving   grace   or   her   worst   nightmare."

CHAPTER THIRTY
THEN
APRIL
One Week Later

To: All Forest River Elementary Parents
From: Forest River Elementary School Principal, Harrison Owen Williams, Jr.
Date: 04/3 @ 1:42 PM

Subject: Anticipating the Storm

Greetings and Salutations Parents and Guardians,

By now, you're all aware of the nor'easter threatening to wreak havoc on Forest River and the surrounding towns. As reported, experts expect gale force winds, coastal flooding, and rainfall in excess of two inches per hour for a twenty-two-hour period, beginning mid-morning tomorrow.

To err on the side of caution, we have decided to heed the meteorologists' warnings. Pursuant to the school district, all Forest River Schools will be closed tomorrow and the following day.

While we pray for the best, we must prepare for the worst.

I urge all Forest River families to take the predictions seriously. Avoid the roads for all non-essential travel. Make sure you have at least three days of food and water, and a first aid kit available. Also, be prepared for a loss of power. I have attached a workbook of fun activities you can do with your children in the event you find yourselves without power. Please review and print out prior to the storm.

If anyone has any further questions, or concerns, please reach out to me directly.

Stay safe. Stay home. Stay smart.

Sincerely,

Harrison Owen Williams, Jr.
Principal, Forest River Elementary School

Headset in my ear, I opened my SubZero refrigerator and pulled out the bag of broccoli and head of garlic I had picked up at the grocery store earlier this afternoon. I expected the place to be busier than usual, but it was like walking through a war zone. Even though a few hours passed since I peeled away from the parking lot, I was still a bit twitchy from the antics I witnessed.

Yes, I understood a storm was brewing, but no one announced there was a remote possibility of the world coming to an end. People I witnessed were ruthless, as they grabbed everything in sight. Most of them, despite their regimes of countless hours in the gym, didn't have the upper body strength to push their overflowing carts. You think I'm kidding? Well, the paper goods aisle was decimated, with only one lonely roll of half-opened toilet paper remaining on the shelf. And when I thought things could not get worse, I watched as two middle-aged ladies practically got into a brawl over the last box of strawberry Pop-Tarts. The store's manager had to physically separate the two before there was bloodshed. I seriously worried the experience might have left me with a touch of post-traumatic stress disorder.

"Want a good laugh?" I asked Donna as soon as she answered the phone.

"Sure, I can use one." She sounded exhausted.

I began to peel the garlic. "Seconds after Harry sent out the email about the school closure, Mia Montgomery called me. She asked if Hayley was up for a slumber party. At first, I was shocked and excited at the same time since I can't remember the last time Mia invited kids over to her house. Yet alone for a sleepover, but —"

"But before you could even reply, she told you she'd drop Melissa and her overnight bag off by five-fifteen?" Donna snorted.

"Yes, how did you know?"

"Because Mia made the rounds. She even called me! I was probably her last resort, though. I just hung up with her, telling her I had a lot on my plate and I couldn't help. The poor woman, she sounded so desperate. I almost felt sorry for her."

"You have a big heart, Donna Warren." I began to dice the garlic.

"Yeah, I try. Seriously, I don't think I will ever understand the woman. She's sure a piece of work. Oh, and by the way, thanks for defending me at the meeting."

I almost cut myself. "What do you mean?" I never mentioned Mia's snide comments to Donna. I didn't want to hurt her feelings.

"I bumped into Claire yesterday at the dry cleaners. She gave me a play-by-play."

"Oh, sorry. You need to take everything that comes out of Mia's mouth with a grain of salt."

"Yeah, you're right." Donna let out a deep sigh. "Thanks for not sharing any details."

"I'd never talk out of school. I'd never repeat anything you told me in confidence," I said.

"Thanks." She let out a slow whistle. "If Mia had a real problem, I don't think she'd be able to cope."

"I know. It's crazy. I can't believe how she must have worked trying to pawn off her kids for the next couple of days. I wonder what she has going that she doesn't want them around? She probably just wants someone else to entertain them so she can concentrate on Jacques. Knowing her, she probably asked him to sleep at the house instead of risking missing a session." I paused. "I probably shouldn't admit it, but I'm excited about the storm."

After almost a month in Forest River, Stan and Joan returned to Florida last week. While I missed my mother-in-law, it was a relief not to have the added worry about her facing the storm, even though physically, she was doing better than she expected. I added, "As far as I'm concerned, the bad weather is a great excuse for some family bonding. Scott even arranged to work from home, which he never does."

Donna met my comment with silence.

I tapped my headset. "Are you still there? Did I lose you?"

"No. Sorry, I'm here." She sniffed loudly. "I wish I felt the same way as you do. You're so strong. I'm freaking out over here."

I put my knife down and sat down at the island. "Why? What's wrong?"

"Everything." She paused. "Never mind, it's nothing. Forget I said anything."

"Are you crazy? I can't forget it, and I won't. I'm your friend. Tell me what's troubling you."

She exhaled deeply again. "Christie is still scared of thunder and lightning, which is manageable under normal circumstances. But then, there's Julia who spends most of her waking hours screaming at the top of her lungs. And while dealing with those two won't be a cakewalk, I can handle that in my sleep. What I'm not so sure about is everything else that might accompany this storm. You know, we live on one of the lowest streets in all of Forest River. If the weather is anything like they predict, and the river surges, we'll probably flood. I fear our first floor may be damaged, especially if we lose power, and our sump pumps can't run."

I crinkled my face. "Didn't you get a generator? Thomas grilled Scott about ours every time they spent more than thirteen seconds together. I believe Scott even got the name of the contractor who installed ours from your husband."

The frustration in her voice was palatable. "Yeah, Thomas talked about getting one until he was blue in the face. He was supposed to schedule a time with the contractor to meet, but did he? No! You know how that goes. Everything else took priority." She groaned. "And speaking of Thomas...he refused to cancel his business trip as I begged him to do last night. He's conveniently in Cincinnati now and isn't due back home until Tuesday afternoon. I'm left handling everything on my own, as usual."

I clenched my fists. On the surface, it seemed as if Donna

and Thomas had a rock-solid union, but, now and again, my friend allowed the cracks in their relationship to show. What I saw in those moments broke my heart. Donna was a beautiful woman, inside and out. She was a wonderful wife and mother who put her husband and family first every day. Unfortunately, I noticed he didn't seem to return the favor. I'd never say anything, but I've suspected for quite a while that he cheated on her.

"Well, this time, you're not flying solo," I said.

"What do you mean? I always am." She sounded so defeated.

"No, you're not. You're going to pack a bag right now and head over here with the girls. I'm making my chicken francese almondine with sautéed broccoli. We'll have a delicious dinner and then we will ride out the storm together. It will be like a party."

"Oh, yeah," she said. "The Warren girls will be a barrel of laughs. You're sweet, Jackie, but you and Scott need our drama like a hole in the head."

"We do!" I exclaimed a bit too loudly. "You guys will keep things fun! Hayley, Brittany, and I will be bored to tears without you, especially while Scott is stuck staring at his computer all day long. Come on, and say yes. Please!"

Her laughter sounded like music to my ears. "Are you sure Scott won't mind?"

"Mind?" I scoffed. "He'll be delighted! With you keeping me company, he'll be off the hook! He can crunch numbers on his computer all day long and then watch sports at night. He'll be in heaven."

I hated to lie to Donna, but I felt my fib was necessary. I wouldn't be able to live with myself if I let her stay home alone and something happened to her or the kids. I knew Scott would understand.

CHAPTER THIRTY-ONE
THEN
APRIL
Three Days Later

"READY TO VENTURE out?" I asked as I gazed out my living room window for what felt the thousandth time in days. Once again, the meteorologists were wrong. They underestimated what felt to me like the "storm of the century." Mother Nature had raged for close to forty-eight hours, and she took all of her frustrations out on Forest River. I never thought the torrential rain and gale-force winds would stop, but finally, now glorious sunshine peeked through the thick clouds.

"If you're sure Brittany won't mind staying alone with the kids."

I left my perch and walked toward the hall closet and pulled out my bright yellow rain slicker and matching galoshes. "I'm positive." I put on my outerwear and then grabbed her coat. I handed it to her. "Shockingly, both babies are napping, and the girls are watching a movie. It'll be like a break for her," I joked.

The last few days were rough for all of us and Brittany had been a godsend. To thank her, I surprised her this morning with a plane ticket home. I knew she was dying to see her family, and so, next month, she'd be able to spend a full week with them. I also handed her a bonus check for one thousand dollars as a token of our appreciation.

Peer pressure, on occasion, could be a great motivator. When Christie saw how much fun Hayley had watching the sky light up, she must have been embarrassed to let her friend see her fear. Except for Christie's quivering lips, Donna was shocked at how well her daughter handled everything, including the loud, constant buzzing noise of our generator, which had kicked on as soon as the storm knocked out our power.

I opened the door and descended down my winding driveway with Donna at my side. She reached for my hand as I stumbled over a thick branch. "Be careful," she warned as she pointed to the left and right.

My breath hitched in my throat as I surveyed the scene. I knew there would be damage, but I didn't expect to see so much destruction. Tree limbs lined the road. A fallen maple tree crumbled my next-door neighbors' garage. And across the street, another neighbor's flooded Alfa Romeo was being hitched to a tow truck.

As Donna and I surveyed the street, I felt like we were two characters in a movie about the end of the world. The whole scene felt surreal. It was so eerie to look at my street and neighbors' homes and see so much chaos.

Donna had been on pins and needles ever since she arrived, anxious how her home would stand up to the storm. I knew I needed to be strong for my friend.

"Scott said the roads are safe enough for us to drive," I said as I walked back up my driveway toward my garage. I was thankful I had a big, colossal gas-guzzling SUV waiting for me inside.

Donna slid into my vehicle and buckled up.

My husband had headed out a half hour before to check out his parents' place. He wasn't too keen on us venturing out alone and made me promise to stay put until he surveyed the situation. I would have preferred he chauffeur us, but I knew Donna would feel more comfortable returning to her house sooner than later. She was already at her wits' end, and I didn't want to give her any more stress.

Donna's anxiety was contagious, and my stomach churned. I prayed we'd find her home in one piece. I stopped at a traffic light and gently placed my hand on her bouncing thigh. "Try to relax a little. I'm sure your house will be fine."

She avoided my gaze. "You're sure?"

"Okay. I don't have a clue. But it's only bricks and stones. You can fix anything. The condition of your home doesn't matter right now."

She turned to me and stopped chewing on her ragged fingernails.

"What's important is that you and the girls are safe and sound. Your lives are the only thing that matters right now," I said. I thought about the poor family a few towns over, who I heard on the news, died when their home caught fire.

Donna must have had the same thought. "You're right," she said, wiping a tear away from her cheek.

The light turned green, and I gradually accelerated. I drove in silence for a few minutes. I was just about to put on some music when I passed the back of the elementary school. I gasped, and Donna practically jumped out of her skin. "What?"

"Sorry." I stopped my car and pointed. Bile rose in my throat. "Look at the playground. The swing set ripped out of the ground."

Donna closed her eyes and whimpered. I didn't want to prolong her agony one second longer than necessary, so I pulled away, reaching her house a few minutes later.

Before I had a chance to put my SUV in park, she reached for the door handle. I thrust out my arm in front of her. "Wait. Remember, no matter what we find inside, we're in this together. You are not alone. Okay?"

Her eyes once again filled with tears, and I wanted to kick Thomas in the nuts with my pointiest shoes for not canceling his business trip. Donna leaned over and gave me a quick hug. "You are a good friend, Jackie."

I gave her a sad smile. I opened my door. "Come on, let's go." I was thankful I wore my tall galoshes, as her driveway resembled a lake. There must have been about a foot of standing water.

Despite her apparent rush, Donna froze when she reached the front door. It was as if she was petrified to put her key into the lock. Once again, I mentally cursed Thomas for leaving her in this predicament. What would she have done if I hadn't insisted they stay with us?

"Give it to me." I grabbed the keys out of her hands. "I can go and check everything first if you want."

"No. I'll be okay."

"Let's do this then!" I twisted the doorknob. I flipped on the hallway lights, and not surprisingly, they didn't work. Fortunately, enough sunlight shined through the windows, so we didn't have to use the flashlights I brought from home. A quick peek showed that the entranceway and living room were in the same pre-storm condition.

"Ugh." I clutched my throat as I fought the urge to retch, assaulted by the stench.

"It smells like rotten eggs and swamp." Donna cringed.

"Thank you," I mouthed after Donna quickly opened the living room windows and let some fresh air into the house. I might be strong-willed, but I couldn't help but gag. I wished I had skipped breakfast this morning. Bagels and lox had been a very bad idea.

As soon as the vile odor diluted, I marched toward the back of her home. I led the way to her sunken kitchen and dining room. We had to use our flashlight to see as the blinds were drawn in this part of the house. To reach these rooms, we had to descend three small steps. "We've got a flood," I announced. Murky river water reached the bottom step and filled the two rooms.

"Oh, my god!" Donna gasped as she pushed me to the side so she could get a better look. "Everything is ruined."

"Everything is repairable, remember?"

"Yeah, I guess," she mumbled. "I'm going to call Thomas."

I watched as the light drained out of her eyes when he didn't answer the phone. Instead of leaving him a voicemail, she sent him a text. I wish I knew what she wrote. After she slipped her phone into the pocket of her coat, she stood frozen in place like a deer in headlights, so I did what I do best. I took charge. I began to bark orders rapid fire, which she obediently obeyed.

In less than two hours, we snapped at least seventy-five photos of the damage, threw out the spoiled contents of her refrigerator and freezer, and relocated anything salvageable from her kitchen's bottom cabinets to the countertops and her dining room table. Then as I made Donna search for information on her homeowner's insurance, I packed a suitcase with a weeks' worth of clothes for her and the girls since I insisted that they stay with us, at least until Thomas came home, and they had other living arrangements.

When we returned to my SUV, I first scrolled through my text messages before starting my engine. I was so relieved Scott texted his parents' home was unscathed except for a fallen elm tree in their backyard.

I put the SUV in reverse and pulled out of Donna's driveway. "Well, that was fun." I never needed a shower so badly in my life.

"Yep. A real blast." Donna opened up the window and turned on the radio.

"So, I have some good news for you." I lowered the volume. "While we were working inside, I had Scott make some calls for me, and you're all set."

"All set with what?"

"The clean-up, silly. He arranged for a restoration company his parents once used after a pipe burst in their basement. They are set to come to your place on Sunday morning. Joan raved they were terrific, and she's pretty critical when it comes to customer service. Anyway, they'll pump out the remaining water, remove the saturated sheetrock, sanitize everything, and then use industrial-strength fans to dry everything."

"Oh, that's sweet of Scott to do, but I don't know."

I gripped my steering wheel so tightly my knuckles turned white. "Don't know about what?"

"Thomas won't be happy. He likes to handle everything with the house himself."

I glanced over at her. "And how did that work out for you with the generator? Did he even bother to text you back yet?"

She pinched the bridge of her nose and closed her eyes. "No."

My heart pounded like a reggae drum. I prided myself for watching what I said about someone's spouse, but this time there was no way I could control my tongue. And if she didn't like what I had to say, so be it. I refused to remain silent.

"If Thomas wanted to be involved, he shouldn't have left you to deal with everything on your own. You can't wait for him to stroll back to the state before you take action. You have two daughters to worry about. You can't sit idly by and let your home fill with mold. Scott called in some favors to get this appointment quickly. If you cancel, god only knows how long you'll have to wait for another company to show up."

"You're right, but—"

"But nothing. You need to start to stand up for yourself. And if you won't, I will."

CHAPTER THIRTY-TWO
THEN
APRIL
Three Weeks Later

JOAN AND STAN returned to Forest River a couple of weeks ahead of schedule. Thankfully, my prayers were answered. My mother-in-law was doing fantastic. Her test results were excellent. Her hair had begun to grow in and she put on some much-needed pounds. She started to resemble once again the beautiful woman I adored. Who was I kidding? Even when she was at her sickest, she never allowed anyone to see her vulnerable side.

Joan decided it was essential for Scott and me to take a mini vacation alone. Despite my objections, she wouldn't take no for an answer. She flew back home without warning, intent on having the girls spend a long weekend at her place. I had learned a long time ago arguing with her was a useless exercise. So rather than fight, I packed our bags, and I reserved a waterfront suite for Scott and me at Gurney's Inn in Montauk.

Between the romantic, long walks on the beach, the therapeutic spa treatments, and the delicious meals we devoured, we felt like new people. Joan, as usual, had been one hundred and ten percent on the money. My husband and I had been in desperate need of some alone time. Except for missing my daughters, I wished we had been able to stay away from Forest River longer.

I won't try and sugarcoat anything. The past few weeks had been emotionally and physically draining for both of us. Donna and her girls ended up staying with us for almost two weeks. Thanks to Scott, their home was repaired quickly, but it took forever for their power to be restored. As Donna feared, Thomas didn't take kindly to the fact that he wasn't consulted about how to handle the house. In fact, he flat out refused our offer to stay with his family and us. I don't know who he thought he was punishing by being so obstinate. He was the one who had to suffer and live in a construction zone without electricity.

Donna and Thomas had several wicked fights, which I witnessed firsthand. I felt horrible I had contributed to their marital discord, but I didn't regret any of my actions. If faced with the same situation, I wouldn't change a thing.

And while Hayley loved having her best friend living in our home, a part of me worried Donna and the girls would become too comfortable and never go home. Thankfully, Thomas came to his senses and apologized to Donna, and us. He admitted his behavior was juvenile, and he also acknowledged it would have been a mistake for Donna to have waited for him to return home to make repairs.

While I appreciated that Thomas was man enough to say he was wrong, I did lose respect for him. I made sure to keep my feelings to myself. As far as Donna knew, I was back on Team Thomas.

Thomas wasn't the only person whose temper was out of control these days. My grandmother said you learned people's true colors during difficult times. And the storm truly brought out the worst in so many people. There had been so many disagreements between so-called best friends that I couldn't keep track of who was still on speaking terms. And to make matters worse, the seed the ladies and I planted in the community about the PTA's vanity project transformed into practically a full-blown war after the playground suffered so much damage in the storm.

"I should have taken two Advil before coming here tonight," I said, massaging my throbbing temples. I sat sandwiched between Donna and Claire in the elementary school's auditorium. We arrived early at the emergency meeting and were lucky to score seats. Trisha and Aimee stood in the back in a kindergarten mom cluster. Mia managed to find a seat in the middle of the room, but it appeared her attendance was for show. Every time I glanced her way, her focus was on her phone.

"Stacey warned me things could get ugly,' Claire said. "Yet I never expected people to be so passionate—and brutal."

Donna glanced at her watch. "Or ramble on for so long! What is wrong with people? They're acting like it's Principal Williams's fault that there might not be a playground for months."

"I think it is more than that," I said, as yet another mother approached the microphone. She flicked her long blonde hair over her shoulder and faced the principal and the school board on the stage. Our esteemed PTA members were also on the stage, but they sat off to the side. I think they were seated there as a sign of unity, their leader not waiving from her personal agenda once.

Principal Williams raised his hand and said, "Please introduce yourself first."

She cleared her throat and smoothed down her skirt. "Sorry. Hello, my name is Adrian Atkins, and I am the mother of Aiden and Adam, two third graders in Mrs. Floyd's class." She rocked in place as she spoke, a bundle of nervous energy. "I am vehemently opposed to proceeding with the LED sign's purchase and installation. While I originally was neutral about this issue, my opinion changed dramatically over the last few weeks." Her voice grew louder with every word she uttered. "Installing this sign, at this time, would be a slap in the face to every student. The sign offers no benefit to the children! Zero!"

Cheers of support reverberated through the auditorium, and Adrian stood taller. With the apparent support, she railed on. "Not only is it in poor taste to begin construction now, I feel it's an insult to every single child who enters this building. Are you trying to tell our kids that a sign, a sign that is no longer vital, that is simply a grandiose shrine to someone's ego, is more important than what would contribute to their happiness?" She paused. "What message are we trying to send these impressionable minds?"

Pamela looked like she was about to blow a gasket. I poked Donna to make sure she saw what I did.

Pamela propped her elbows on the table. "How many times do I have to say the same thing? For the millionth time, one thing has nothing to do with another. What is wrong with you people?"

"You people?" Adrian fired back. "Why don't you shut up?

No one is interested in your opinion anymore. How dare you act all high and mighty! Last time I checked, I was addressing the school board, not you. I"—she turned around to face the spectators—"and every person in this room deserves the right to speak our minds!"

The crowd erupted in applause as Pamela sat back. "Well, I am the PTA president."

"Well, you are a self-centered witch."

"Ms. Atkins, please"—Harry held up his hands—"refrain from name calling. You've already had your chance to be heard. Thank you for voicing your concern."

Adrian realized she had officially been dismissed and turned away from the podium. Harry continued. "I know I speak for everyone. It's wonderful to see our parents and guardians so engaged and passionate about this issue. As I've said many times, everyone has a right to speak. We have rehashed the same argument for"—he glanced at his watch—"over two hours. Moving forward, I respectfully request you refrain from revisiting the same arguments that were already made by others." He smiled as several members of the audience clapped. "Thank you. Now, if anyone has something constructive to add, please step forward."

Stacey glanced at me from her seat on the stage, and our eyes met for a quick second. She had predicted her brother-in-law would lose his patience and utter these exact words. Clearly, this wasn't the first time an open meeting went off the rails.

"Wish me luck," I whispered to Claire and Donna as I rose to my feet.

In my excitement, I missed the second step that led to the podium. The audience gasped as I practically went flying before I grabbed the wood railing. I dropped a few sheets of paper in the process, and I felt the heat rise to my face as I bent down to pick up my notes. Somewhat composed, I began to speak but instead of my voice projecting through the room, loud feedback disturbed everyone's ears. I wanted the ground to swallow me whole as I figured out how to adjust the microphone.

"Well, I guess I have everyone's attention now. Sorry," I said sheepishly as I tried to regain my confidence. "Good evening, Principal Williams and esteemed school board members. My name is

Jackie Martin, and I am the mother of a kindergartener in Ms. Anderson's class and one of the organizers of the Spring Fling. I feel it is important for me to preface my comments by admitting that I have been vehemently opposed to the erection of the sign even before the storm.

"For those who know me, I'm not quiet or shy. I tend to be quite vocal.

"Call me naïve, but I'm a firm believer that all money raised for the school should benefit our children in a meaningful way. I can't fathom how a sign enhances their educational or leisure experience. I know this is just my opinion. I am just a kindergarten mom, as the PTA president has pointed out many times over the past few months." As the crowd chuckled, the color drained from Pamela's face. "So I'd rather stick to the facts, if I may?"

"Yes, please do," Principal Williams said. "We appreciate facts."

To my delight, Pamela Peterson didn't even attempt to hide her grimace.

"I think the parents in attendance tonight have done a wonderful job of expressing their outrage that the playground will take months to be restored." I placed my hand on my heart. "As I said, I have a young daughter, so I understand their frustration. I have also researched how capital projects like this work." I glanced at the sheet of paper. Even though I knew the information printed on the page like the back of my hand, consulting my notes gave me the reassurance I needed. "Unless the district has excess unreserved cash, which according to the budget, ours doesn't, the district would have to borrow funds to cover the project's cost. As a result, taxpayer money would have to be used to pay the interest on a bond or BAN, potentially for years."

"That is correct," a board member said.

"What's a BAN?" Pamela whispered to Stacey without first covering her microphone.

As Stacey frowned, I faced the PTA president. "It's a bond anticipation note." I focused my attention back on the administration. "While borrowing is common practice, our situation has a slight twist. In this case, the required restoration is a result of a storm. We all know this wasn't a normal storm. This storm was part of a declared state of emergency. From what I gleaned online, it appears the district has already filed a claim with FEMA and expects to receive reimbursement from the agency, which will cover the playground's full replacement cost. Is that correct?"

Several board members nodded their heads, and Pamela looked constipated.

I plowed forward. "From what I researched, when an emergency is declared, it takes much longer to receive funds from the agency since they have so many claims to address. Also, I read, there is no way to know the timing of the payment. It could take weeks or, more likely, months for the money to reach us, which is why you warned we might not have a fully functioning playground next year, correct?"

Again several school board members nodded their agreement.

"Oh, please. Can you get to your point already?" Pamela said loudly.

"Sorry, Pam. I just wanted to confirm my understanding of the facts first. I like to make sure I have all my facts straight before I speak. I wouldn't want to make a fool of myself."

I heard a slight ripple of laughter from the audience, and I smiled.

"So, getting back to my point," I said when the crowd calmed down. "Right now, the pressing problem is the playground. As far as I could tell from my research, there is no rule or regulation to prevent the school from utilizing the PTA's funds to restore the playground. Then, when the FEMA money is received, the school can reimburse the PTA. This way, the children will have a playground much sooner without the district having to incur unnecessary interest expenses. Also, since the sign issue is such a hot topic, the unavoidable delay would provide the stakeholders with additional time to mull over all the facts so they could properly decide if the purchase is a wise usage of PTA raised money or not. In my humble opinion, my plan is a win-win solution for our children."

"I agree!" Donna cheered. I was so thankful for her support.

"Me too," Claire called out.

I turned around toward the audience as more and more people followed my friends' lead and stood up, showing their agreement.

"We need change!" Someone, who I think was Aimee, yelled.

As parents began to chant "change, change, change," I returned my attention to the principal and the school board members. Most had satisfied grins on their face, which I took as a sign of their support. My heart filled with pride as I felt my efforts this year made a difference. I might have begun my fight months ago, but right now I felt like I finally found my stride.

I looked at Pamela and the look she gave me sent chills down my spine.

CHAPTER THIRTY-THREE
THEN

DONNA, CLAIRE, Aimee, Trisha, and I stood in a circle near the gate to the school's parking lot right after the meeting ended. Stacey didn't dare linger with us. Mia snuck out of the auditorium as Principal Williams made his closing remarks; it was a rude move but typical—and brilliant! She avoided the crazy traffic jam of cars attempting to leave the parking lot all at once.

My friends and I were not in any rush to leave the premises. I had no desire to fight my way through the madness to reach my car, and besides, I wanted to rehash the evening with my friends.

"Jackie!" Someone called my name, and I turned around.

"Hi, Elaine." I smiled at the petite mom. I mentally patted myself on the back for being able to recall her name so quickly. We had met briefly, right after the Mothers' Social at the club. I think she said she had a daughter in the same class as Stacey's and Mia's sons. "How are you?"

"Fine, thanks." She gestured to my friends—"Sorry, I don't want to interrupt your conversation, but I did want to applaud you for what you did in there. You have chutzpah, and you brought a much-needed, fresh perspective."

I squeezed her arm gently. "Thanks so much. You're so sweet. I appreciate your kind words."

"My pleasure." She paused and looked over her shoulder. "Um, do you think I can steal you away for a second? I have something I want to ask you in private."

"Sure." I turned to Donna, who stood at my side. "I'll be right back."

Elaine and I walked a few feet away to a quiet spot. "You

have my attention, so shoot."

Elaine once again glanced around the schoolyard. She seemed on edge. "The parents were right in there. Our school needs a change, and fast."

I puckered my lips. "Yeah, I couldn't agree more."

She furrowed her brow. "I know. It's sad. Change is long overdue. Parents have not been happy with the status quo for more years than I can count. You know how it goes. Everyone is quick to complain, but no one wants to do any work or offer any constructive solutions to a problem."

"Yeah, I know and when people step up to volunteer, they are turned away." I frowned. "It is very frustrating. If I live to a thousand, I will never understand the mentality."

"I had a hunch you'd say that, which was why I asked to speak with you. You see, not only am I good friends with Stacey"— she winked—"I'm also on the PTA nomination committee, along with two of my friends"—and she nodded toward two ladies huddled by the fence. "The process has been nothing more than a paper-pushing formality for the past few years. No parent has expressed one iota of interest in taking a position of power. Everyone would much rather bitch and moan instead of act. Don't get me wrong, I'm not trying to judge anyone. I know I'm also guilty."

"Okay…"

Elaine eyed me directly. "You're different than the others, Jackie. You don't sit idly by and wait for results. You are a change agent! And I am talking more than just organizing events. You're new to the school, but you have already made quite the name for yourself, and fast! I've noticed everything you've done, and so have many others. You are tough, smart, strong, disciplined, and caring. You genuinely appear interested to pitch in and help make Forest River Elementary School a better place. If you're half as sincere as you claim to be, and if you are willing to work hard for our children, my friends and I have the power to make it happen."

My stomach fluttered, and my heart raced, but I refused to show my eagerness. "How?" I thought back to the email Pamela sent me when she dangled the potential to join the PTA board in my face like an unobtainable carrot.

"As I said, I am on the nomination committee. In a couple of days, I will be sending out the emails to get the ball rolling. Change is possible. All it will take is a few phone calls from my friends and me and, like that"—she snapped her fingers—"you and your team will be on the ballot. Jackie, this could be your moment. Would you like that?"

I felt an adrenaline rush as I looked at the school. "Yes, I'm game, Elaine. Let's do this! Make your magic happen."

She clutched her hands in front of her chest. "You won't regret this," she said. "So, tell me, if you had your choice, who would you pick as your treasurer and secretary?"

CHAPTER THIRTY-FOUR
THEN
APRIL
A Couple Of Days Later

To: Forest River Elementary School Parents
From: Elaine Poole
Date: 04/29 @ 6:42 PM

Subject: PTA Nominations

Hello Parents and Guardians!

Can you believe it? It's that time of year again, where we must reflect on the past few months and look forward to the future.

Come on, people! Let's make magic happen this year! Don't be shy! Speak up! Let your voices be heard! Our children need you.

The new school year is right around the corner, and the PTA of Forest River Elementary School is once again seeking individuals who are willing to serve as leaders on the executive board.

Officers included in this election:

Mandatory Officers (Check all that apply):

President

Recording Secretary

Treasurer

Non-Mandatory Officers (Check all that apply):

Vice President

Corresponding Secretary

Executive Officer

Nomination Process: To nominate yourself or someone else, for any of the open positions, please write a short letter of intent or recommendation. Submit your nominations by email to ForestRiverPTA_Elected Officers_Nominations@gmail.com or submit in person to Elaine Poole, Sophia George or Lynn Andrews.

To stay up to date on the nominations visit our website - ForestRiver_PTA_Nominations.com. The nominations will be logged and uploaded to the site in real time!

Deadline to submit is May 7.

All parents and guardians are eligible to hold office unless they are employees of the school.

As a reminder, the election will be held on May 12 in the school gymnasium between the hours of 7:30–11:45 AM. If you are unable to be present for the voting process, absentee ballots can be provided upon request.

Important! If you intend to take advantage of an absentee ballot, you MUST have your signature notarized before submitting in a sealed envelope. Failure to do so will result in your vote being disqualified.

Thank you!
Elaine Poole, Sophia George or Lynn Andrews

"How are you holding up?" Donna asked as soon as I answered the phone.

"What do you mean?" I spread mustard on a slice of bread as I prepared Hayley's lunch for tomorrow.

"The PTA nominations, silly." She groaned. "I just checked the website and saw only Pamela and her pals' names were listed. I know you got your hopes up after your chat with Elaine. I'm sorry if it was all for nothing."

I placed three slices of low sodium turkey breast on the bread and then began to slice a tomato. "So you've been obsessively hitting refresh on the website too?"

"How could I not?" Donna replied. "I was part of this plan of yours too."

As soon as Elaine and I finished our conversation, I rushed back to my friends and reported our conversation, practically verbatim. The ladies took the news in stride when I admitted how I offered them up to serve on the PTA with me. Sure they all seemed excited to be part of a change at school, but I worried if they were sincere. I knew I had put Donna, Claire, Aimee, and Trisha on the spot when I informed them how I *volunteered* them. When I rehashed the story with Joan the next morning, I realized, even though they had been extremely supportive of all my efforts related to the school, I should never have broken the news to them all at once. It would have been uncomfortable for one of them to back out or express their lack of interest with the others seeming so supportive and eager.

"True."

"Are you sure you are feeling okay?" Her voice raised a few octaves.

"Yeah, why wouldn't I be?" I wrapped the sandwich in plastic wrap.

"You seem so calm. I was convinced you'd be a wreck by now with the uncertainty. I know you'd love to be more involved, but it will be a huge responsibility. Maybe it is all for the best if it doesn't work out."

I placed the knife in the sink and closed my eyes. "Donna, do you not want to serve on the PTA?"

"What?" she gasped.

"You heard me. Do you not want to participate? Please tell me the truth. I know I pull you into doing a lot of things that maybe you wouldn't choose to do on your own…"

"It's a moot point anyway. We haven't been nominated. Elaine made you a bunch of empty promises."

I sat down at the island in my kitchen. "I don't believe she did. It's only been two days since she sent out her email. I have full faith the site will look completely different in a day or so."

"Really? You do?"

"Yes. I'm fully confident we will be on the ballot." Elaine had called me earlier in the day to let me know nominations with our names were rolling in fast and furiously. She swore me to secrecy when she shared her plan on waiting a few days before she posted our names on the site. She wanted to give her friends sufficient time to contact more people and sing our praises.

"Oh."

"Please answer my question, Donna. Do you want to participate in the PTA or not? If you aren't interested, don't worry. I understand public service isn't for everyone. There is no reason to feel ashamed or pressured. No one, not me or any of the members of the nomination committee, has the power to force anyone to join the PTA. Just because your peers nominated you, doesn't mean you have to be part of the election process. Before the vote, the committee members will call everyone who was nominated and provide them with the opportunity to decline the initiation. So please, be honest with me. Do you want to be part of my team?"

CHAPTER THIRTY-FIVE
THEN
MAY
A Week Later

To: Jacqueline A. Martin
From: Stacey Williams
Date: 05/06 @ 7:30 AM

Subject: Fwd: WTF is happening here?????

Hey Future President!

I'm getting sooooo excited! I know you are too!

And not only about the Spring Fling, which is right around the corner!
I figured you'd get a kick out of this message...
Let the games begin!!!!

XO,
S

BTW – I hope I live long enough to work with you. I'm worried when Pamela realizes I've jumped ship and have been working behind the scenes to support you she'll probably skin me alive. ☺

To: Forest River PTA Members
To: Pamela Peterson, Forest River President
Date: 5/6 @ 2:37 AM

Subject: WTF is happening here?????

Ladies,
Someone please tell me what is going on here? NOW! How could something like this happen????

As usual, after drifting off for an hour, I woke up wired. I twisted, turned, and then I caved and popped a Xanax. As I waited for the power of the pill to kick in, I picked up my phone to distract my stressed-out mind. Well, that didn't work!

As soon as I unlocked the phone, I found myself on the PTA Nominations webpage. Out of habit, I clicked refresh. I didn't expect any data to change. I know we own the PTA! No one in their right mind would be foolish enough to want to go up against me (oh, and you guys too - LOL).
I should have known once Elaine sent out her email, the witch wouldn't be able to resist. Jackie Martin is a vulture, lusting for power, and we must STOP her!
And to make matters worse, not only did the bitch brazenly and boldly back herself for the presidency, she had the audacity to endorse her entourage! How dare she toss these nobodies into the mix!
We need to act now and nip this insanity in the bud! While I am confident Jackie and her pals don't stand a chance in this election, I refuse to sit idly by and allow her to sway even one vote against us.
You know what to do! I don't care if you have to lie or concoct stories. We only have a week left before the election, and we need to make every second count! It is our duty to protect our rightful place of power. Forest River PTA is ours!
Pamela

I minimized my inbox, opened up Facebook. I was delighted to see my post on the Forest River Mom and Dads group had practically gone viral. In only a couple of short hours over two hundred people shared my words and there were four hundred and fifty-six mostly positive comments.

Parents and Guardians of Forest River Elementary...

I know that this has been a difficult and challenging time for many in Forest River. The storm was far worse than any of us ever expected. It saddens me deeply to know so many people are still struggling with the aftermath. I believe difficult times like these should bring us closer as a community, not further away.

I am well aware of the rumors and speculations flying around Forest River, and I want to set the record straight. Contrary to the smear campaign, Pamela Peterson has posted on various social media platforms, I have no personal agenda in my quest to join the PTA. I am simply a concerned mother who wants to offer my time, energy, and experience to help make Forest River Elementary School the best place possible for our children. I also want to help foster a sense of community for us parents and guardians, which is why I spearheaded the first Spring Fling.

I refuse to stoop to Ms. Peterson's level and attack her or her team personally or professionally. Instead, I would like to take a moment to applaud the current PTA. During their tenure, they have accomplished a lot for the school and our children. Times have changed, and our children need new energy and fresh ideas. I am confident that if you place your trust in me, you won't be disappointed. Together we can make Forest River amazing again.

As for Pamela's claims, while she clearly embellished some details (and resorted to name-calling), I am proud to say the crux of her allegations are correct:

I am a high energy multi-tasker who demands stellar results from myself as well as others. I fight hard for what I believe in, and I refuse to stay quiet when I see an injustice, even if it contradicts popular opinion. I am a workhorse, not a delegator. I get my hands dirty—there is no job I would ask anyone to do that I would not do myself. I'm detail-oriented and live by the adage "Proper planning prevents poor performance."

I believe everyone has a voice and deserves to have their voice heard. Under my leadership, Forest River Elementary School will be a democracy, not a dictatorship. Unlike the current regime, I would never turn down the assistance of any parents. Instead, I would encourage and embrace all volunteers. I learned a long time ago that teamwork makes the dream work!

When you cast your votes tomorrow, please take a moment to ponder this question. What do you want for you and your children? Do you want more of the same, or do you want creativity, determination, heart, and collaboration? I hope the latter. I know, together, we can redesign and reimagine Forest River Elementary School!

CHAPTER THIRTY-SIX
THEN
MAY
Election Day

"ARE YOU SURE your mother-in-law won't mind?" Donna asked me the same question for what felt like the thousandth time in fifteen minutes. (Brittany was in the Netherlands this week with her family. She's been having a blast, and every night since she left, texting us dozens of pictures. Surprising her with the plane tickets was probably one of the best things I did all year.)

"Stop worrying. Joan's excited to spend time with the girls," I answered honestly.

Once Joan and Stan returned to Forest River from Florida for the season, Joan was determined to make up for all the time she lost this year with Hayley and Cassidy. Her energy returned in full force, and she put it to good use. Hayley has been having the time of her life being spoiled and doted on, and Cassidy is bonding beautifully with her grandmother. Joan has also joined me on the sidelines for many of Hayley's ballet and soccer practices. And on days like today, when I needed a helping hand, Joan was ready and eager to pitch in. I probably should swipe her passport to prevent her from traveling next year.

Donna pinched the bridge of her nose. "Christie is a breeze, but Julia is a handful. She's so colicky."

I topped off her coffee cup. "Stop worrying. Joan can handle the baby. She loves to tell me how Scott spent the first six months of his life screaming his lungs out and never sleeping a wink. Thank goodness, he grew out of his temper tantrums before he met me." I snorted. "There's only room enough for one diva in this house."

Finally, Donna laughed for the first time since she arrived at my doorstep. I also knew Donna's drab mood was caused by more than the election, and I felt sorry for my friend. Since we were up for election, we needed to be at school a half-hour before the doors opened to the public. Thomas had promised Donna he would take the morning off work to stay with his children since the college girl who helped her out occasionally had a final this morning. Unfortunately, last night he sprang the news that she'd have to figure out alternate arrangements. She was embarrassed and livid, and desperate enough to turn to Mia for assistance since she was the only mom in our circle who wasn't a candidate. Even though "Dina" had bent over backward this year driving Melissa around, I'm sure you can imagine how receptive Mia had been since she had a previously scheduled training with Jacques.

When Donna finally reached out to me last night, she was borderline hysterical. It hurt how she didn't come to me first, but I could understand why she tried to make alternate arrangements on her own. Donna was such a good person, yet she allowed people to take advantage of her, over and over again. I wish she stood up for herself more; her lack of strength broke my heart.

Still, today was a big day for both of us, and we were both excited. In about an hour, the PTA election would begin. I, for one, wasn't too proud to admit I was a nervous wreck. I woke up in the middle of the night in a cold sweat. I had a nightmare that not one single person voted for us. Life would have been so much less stressful if the election was held online using a service like Survey Monkey or something. But the moms of Forest River were old school and loved an excuse to gather and kibitz in person.

The polling opened at seven-thirty in the morning. I believe they set the hours to provide an opportunity for the parents who worked outside of the home to vote before they had to head off to jobs. According to Stacey, however, most of the "working moms" took advantage of the absentee ballot option. The early bird voters instead were made up of the spandex-clad gals who spent the majority of their mornings running, spinning, or doing Pilates.

"Knock, knock!" Joan called out as she opened my front door and entered the hallway. Donna and I left the kitchen to greet her.

"Nana!" Hayley squealed as she ran toward the door with Christie trailing behind her.

"There's my brilliant girl!" Joan bent down and hugged her.

"Want to hear me sing?"

"Hi, Christie," Joan said as Hayley burst into song.

Christie waved and Joan asked, "Can I give you a hug too?"

"Yes," Christie said sheepishly and fell into Joan's embrace.

Joan waited until Hayley's number was over before she asked, "Where are your little sisters?" Christie took Joan's hand and led her to the two bassinets in the living room.

I poked Donna in the ribs. "See, stop worrying. They'll be fine. Scott will drop the girls off at school, while Joan stays here with the babies. There's only one problem"—I tilted my head in my mother-in-law's direction—"you may have to pry Julia out of Joan's hot little hands by the time we get home."

Joan stopped cooing over the babies and walked over to me and kissed me and then faced Donna. "Jackie is right, I'm going to have so much fun today with these little ones. There is no need for you two to rush home today. Enjoy your time, and cherish the moment. You've both already done amazing work so far. I have full faith the voters will do the right thing this morning. But if they don't, it will be their loss, not yours. You are both stars in my eyes. Speaking of which, I have a little something for you, Jackie."

"Oh, Joan, you shouldn't have."

She winked and then sat down on the couch. "I know, but when has it ever stopped me?" She placed her oversized Bodega Veneta bag on her lap and began to rummage through it and then pulled out a long, expertly wrapped box.

I sat down next to her and unwrapped the package. Inside I found a delicate gold necklace with a charm. I took it out of the box and held it to the light and saw she had the words "Mom Boss" engraved on the charm. "Oh, Joan. I love it," I gushed as I recalled a conversation we had right after my first parent-teacher conference when she joked and called me that name.

Joan took the necklace from my hands, and I lifted my long hair off my neck. She closed the clasp, and I turned around to face her. Her face glowed. "Perfect." She kissed my cheek once more. "Now get out of this house, you two. You have an election to win!"

***

The mood at the school was electric and the complete opposite of what I imagined, even though Stacey tried to warn me. Like many schools and municipal buildings across the country, this space served as a polling place for governmental elections. I automatically assumed the room would look similar to how it appeared when Scott and I voted for the presidential election this past November. I couldn't have been more wrong.

"Oh my god." Donna and I gasped as we approached the gym's doorway.

"Wow," Donna said in awe. "Look at this place."

I waived to Aimee and Trisha, who were already inside the room. "Elaine and her friends outdid themselves." Multicolored balloons floated around the space, and party music blasted through several speakers scattered around the room. There was even gourmet coffees and teas to sports drinks, green smoothies, gluten free muffins, yogurt, and fresh fruit stands scattered throughout the room.

Three long tables were set up in a u-shape toward the back of the gym. The first one was against the back wall and designated for the nomination committee. From their table, these ladies would sign in the voters. It was their job to ensure only one parent or guardian per household, cast a vote. The committee members also were in charge of collecting the completed ballots, which they placed into several locked mailboxes behind them. The other two tables were reserved for the candidates. We didn't have assigned seating, but Pamela and her posse filled one of the tables. My group and I sat at the other, which was great because the thought of sharing a table with Pamela right now was about as appealing as the thought of having a colonoscopy and a double root canal on the same day.

All candidates were required to be present and easily approachable if a parent had a last-minute concern or question. I had no doubt Pamela planned to use the opportunity to continue her campaigning. She wasn't going down without a fight.

After Donna and I got situated next to Aimee, Mia, and

Trisha, I walked over to one of the stands and helped myself to an iced green tea, greeting Elaine. I was careful to keep the conversation light and avoid any PTA talk. Then I headed toward my opponent.

Pamela stood against the back wall, surrounded by her team. I took care not to even glance in Stacey's direction. I kept my eyes focused on the leader of the pack. As I approached, the other women dispersed slightly, allowing me some room. I extended my right hand. With a broad smile on my face, I said, "I wanted to wish you good luck today, Pamela."

Instead of shaking my hand, like a civilized human being, Pamela dramatically crossed her arms across her chest. "I don't need luck."

"You're lucky, Pam. I wish I had your confidence. It must be so freeing to feel so secure. I've been a nervous wreck all week. I can't stop worrying no one will vote for me."

She laughed. "I guess that is what separates a true leader from a wannabe."

I fingered the new chain around my neck. "Alrighty then. I guess I just wanted to wish you well, regardless of the outcome. May the best candidate win." I locked eyes with Donna's as I began to walk away, mouthing the word "bitch."

My exchange with Pamela didn't anger me as much as it motivated me. I knew I had given this election my all from day one. I refused to rest on my laurels like the incumbent. I didn't sit like a statue during the voting process. I made sure to walk around the room often. I greeted and conversed with every person who entered. Not only did many people voice their excitement about the Spring Fling, at least fifteen women offered last minute donations. By the time the clock struck eleven forty-five, and Elaine and her crew began to usher the voters out of the gym, my jaw was killing me from smiling, and I had to pee so badly I didn't know if I could make it to the bathroom.

I returned to the room slightly out of breath from my mad dash right before Elaine closed the doors to the public.

"So, what happens now?" Aimee asked me.

I winked at the women and said, "The fun begins.

CHAPTER THIRTY-SEVEN
THEN

AS THE VENDORS packed their display tables, Elaine and her team fetched enough water bottles for all the candidates and handed them out. Once her hands were empty, Elaine looked around the room and asked, "Are you all ready to find out the results of the election?"

Pamela stood up a bit straighter and flipped her hair off her neck. I wanted to rip her smug smile off her face. She snorted and said, "I, for one, can't wait to put this experience behind me."

I considered censoring my reply for a second. But then I thought better of it, as I no longer cared about playing nice. "Really? Hmm, I honestly thought you were eager to serve another term."

Pamela seethed. "I'm counting the seconds until I can finally get you out of my hair for once and for all. This little power struggle of yours has gone on long enough. You've been nothing but a nuisance. You've stuck your nose everywhere it didn't belong. I'm sick and tired of wasting time dealing with you and your antics. After the votes are tallied, you'll finally realize what the parents of Forest River really think about you."

I jutted out my chin and raised my eyebrows in reply. I rested my hands on my hips. "I guess we'll see soon enough."

Pamela opened her mouth to speak, but before she had a chance, there was a loud knock on the gymnasium's door.

Elaine glanced at her Apple Watch and clasped her hands. "They are right on time." She opened the door and said, "Come in, come in," gesturing for the two men and one woman, all who wore impeccable business suits, to enter the room.

"Ladies, can I have your attention, please?" Elaine asked before she pointed to the taller of the two men. "I'd like to introduce you all to Jack Powers and his team. Jack is a partner in the accounting firm of Powers, Wilson, and Monroe. Their highly regarded firm audits the school district's books, as well as loads of other municipalities across the state."

"So nice to meet you all." Jack flashed a toothy grin. The three auditors began to work the room, shaking our hands. "This is Julie and Bob. They will be working with me today."

After the introductions were completed, Pamela huffed. "Why are these outsiders here?" She jabbed a finger in Elaine's direction. "You and your team have tallied the results in the past. So why did you incur this unnecessary expense?"

"Because it needed to be done. For the past few years, there had been only a couple of challengers, if any. This year"—Elaine motioned around the room—"look at all the people running. I'm not naïve. There was no way I'd risk allowing someone to claim ballot tampering or allege improper calculations in the tally if they didn't like the outcome. Bringing in impartial experts eliminates any doubts for everyone."

Pamela clenched her fists. "I didn't authorize any PTA funds to be used for this dog and pony show."

The auditors looked mortified. I'm sure they never expected this level of hostility when they signed up for a PTA gig. Elaine didn't seem fazed. "We're not using PTA money."

Pamela's face flushed. "Don't you dare tell me you are throwing taxpayers' money down the drain"—she tipped her head in my direction—"to pacify her and her pals when things don't go their way? I've known you a long time, Elaine, and I'm shocked to learn you are placating her."

I had to give Elaine credit. If I were in her shoes, I didn't think I could keep my temper in check the way she did.

Elaine said, "I think it's time you settle down now, Pamela. I appreciate you voicing your opinions and concerns, but you need not worry. The firm was compensated privately. The nomination committee has all chipped in to pay for the services." She then turned to her team members. "Won't it be nice to sit this one out and relax while the experts do their job?"

Sophia George nodded, and Lynn Andrews said,

"Absolutely."

"Excellent," Elaine said. "Jack, we'll let you get to work."

"I hope they make it snappy," Pamela mumbled half under her breath. Then louder, she added, "I don't want to have to change our reservation at Bistro Baron." Her loyal followers bobbed their heads like puppets. Regardless of the outcome, Pam would have to call the restaurant. Stacey was going to join my group for lunch.

Eventually, we all returned to our seats. The atmosphere was thick with animosity. Not one person uttered a single word. It felt surreal. Everyone's eyes were laser-focused on the auditors who shuffled papers and typed feverously on laptops. The only other sound in the room was the tick of the clock's second hand.

Finally, after what felt like a lifetime, Jack raised his arms over his head and stretched in his seat. He then glanced left and right at his teammates. "Have you both completed your calculations?"

Julie and Bob simultaneously replied. "Yes." They then closed their laptops.

"Excellent." Jack stared at his screen for a few moments before he turned his attention back to us. "Okay, ladies, thank you all for your patience. I won't delay any longer. The turnout for this election was remarkable. Three hundred and four parents placed their votes, which equates to—"

"Over ninety-seven percent of the eligible voting population," Julie said, "which is —"

"Please spare us electoral statistics," said Pam. "We've been cooped up in this room for hours. We saw the parade of parents firsthand. We know there was a tremendous turnout. Please, just read the results so we can just move on with our day."

"Rude!" I whispered to Donna, who sat to my right.

Donna squeezed my leg. "It's fun watching her squirm."

Jack cleared his throat. "Fine. So with no further ado, we'll proceed. We'll begin with the non-mandatory officer roles, for the position of vice president, two hundred and ninety-nine people selected Stacey Williams."

Mia yawned and asked, "Can I go now?"

Before I could shush her, Pamela jumped out of her seat. As

she yelled "Her team members cheered and yelled, "Yes!" er team members cheered. "What a landslide!" She did a little celebratory jig. "Way to go, ladies!" Then she walked around the table so she could face them and high fived the group. "I told you all we had nothing to worry about, and here's the proof. We're golden."

"Ladies, please," Elaine said, "there are five more spots left to announce. Let Jack name all the winners before we celebrate, okay? We'll save time this way"—she winked at Pamela—"since you've made it clear you are in a rush."

"Whatever," Pamela replied as I clasped Donna's hand under the table so tightly, I prayed my nails didn't dig into her skin.

"Okay, the next role is for the corresponding secretary. Two hundred and seventy-five people cast their vote for Aimee Roberts."

"Yes!" Pamela yelled and raised her fist high. It took her a few seconds to realize she was the only person reacting. Her eyes blinked in rapid succession as she paled. She pointed a finger at Jack. "What did you say?"

"I said Aimee Roberts, by an overwhelming majority, has been elected to the role of corresponding secretary."

Pamela banged her fist on the table and her teammates startled. "How the hell did that happen?" Pamela asked everyone and no one in particular.

"May I continue?" the auditor asked.

"Yes, please," Elaine said.

"Next is the executive officer role. Two hundred and seventy-three people selected Trisha Dickens."

Pamela began to pace and tug at her ponytail as my side of the room began to clap and cheer. She downed a bottle of water almost in one gulp when Claire was elected secretary. When Donna was named treasurer, Pamela began to fan herself. While I wanted to cherish every moment, I was thankful Jack was swift. Based on Pamela's reactions, her stress level was reaching an all-time high. I worried if he dragged the process out, we'd have to call the paramedics.

"This is remarkable"—he pointed at his screen—"only one voter was in opposition of selecting Jackie Martin for president."

Tears of happiness streamed down my face. Donna leaned

over and engulfed me in her arms. "I'm so proud of you."

"I don't believe this!" Pamela yelled. "The vote was fixed! I demand a recount!"

"I'm sorry, ma'am. Every form was reviewed and tallied by three independent CPAs. The facts don't lie. Of course, if you want to quadruple check our work, we'd be glad to make you photocopies of the ballots, as the originals, as you know, must be given to the committee for safekeeping."

Donna handed me a tissue and I wiped my eyes. I knew I probably had mascara running down my face, but I didn't care. I stood up, and one by one, the ladies at my table hugged me.

As Jack's words sunk in, Pamela collapsed in her seat. She looked shell-shocked. I can't even imagine how betrayed she must feel knowing her team had turned on her and helped vote her out of the PTA. Stacey practically skipped across the room and twirled me around in a circle. "We did it, Jackie!"

"You!" Pamela jumped out of her chair, bolting over to Stacey. She poked her in the chest. "You did this! You sneaky, self-centered piece of crap! How dare you! I was so good to you, and this is how you repay me? You, backstabbing bitch! You should be ashamed of yourself."

Stacey opened her mouth to speak but Pamela didn't give her a chance. "Don't bother saying anything. I'm out of here." Pamela slammed the gymnasium door with so much force the room shook.

I hugged Stacey once more before turning to my friends. "Come on. It's time to celebrate."

CHAPTER THIRTY-EIGHT
THEN
Election Night

To: Forest River PTA President, Pamela Peterson
From: Forest River PTA President Elect, Jacqueline A. Martin
Date: 5/12 @ 11:08 PM

Subject: PTA Presidency

Hi Pamela,

Today was a whirlwind of a day for both of us. I am incredibly honored and thankful the parents of Forest River feel I am up to the challenge. I know how important a job this is, and I am determined to give it my all. I vow not to let the office or anyone down.

I would love the opportunity to meet with you and go over any open or pressing issues, so there might be a smooth transition. I will make myself available any time you are free.

Also, I want to thank you for your years of service. You have been an integral part of the school. From everything I have seen and heard over these past months, following you as president, the expectations are high for me. I am hopeful I can continue not only the good work at Forest River but also enhance your efforts with my new team's fresh ideas.

Unfortunately, there is not an official role for you on the team. Yet, I am not one to turn away help, especially for a good cause. I welcome you to participate in any capacities you see fit!

See you at the Spring Fling!

Warm best,
Jackie
Forest River PTA President Elect

"You have no idea how proud I am of you, Jackie. I love you." Scott reached across the bed and took the phone out of my hand, right as I hit send. He placed the device on his night table, far out of my reach.

"Hey." I pouted and pretended to sound annoyed. "I'm working."

"You know what they say about all work and no play...?" He leaned over and kissed me deeply.

CHAPTER THIRTY-NINE
THEN
MAY
One Week Later

"ARE YOU SURE you're ready for this?" I was squatting on the hardwood floor and looked at Hayley intently.

"I've been born ready for this moment!" my daughter exclaimed. Despite my worry, I had faith she was right. Ever since Scott and I discussed the concert with Hayley, she's been beyond excited. At her insistence, we purchased a huge calendar for her wall so she could count down the days. And in the last week alone, she must have belted out her solo verses fifty-seven billion times. I now hear the words in my sleep.

Donna approached with Christie, and I stood up. "Well, then, break a leg, sweetie." I kissed the top of Hayley's head. She looked so beautiful and sweet with her hair slicked back in a tight ponytail, a white tee-shirt, and a hot pink sequined skirt like all the other girls in her class.

She blinked rapidly and her joy faded. "Why, Mommy? Wouldn't that hurt a lot?"

Donna chuckled, which caused Christie to burst into hysterics. Poor Hayley looked so confused. She matured so much over these past months, sometimes I forgot she was still a child.

"Yeah, you're right. A real broken bone would hurt a lot. But I don't want you to actually break a leg. The expression is something people in show business say to wish performers good luck."

Hayley pouted. "Well, that's dumb. Why don't they just say good luck?"

"You know" — throwing up my hands — "I have no idea. All I know is you are going to do great."

I glanced toward Ms. Anderson and the other children. "Go on, girl, and join your friends. It's almost showtime, and Donna and I have to find our seats. We don't want to miss one second of the show."

"Okay, Mommy," she replied, trotting back to her classmates with Christie in tow.

I took one more glance in my daughter's direction before Donna and I exited the area.

"Run, Melissa, run!" Mia yelled.

"Guess someone is tardy, again," I said as the little girl rushed by, followed by her mother.

Mia stopped in front of us. "Jackie! Hi! I'm so glad to see you."

"Hi Mia." I cleared my throat and angled my head slightly in Donna's direction.

"Oh, yeah. Hi, Dina."

"It's Donna," Donna replied with a curt nod.

Mia batted away an imaginary fly. "Oh, right." Then she turned back to me. "Melissa told me some very unsettling news on the way here tonight."

"Oh? What?"

"She said Hayley has a solo."

Butterflies once filled my stomach. Hayley might be super excited for her moment in the spotlight, but I was still uneasy. "Yes, she does."

Mia's eyes widened. "How did that come about? I know you're new here, but it's very unusual for a kindergarten kid to be awarded a solo. Did you pull any strings?"

"No, of course not."

Mia put her hands on her hips. "Just because you'll soon be the PTA president, you don't have the right to get preferential treatment for your kid, you know."

"I know," I said. "And I would never think otherwise. Ms. Anderson approached me months ago about this, long before I even ran for office."

Her eyes darted around. "I don't understand. There must have been a mistake. Why did she ask Hayley and not Melissa?"

I lifted my hands, opened palms.

"Melissa should have been picked." Mia frowned. "My daughter is incredibly popular and can also carry a tune."

"I'm sure Melissa has a lovely voice," I said. "Ms. Anderson had her reasons." I tried to keep a straight face as I added, "Maybe you should ask her next time you volunteer for class mom duties. Sorry, but we have to run. The concert will begin any minute."

I grabbed Donna's hand, and we walked briskly down the hallway toward the auditorium. "Do you believe that woman?"

"I think it was funny," Donna said. "She stopped shocking me months ago. She's a piece of work. I'm sure she's smarting over the fact that Hayley is the most popular kid in class these days."

I threw my head back. "Who would have thought our kids would come so far in such a short time?"

"Certainly not me," Donna said. "Look at everything that has changed already. Speaking of changes, did Pamela ever reply to your email after the election?"

"Nope. I never expected her to. The note was more for me than her. I wanted to do the right thing, and offer an olive branch, and let her know if she did want to participate, I would embrace her efforts. It's funny and sad at the same time, if she had only been a tad welcoming to me when I first reached out, I probably never would have thrown my name into the mix this year."

"I know, but everything worked out for a reason. You've already done so much for the school. You're going to love every second of your new role."

I opened the auditorium door. I waved to Claire who sat next to an empty seat. I wondered if Kevin would show up tonight or disappoint Claire and the kids again.

"Totally," I said as we approached our third-row seats. Our party stood up to make room for us. Joan handed Stan the giant bouquet of long-stem pink roses she planned to give my daughter after the show and then hugged me tightly. Then I took my seat in between her and Donna, just as the lights went down.

As Principal Williams took the stage, I whispered in my mother-in-law's ear, "I'm so worried."

She reached for my hand. "I know you are, but she'll be fine.

She's so excited."

I felt a jab in my back as the person behind me whispered "shush," much louder than how we whispered.

I peeked over my shoulder and wasn't surprised to see Pamela Peterson was the person who poked me. I decided to kill her with kindness instead of stooping down to her level. I didn't acknowledge her action. Instead, I waved daintily before turning my attention back to the stage.

"And now, without further ado, let's get this show started!" The crowd went wild as the curtain began to rise. Scott, who sat at the end of our aisle, had his phone angled ready to capture every second of our little girl's five minutes of fame. "First up, let's welcome Ms. Anderson's kindergarteners."

I raised my hands to my face as I took in their adorable outfits and big smiles. "They look amazing," I gushed to Donna. Hayley clasped Christie's hand on stage.

Ms. Anderson counted to three. Then, right on cue, the group belted out "Here Comes the Sun" by the Beatles. Hayley's face fell as she looked to her right and left and saw how packed the room was. Then the spotlight shined on her face, and I felt my heart in my throat. Tears filled my daughter's eyes as she opened and closed her mouth, unable to make a sound. My heart shattering, I knew I shouldn't have allowed her solo. I was the worst mom in the whole wide world!

I jumped out of my seat like a rocket and screamed at the top of my lungs, "You can do it, Hayley!" Yet, my outburst seemed to cause my daughter to look only more panic-stricken.

Donna stood up and started to sing Hayley's lyrics, which somehow, I managed to momentarily forget. Joan stood up and added her voice. I bit back tears as the words came flooding back to me and began to sing as well. The three of us had our arms around each other's shoulders as we swayed back and forth to the music. We weren't alone. Throughout the auditorium, numerous parents also stood up and joined in. Melissa walked over to Hayley on the stage and put her hand on her shoulder. Christie did the same. Finally, with everyone's support Hayley found the courage and confidence she needed to go on with the show.

"Sit down already." Pamela's hissed when my daughter's solo ended, and the class sang in unison. I ignored her request. I felt like I still needed to support my child.

"I said, sit down," Pamela said much louder. Then she did the unspeakable. She shoved me.

"Hey!" I exclaimed.

"Are you crazy?" Donna spun around. "How dare you!"

Pamela crossed her arms defiantly.

Joan put her hand on my shoulder and said to Pam, "It's a shame your husband wasn't able to break free for the show tonight. Hopefully he can attend the Spring Fling. Where is he again? Oh, yes. Virginia. I do hope orange is his color."

Pamela's face turned red and she clenched her fists. In one swift, fluid motion, Scott passed the camera phone to his father and pulled me toward him before either of us could draw blood. Then, his mom switched seats so he could sit at my side. He kissed my cheek and placed a protective arm around me. Donna took hold of my right hand as we watched all the other performances. By the time the last act completed, my heartbeat had returned to a somewhat normal pace. All of the children flocked the stage and took one final bow.

Later, when the curtain rose, and the lights came up, Scott ended his embrace. "Can I trust you to be on your own for a few minutes and not get in a fistfight, Rocky?"

I made a face. "I think so."

"Good. She's not worth it," he whispered in my ear. And he gave me another quick kiss. "Now, please, pull yourself together before we get Hayley."

"Okay." He stood up and greeted a few of the other dads.

Joan returned to her original seat. "Are you all right, Jackie?"

I exhaled. "Yes, I am now. I love you so much, you know that, right?"

"Of course I do."

Then I turned to Donna and gave her a huge hug. "Thank you, my friend. It was your quick thinking that saved Hayley's performance. I don't know how to thank you, and not just for this. For everything." I wiped a tear away from my eye. "

"I'd do anything for your girl, Jackie." I saw she too was crying. "You have done so much for me this year. I don't know how I would have survived without you. You've been my rock."

"And you've been mine." I sniffed. I grabbed both of Donna's hands and held them tight. "Please promise me no matter what, we'll be there for each other, and we will make sure to look after each other's children like our own."

"I promise."

I threw my arms around her. It was freeing to know I finally had the best friend I desperately wanted.

CHAPTER FORTY
NOW
AUGUST
Five Years Later
Back to the Beginning

To: Jackie Martin

From: Forest River Elementary School Principal, Harrison Owen Williams, Jr.

Date: 8/25 @ 10:04 AM

Subject: Meeting request

Salutations Jackie,

I hope the summer has treated the Martin family well, and you have all enjoyed your much-needed holiday away from the demands of Forest River Elementary School.

Maybe it's me, but the breaks seem to fly by faster with each passing year. I am sure that both Cassidy and Hayley are excited to embrace another exciting term just like my staff and I are.

Unfortunately, I have had to make a change to Hayley's placement. She will no longer be in Mrs. Epstein's class, as initially indicated. Instead, she will spend her final year in Mr. Smithstien's fifth-grade class.

I'm sorry to inform you of this change at such a late juncture. I would love to meet with you in person to go over the motivation for this action. I will not be in the office or available by phone at all today. I know you'll be eager to discuss this matter, so I have cleared my calendar tomorrow and we can discuss this matter any time after 9:00 a.m. Please let me know what time works best for you.

Send my regards to Scott.

Sincerely,
Harry

Harrison Owen Williams, Jr.
Principal, Forest River Elementary School

I have no idea why I felt the overwhelming desire to re-read Harry's email yet again. During the past twenty-two hours and thirty-seven minutes, I must have stared at the note so many times I could recite the words verbatim. I pulled down my sun visor and examined my reflection in the mirror. No shock here; I looked even more horrible than I felt. My eyes were puffy and red from crying and lack of sleep. Donna had dodged my calls yesterday. After I put Cassidy and Hayley to bed, I caved and called Thomas. No shock, he wasn't home. I caught him at a business dinner in Alabama, even though Donna previously told me he'd be in Toronto this week. He offered no explanation for why I couldn't reach Donna, but he did assure me she and the girls were alive and well, because there was an excessive amount of activity on his credit card. And while I was thankful that they were in one piece, her peculiar behavior reinforced my nagging hunch about what was happening.

Claire, on the other hand, as usual, had been a wealth of information. I was a tad upset she didn't come to me sooner. But I couldn't really hold a grudge that she kept her suspicions to herself. Firstly, she was not involved in the situation. Secondly, she had enough of her own drama to handle. Speculation surrounding Claire Conroy's sex life has fueled the rumor mill. Everyone knew she had been stepping out on her husband with his best friend from college for a couple years now. The allegations had recently become even more detailed and vicious as the lovebirds no longer tried to hide their romantic rendezvous. Even though I didn't condone extra marital relations, I couldn't judge her either. You really never know what happens behind closed doors. The one thing I was sure of: I never wanted to find myself married to Kevin Conroy!

The real reason I wasn't upset with Claire is she didn't have any hard facts to support her outrageous theory. When I called her in a panic yesterday, she shared the little bits and pieces she knew about what happened this summer. She had been able to fill in a few blanks for me, but her speculations and observations managed to leave me with more questions than answers.

I glanced at my watch. Thankfully, my wait for answers was almost over. I only had a few minutes more before my appointment with the principal.

As I touched up my mascara, my cell phone rang. As I reached for my phone, I said a silent prayer that Donna would be on the other end of the line. Instead, my mother-in-law's landline flashed on my screen. I quickly declined the call and fought off a fresh set of tears.

I would do anything to speak to Joan one more time, but she lost her battle with cancer three years ago. I miss her every day.

Scott's dad, Stan, didn't waste any time mourning the loss of his wife. Less than a year after he buried his bride, he met a bikini-clad bimbo on vacation in Bermuda. She was almost fifty years his junior, and the age difference didn't stall the love affair in the slightest. Stan rushed her down the aisle like five minutes later. Don't get me wrong. Zoey is a nice enough kid, I guess. We've never had anything in common. All of our conversations felt so stilted. It didn't help I felt a fierce loyalty to Joan, and my kind, amiable Scott was downright hostile around her. He was very verbal about his belief she manipulated his father for his money. I didn't think Zoey was bright enough to pull the wool over Stan's eyes, but only time would tell. And to add fuel to the fire, she recently found out she's expecting their first child and I suddenly became her go-to person. She now called me at least twenty times a day for tips and advice. Hopefully, when the baby comes, we will all find some common ground.

"Hi, Jane," I said as I handed the receptionist a cup of iced vanilla, sugar-free, soy latte, which I know is her favorite. I glanced at the wall clock. I was fifteen minutes early for my nine o'clock appointment.

"You are the best, Jackie." She poked the straw into the top of the cup. "How did you know I needed a caffeine fix?"

"Just a hunch." I angled my head in the direction of Harry's door. "Is he in his office? We have an appointment."

"Yes, he's waiting for you. Go right in."

I pressed my hands down the gray pencil skirt I wore before I pulled open the thick wood door. Unlike many parents, who conducted school business in their gym attire, I liked to look professional when I had official business with the principal.

"Greetings, Jackie." Harry rose from his large wooden desk, which was covered by loose papers and file folders. He looked so relaxed and tan in his white polo shirt and khakis. "How has the summer treated the Martins? I know you spent some time in Spain. The pictures you posted on Instagram were lovely. The family and I went a few summers ago. Did you have a chance to see—"

"Harry, please." I cut him off as I collapsed in one of the leather seats opposite his desk. "Can we save the chit-chat for some other time? I am sure you don't need me to tell you how troubled I have been by your email."

He sat down and took off his glasses and massaged the bridge of his nose. "No, you don't. I know my message must have come as quite a shock to you. I'm sorry, but I felt it was important to address the matter as quickly as possible."

"Thank you. I can't take the uncertainty anymore. In all my years of service here at Forest River, I never heard of a situation like this. Please, Harry, tell me what happened."

He put his glasses back on and shuffled around his desk. Finally, he found the folder he was looking for. "I'm sorry to have to tell you, over the past few weeks, we've received numerous calls about Hayley."

My voice was shaky. "What kind of calls?"

He propped his elbows on his desk and steepled his hands. "There is no easy way to say it, and I don't want to sugar coat anything. The calls were complaints."

"Complaints?" I bounced out of my seat. "What kind of complaints?"

"There have been numerous allegations, made by mothers of girls in Hayley's grade, claiming your daughter is a bully."

"A bully?" I screeched and grabbed the edge of the chair for support.

"Yes. Jackie, you of all people know Forest River Elementary School has a zero bullying tolerance. We must take all claims seriously."

"Harry, come on!" I banged my fist on his desk. "You have known Hayley for almost five years. Have you ever once seen her be unkind to any child? In fact, you"—I pointed a freshly French manicured fingernail in his direction—"were the one who insisted she hold the role of"—I made air quotes—"buddy-buddy greeter girl, and welcome all new students to the school."

He threw his hands up. "I won't argue with you, Jackie. I was as shocked as you are when I started getting calls. Never, in a thousand years, would I ever expect behavior like this from Hayley. From her first day, she's been an exemplary student."

I sat back down across from him. "So what makes you think she changed now?"

"Is there any trouble at home?"

My heart threatened to escape my chest. "Really, Harry?"

"I'm sorry." He rubbed his forehead. "Don't get mad. I have to ask. It is the logical question, after all."

"Maybe in most cases, but you know us better than that. You know in your heart Hayley isn't capable of being cruel to a fly."

"I certainly never expected feedback like this about your daughter. Truthfully, I have no idea what to make of this matter. I find it unfathomable that Hayley's personality could have taken such a drastic turn for the worst. Sadly, I've learned the hard way that you never really know what someone is capable of doing. And while my gut tells me there must be a mistake or misunderstanding, I can't rely on my intuition or emotion in a situation such as this. I must follow the facts." He pulled a wad of paper out of the folder and flipped through the pages. "And the facts clearly state numerous mothers contacted the school psychologist, too, and voiced their concerns about having Hayley placed in their daughters' class."

I jutted out my chin. "I want to see transcripts of those calls."

He shook his head. "I'm sorry, Jackie. I can't release them to you. All complaints regarding children are considered classified information. You, of all people, know we have to make Forest River a safe haven. All students and their parents and guardians should feel comfortable to speak their minds without any fear of retaliation."

"But what about the falsely accused? Who represents them?" I mentally kicked myself for spearheading the initiative of this privacy policy three years ago. I never expected my do-gooding nature and hard work to come back and bite me in the butt. "Fine. But can you please give me more information about what these mothers claim my daughter did to these children?"

Harry gave me a sad smile. "I'm sorry, no, I can't."

I buried my head in my hands and fought back my tears. Harry must have taken pity in me.

"Fine, I will tell you this."

I looked up, and he pointed to the sheet of paper in front of him.

"All of the mothers claim Hayley acted out following an altercation between her friend group right before the term ended last year."

"Come on, Harry. That's ancient history. Yes, Hayley and Melissa Montgomery disagreed, and the rest of the group took sides. As quickly as tempers flared, the argument blew over, and the girls reconciled. In fact, between day camp and play dates, they have been practically inseparable this entire summer. It's as if this little spat never happened."

"I wish that was the case, Jackie." He closed his eyes for a second. "The calls didn't come from the concerned parents in June after the altercation. The calls started coming around four weeks ago. Unfortunately, due to time constraints and my summer vacation in Italy, I wasn't able to address the matter sooner."

"What?" I felt like someone had just sucker-punched me in the gut again.

"You heard me. It's been over a month since the first call, and there have been follow-up phone calls since, which was why I had to act so swiftly." He closed the folder and looked me square in the eyes. "I know how challenging this is for you to grasp. You must be incredibly upset, and I am sorry. But since this happened outside of school, there's really not much I can do but appease parents and smooth the transition for Hayley. Hopefully, you can expeditiously clear Hayley's good name. I know setting the record straight would give you a bit of peace. I have no choice with so many parents calling me. My hands are tied. I must place Hayley in a different class than the other girls."

I let out a deep sigh. I was defeated, and I didn't care that it showed. I knew nothing I said or did now would have the power to sway him. He had made up his mind. For a moment, I contemplated voicing my suspicion of what prompted these phone calls, thanks to Claire's keen insight, but thought better of it. Even I had thought her theory sounded far-fetched yesterday. Logical and strait-laced Harry would think I had lost my mind. He'd probably rush *me* off to the school psychologist for an impromptu evaluation. No. I needed proof before I could make any counter-allegations.

"You know I am not happy, Harry. I don't like this at all, but I respect you and your position. I know you are trying to do the right thing."

"I knew you would understand, Jackie."

I nodded. "Mr. Smithstien is a wonderful educator with a stellar reputation. I'm sure Hayley and Christie will love being in his class together."

Harry looked like he'd seen a ghost. "I'm sorry. I should have been clear. Christie will not be in Hayley's class either. Donna Warren gave me no choice. I had to separate them as well."

CHAPTER FORTY-ONE
NOW

"*IS SHE THERE?*" I fired off a text to Claire as soon as I walked out of Principal Williams's office.

"*Yes,*" she replied immediately.

I was a mix of emotions. I was enraged that she was capable of carrying on with her life as if today was a typical Tuesday. Well, she'll soon find out it wasn't going to be business as usual!

"*Good! I'm on my way. Don't let her leave. Please!*" I replied as I walked briskly to where I had parked my car. Then I added, "You were right. I owe you big time!!!"

"*Sorry. I had hoped I was dead wrong...Hugs.*"

I acknowledged her text with a heart and then drove home. I hurried into my house, shedding my business attire as I made my way toward my bedroom. I didn't bother to pick up one discarded item. I'd deal with my mess later. I shimmied into my black Lululemon yoga pants and a white and pink spandex shirt.

After my call with Claire yesterday, I had spent most of the night preparing for and dreading this moment. I desperately hoped I wouldn't have needed to put my plan into action, but the constant nervous churning of my gut had warned me otherwise. And while I wasn't happy about having this conversation, I was braced for whatever happened next. I pulled my hair into a high ponytail as I quickly made my way back downstairs and out my front door.

When I parked seven minutes later, a shiver ran down my spine. It scared me how I had managed to drive to the Pilates studio in record time as if on autopilot. I didn't remember making one single turn or stopping at one red light. My mind had been everywhere except on the road. It was a minor miracle I had made it here in one piece.

I entered the brightly lit building and gave the pink-haired girl at the front desk a quick wave. Another glance at my watch confirmed I had made it here right on time. I trotted toward the back of the building, where my usual Tuesday morning class had just let out. My pulse raced as familiar smiling and sweaty faces headed in my direction. From experience, I knew the women were eager to cool down with a little gossip and a green smoothie. Little did they know they were walking away from the action, because sadly, a show was about to start.

I approached the doorway and I let out the breath I had been holding. I knew I needed to look more composed than I felt. Fortunately, only a few women remained in the room, and thankfully Claire was one of them.

"Jackie, hi! We missed you in class today," Tania Walden, the mother of one of Cassidy's classmates, and a member of the first-grade carpool, enthusiastically greeted me.

"Thanks." I squeezed her arm and flashed her a quick smile as I sprinted away. I knew it was rude of me not to stop and make small talk, as I usually did, but I didn't have a choice today. Tania must have sensed something was amiss, staring as I strode over to Claire and Donna. Some other moms followed Tania's lead and lingered in the room. I felt all their eyes on me. I would have preferred to hold this conversation in private, but I had to seize the opportunity presented to me. It was unfortunate we had an audience to hang on every word, but I didn't see any alternative since she was the one who had been avoiding me.

"Hi guys," I said, surprised how steady my voice sounded to me. If my best friend, the one woman I had trusted implicitly in this world, was nervous to see me, she didn't let it show. Her face was emotionless, which infuriated me even more.

"Hi, Jackie," Claire said as her sympathetic eyes conveyed so many emotions to me. "Well, I've got to bounce. I'll leave you both alone."

"Please, don't go," I implored her. I needed an ally nearby. I feared I was too emotional to process and remember the words in this exchange. Despite Harry's parting words reinforcing my worst fears, I desperately clung to the chance Donna was not complicit.

"Okay." Claire looked incredibly uncomfortable. As she inched backward, she added, "I'll just be over here."

Donna said, "I was surprised you weren't in class today. You never miss Pilates." She took a swig of water from her Forest River PTA hot pink water bottle.

I counted to five, silently. I knew I had to calm myself down. I couldn't let my raging emotions get the best of me. I needed to keep my wits. I still didn't have any evidence yet. And I cared too much about Donna, our friendship.

"You're right. I never miss class. Unfortunately, this morning I had to meet with the principal."

"Oh." She looked down at her sneakers.

"Yeah. I tried to call you like a billion times yesterday. You never called me back. Why?"

She nibbled at a cuticle. "The day ran away from me, I guess. You know how busy things are this time of year."

I looked around the room at the pampered women who remained in a huddle, their eyes laser focused on us. "Yeah, I know. We moms, we never have a moment for ourselves. It's just work, work, work for us!"

"Speaking of which"—she glanced at her Fitbit—"I've got to run. I have so much to do today."

I locked eyes with Claire and willed my tears not to fall. If I had any lingering doubts, Donna's rush to leave caused them to disappear instantly. "So, you're not going to ask me why I had to go to school?"

Donna rocked back and forth on her heels.

I stared at the woman I had considered my confidant and best friend for over five years and exhaled deeply. "Are you not asking any questions because you already know all of the answers?"

Donna glanced over at Claire, and fury flashed across her face. Even though years had passed, despite all Claire's best attempts to deepen their bond, Donna remained aloof around Claire.

I waited for a response that didn't come. "Nice. So, now you're going to give me the silent treatment?" I snorted. "Well, isn't that rich? Come on, Donna, after everything we've been through together, this is how you want to play?"

"I don't know what you want me to say."

I looked down at my Golden Goose sneakers, counted to five once more, and then said, "You can start with telling me the truth."

"The truth?"

"Yes, Donna. The truth. I know what happened this summer when we were in Spain. I know what you all did. Now I want to know why." I pointed my index finger in her direction. "Please, look me in the eye and tell me why you sold out my daughter so yours could go on an all-expense-paid fancy trip to the Caribbean. I can't believe you allowed *Mia Montgomery*, of all people, to manipulate you in her attempt to boost Melissa's popularity this term."

I had tried to keep my voice low, but I didn't succeed. I heard a collective gasp from the peanut gallery of nosey moms who remained in the room.

Donna's nostrils flared. "How did you find out?"—glaring at Claire—"Oh, you. I should have known you'd stick your nose where it didn't belong. You can't help but worm your way into something *or someone.*"

I had to give Claire credit; she didn't respond or flinch. She stood like a statue. Donna had been very vocal about Claire's alleged affair. I think she was so offended by Claire's extramarital relationship because she feared Thomas was unfaithful to her. Yet, even if I always suspected Thomas stepped out on her, I never dared utter a word. I had been close enough to see firsthand all the fissures in their relationship. It broke my heart.

"This has nothing to do with Claire." I clenched and unclenched my hands. "In a town like Forest River, did you honestly think this little stunt would remain a secret forever?"

She shrugged once more, and I wanted to grab her by her shoulders and shake her. I needed to hear the words from her mouth. I asked again, "Donna, is it true? Did you stoop so low as to contact the school psychologist and Harry and claim Hayley bullied your daughter, at Mia's request? In exchange for her to include Christie with a bunch of the other girls on a trip to Turks and Cacaos?"

Donna let out a deep breath and raked her fingers through her hair. "I don't know why you are making such a big deal about this, Jackie."

Black dots blurred my vision. I felt faint. "What did you say?"

"Come on, Jackie." She frowned. "You know you and Hayley will come out on top. You always do. So, Hayley had to change classes. What is the big deal? The school year didn't even start yet. It isn't like Hayley's going to suffer in the slightest. Everyone adores her. She'll be fine. She's just won't be in the same class as the other girls, but what difference will that make? They'll still be friends."

I heard Donna's words, but I couldn't decipher them through the buzzing in my head. I felt like I had entered an alternative universe and was suddenly standing in Bizzaro Land.

"It's more than just being separated from the group, Donna. You said my daughter is a bully! That's on her record. I could sue you and the school!"

"You could, but you won't. Garnering negative attention is so not your style."

This was a mistake. "Let's get out of here." I reached for her hands. "Let's talk this over in private."

She released a slow deep breath. "I'd rather not. I don't think Hayley even knew about the trip. The girls kept the details to themselves. It's a shame some mothers can't do the same." She tipped her head in Claire's direction and rolled her eyes. "Mia brought the girls down to the island while you and your family traipsed around Spain this summer. What was wrong with the other kids enjoying a vacation too?"

"First off"—I raised my index finger—"how many times did I offer to take Christie and Julia along on one of our vacations? I've even invited you more times than I can count to join us, too, but you declined. I knew it upset you how Thomas refused to travel for leisure since he is constantly on the road for work."

"I never wanted your charity," Donna said softly.

"It never was charity, Donna. You were my best friend. I would have loved nothing more than for you and the girls to share those magical moments with us."

Donna looked down at her shoes once more. I wondered if she caught my use of the past tense.

"But you could accept a trip from Mia, *Dina*? It was more than just a beach vacation, wasn't it?"

When she didn't respond, I continued. "When Mia concocted this cockamamie plan, why didn't you come to me instead of joining the bandwagon?"

Donna dismissively waved a hand. "As I said before, I don't know why you are blowing this out of proportion. They are in fifth grade. So Hayley missed out on a girls' trip, so what? She's already seen half the world twice over. The girls are all bosom buddies again, and even though Hayley will be in a different class, they'll still see each other all the time. And Mia said—"

"*And Mia said*"—I shook my head. "I can't wait to hear this one. You make me die laughing, Donna. After five years, Mia Montgomery finally managed to miraculously remember your name, and you now treat her words as gospel?"

I reached for her hands again, as my heart softened slightly when I saw tears fill her eyes. "Please, Donna. Talk to me. Help me understand what happened. Let's get everything out in the open once and for all."

As quickly as she let her guard down, she built her wall back up. She stood straight as a pencil. "There isn't anything to discuss," Donna said. "I'm not upset at all."

"Okay, good." A genuine smile returned to my face. "We'll head back to school together. You'll explain to Harry what actually happened, and Hayley will no longer be branded as a bully." I reached for her hands. "I accept your apology."

Donna jerked her hands behind her back and her eyes protruded. "My apology? I didn't do anything wrong, so I have nothing to apologize for."

Whatever peace I had found vanished in an instant. My heart pounded so fast I heard it beat in my ears. "What?"

"Everything I told the psychologist was true. Melissa and Hayley did fight. The other children were encouraged to pick a side." She added, "I can't be held responsible how she interpreted my words."

"I don't believe this," I said as I looked toward the ceiling and willed my tears not to fall. "You're a grown woman, and you knew exactly what you were doing, and you don't have one iota of remorse? What is wrong with you?"

She didn't say anything.

"I was furious when I came here today, but I still gave you the benefit of the doubt. Even though I knew in my core you sold out my child, I didn't want to believe what I heard. All night long, I told myself if I found out the rumors were true, I'd figure out a way to forgive you. Sure, it would have taken a long time for you to fully regain my trust. I wanted to think the best of you, Donna. I didn't want to think you'd willingly throw away all our years of friendship. All you had to do was own your actions." I held up my thumb and index finger so they practically touched. "A sliver of sincerity would have gone a long way. But you couldn't do that, could you? It's pathetic how you can spend years with someone, and feel you know them inside and out, and then realize you never knew them at all. After everything we've been through together, I can't believe this is how you repay me?"

"Repayment?" She looked around the room and didn't even seem bothered by the audience. "A very interesting choice of words, don't you think?"

"What do you mean?" I couldn't help glance in Claire's direction.

"Fine, I'll spell it out. I'm tired of being your sidekick."

"My what?"

"Come on, Jackie. I'm not a fool. I know you got where you are today because of my misfortunes. My shitty luck came in handy for you. Your social standing was boosted every time you had the opportunity to play the hero. I'm tired of being your charity project."

I pointed at my chest. "So, you hurt me and my daughter because you resent how I was a friend to you? Are you trying to say you can't handle the fact I had your back and showered you and your children with kindness?"

"No. I'm not saying that at all. I'm saying I'm tired of constantly standing in your shadow. I'm fed up feeling like your pet project. And I'm sick of my kids and I being second best. And I am not the only one. Mia feels the same way. It's frustrating how you and Hayley can never do anything wrong. Like I said before, I am sure you'll figure out a way to spin this situation so Hayley and you both are painted in the perfect light. Like they say, all's well that ends well."

I slapped my hands against my face. "Oh my god, you are seriously disturbed! How did I never see this side of you?" Years before I had thought her sister was nuts, and now I realized Donna was just the same.

"You must have been too busy looking in the mirror, calculating your next plan of attack."

I blinked rapidly. "I can't believe I am having this conversation with you. I can't believe you are standing here saying these horrible things to me right now. If I did something to hurt you, why didn't you say something at the time? Why did you wait five freaking years to express your feelings? We didn't have to get to this point. None of this had to happen! We promised each other a very long time ago how we'd be there for each other and protect each other's children. I took my vow seriously. Everything I ever said or did was out of love for you and your girls. I would never in a million years hurt you. I never had a best friend like you in all of my life. But you were never my friend." I swallowed the hard truth. "Besides Scott, you were the only person I spoke with every day. Good or bad, you were the first person I turned to. I trusted you completely. Our relationship meant everything to me, but now, I see it meant nothing to you. I can't believe I was so wrong about you. I have never felt so betrayed in my entire life."

I turned around and fled the studio. I refused to give Donna, or anyone else, the satisfaction of seeing me weep.

CHAPTER FORTY-TWO
NOW

"THE SHOW IS OVER people. Give her some space," Claire called out behind me. I didn't turn around. Instead, I increased my pace.

Claire caught up to me as soon as I stepped out of the building and onto the curb. I was about to unlock my car door when she pulled me to the side and practically dragged me into the seedy bar located in the strip mall, next to the Pilates studio.

"Come on. It will be safe in here," she said as she held open the door for me.

I arched an eye at her. I didn't feel like my voice would have been steady enough to speak.

She snorted. "I'm not being ironic. Look around. No nosey Forest River mommy would ever be caught dead in an establishment like this on a Tuesday morning at ten-fifteen."

Even though I wouldn't have thought it would be possible, she made me laugh. I hugged her, and then I couldn't hold back the emotional storm I had tried so hard to suppress. I sobbed into her shoulder as she gently rubbed my back.

The barman cleared his throat, and we pulled away. "Can I get you something, ladies?"

I was about to say no but Claire spoke. "Yeah. Two shots of Casamigos Silver, please." Then she took my hand and led me to the bar.

"Are you crazy?" I asked, still shaking slightly.

"Sometimes." She gave me a sad smile, as she placed a twenty down in front of us. "But not right now. You need this."

I sat down on the stool next to her as the burly man in a shirt two sizes two small wiped down glasses. I propped my elbows on the mahogany bar and rested my head in my hands. "I think you're right."

"Here you go, ladies." The bartender placed the shots in front of us and handed me a wad of napkins so I could wipe my tear-stained face. He gestured to the back of the building and said, "I'll give you two some space. Give me a holler if you need anything else."

"Thanks," Claire said and raised her glass. I did the same and clinked her drink. Then we both threw back the shot.

I guess the smooth vanilla burn of the tequila took a tad of the edge off, but it was insufficient to counteract the outrage I felt bubbling through my veins. I probably could have chugged the entire bottle in one big gulp and not managed to feel a buzz, I was that rattled.

I turned to Claire as I undid my ponytail. "I don't understand. What the hell happened in there?"

Claire shook her head. "I don't know. I'm as shocked as you are. Donna didn't show even a tinge of remorse."

I rubbed my eyes and said, "I know. Who was she?"

"I'm sorry, Jackie. I should have told you the moment I suspected Mia was up to no good. But the snippets I heard at the beginning of the summer didn't sound my alarm bells. I just figured Mia was simply buying Melissa's popularity, and you guys weren't going because of your Spain trip. I guess I underestimated Mia because she's usually so lazy and self-centered. Hatching such a plan to alienate Hayley and you seems like way too much effort for Mia."

"Yeah, I wish you told me sooner. "

She reached for my hand and squeezed it. "It was a mistake, and I'm sorry. I really am. I never thought Donna, of all people, could hurt you and Hayley like this. Sometimes I feel like you can't trust anyone in this town."

I wiped another tear and closed my eyes. "I know. We are all so worried about keeping up appearances. Why?" I sniffed. "I feel like I put on a mask every day. People look at me and see a feisty woman who strives to get her way. But that isn't me."

"Oh, really?"

I frowned. "Sure, I have made it clear I won't suffer fools.

And fine, I will be the first one to admit, I easily lose my patience if things don't go my way, but that isn't the full me. I have fears and insecurities too! Lots of them! I don't feel the need to broadcast them to the entire town. I try to keep my concerns to myself. I only ever really confided in Donna."

Donna. Donna had been my friend through some of my darkest days. I was devastated by my mother-in-law's death. Some days I struggled to even get out of bed. Donna stayed at my side and prevented me from collapsing. She rallied the troops and covered my pressing PTA duties. She encouraged me to talk to someone and convinced me to take the medication I was prescribed when I was scared to.

I let out a slow breath as I looked around the empty bar. "This is how she behaves? Forget about how she treated me. How could she do this to Hayley? I thought she loved her. I hate her for this!"

Claire took my hands. "No, you don't. You're angry right now, I know. Come on. You two have been inseparable for years. I'm sure she'll come around and apologize."

I stared at my thumbnail. "At this point, after everything she said, I am so hurt and betrayed I don't think I want her to."

"I know, but you are letting your emotions get the better of you. Are you really ready to lose years of friendship?"

I contemplated calling over the bartender for a refill, or five, but thought better of it. "It doesn't matter what I want or what I'm ready for. I had no say in this situation. Our friendship is over—if we even had one to begin with. Donna destroyed it."

Claire studied the empty glass before her in silence.

Even though the bar was sweltering, a shiver ran down my spine. "Donna was so full of rage and hate. How could I have been so blind?"

Claire leaned in. "Don't berate yourself. She never gave you, or anyone else, an inkling of what was going on in her head. Who knows?" She shook her head. "Maybe her resentment built up little by little each year, and she snapped? Or maybe something else happened in her life, and you were an easy target for her to take her frustrations out on."

"Maybe. I know Thomas has been traveling more than usual."

"Oh, please. Don't be naïve. We all have our marital issues. Half the marriages here are probably on the rocks. Thomas' excess traveling is no excuse for what she did to you."

"You're right. I wish I knew the reason. Everything I did for her was out of love."

"I know, Jackie. You have a huge heart and you have helped so many people out over the years. Like the time—"

I raised my hand and cut her off. "Don't." I knew she was trying to help but I wasn't in the mood to take a trip down memory lane. "I have a question for you. You and Donna never really connected, and I never asked you why. What do you honestly feel about her?"

Claire shrugged. "We just never clicked. Besides, I'm not going there. I've kept my feelings to myself all these years, and I'm not going to bash your bosom buddy right now to make you feel better. You need to focus on what you feel now, not what I think."

I looked deeply into her eyes, curiosity killing me, but I didn't want to push her. "Do you think she'll apologize?"

"Honestly? No."

I closed my eyes and fingered the Mom Boss charm I wore around my neck. I pictured Joan's face and sent her a silent prayer. I knew I couldn't waste any more time dwelling on my feelings. I had to focus on my daughter's needs. I stood up as a plan of attack rapidly formed in my mind.

CHAPTER FORTY-THREE
NOW
Later That Afternoon

"Mommy, we're home!" Cassidy yelled at the top of her lungs as she raced up the driveway waving a painting.

I squatted down and gave my baby a big hug as the camp bus pulled away. She was babbling a mile a minute about her day. As usual, I could only understand about every third word she said.

I glanced over the top of her head and locked eyes with Hayley.

"What's wrong, Mom?"

I should have known my daughter would notice my unease right away. "Nothing." I stood up and then kissed the top of her head. "But we need to talk. Let's go into the backyard. I'll meet you there in a few."

"Okay." She headed toward the yard, kicking a rock along the way.

I turned to my other child and asked, "How about some iPad time?"

"Yeah!" Cassidy raised her arm into the air and ran inside to where her device was charging.

I went into the kitchen and poured three large glasses of lemonade. I took my time going outside. Scott had wanted to be part of this conversation, but I felt it was better if I did it alone. What girl wanted to have a heart-to-heart with her dad standing by?

"Thirsty?" I asked as I placed an icy glass in front of my daughter.

She took a sip. "Not really. What's going on? Is Poppy sick? You're scaring me."

"No. Sorry, sweetie. Everyone is fine." It was uncanny how much my daughter was like me. "We need to talk about the girls and school."

"Okay." She let out a sigh of relief and pushed her hair away from her forehead.

Even though I had hours to plan this conversation, I was still unsure of how much I should tell my daughter. I didn't want to lie to her, but I also didn't want to shatter her confidence either. I knew she was a mature kid, but I feared she was still too young to learn how cruel and calculating people could be.

"There has been a change in your schedule. You're going to be in Mr. Silverstein's class."

She seemed to study my face. "That's no biggie. Kyle's in his class, right?" Ever since kindergarten, those two children had such an adorable relationship. I secretly wondered if one day the young man would end up being my son-in-law. *Ha!* I better keep Claire on my good side, otherwise, Thanksgiving dinner would be extremely awkward.

"Yes."

"Cool." She propped her elbows on the table. "I know there is more, Mom. Spill it."

I laughed and I took a sip of lemonade. "None of the girls are going to be in the class. You are going to be separated."

Her face was emotionless as she processed what I said. I opened my mouth to speak but I didn't utter a word. I wanted to give her a chance to think.

"None of them? Not even Melissa or Christie?"

I reached for her hands. "No."

She played with a leaf that fell on the table. "Well, that's not the worst thing in the world. I spend so much time with them as it is, it will be nice to get a bit of a break."

My eyes bulged. "Really? You're okay with this?"

"Yeah, why wouldn't I be? It's just a class. We'll still be friends."

I should have been relieved she took the news so calmly, but I wasn't. My Spidey-senses were on high alert.

"Hayley, did something happen with you and the girls?"

She avoided my gaze.

"Hayley Charlotte Martin, answer my question."

"It's nothing."

I wrapped my arms around my waist. "I'll be the judge of that."

She looked everywhere but at me. "Fine. Remember the little fight I had with Melissa in the summer?"

"Yes. And you made up like five minutes later," I said as my stomach cramped.

"I thought everything was fine, but when we were in Spain last month, Melissa's mom took all the other girls to the Caribbean. I was the only one who wasn't invited."

I closed my eyes. "Did you just find this out?"

"No." She shredded the leaf into a million little pieces. "I knew before they left." Then she pulled her cell phone out of her back pocket and started to scroll.

Toward the end of last year's school term, many of the moms who had children moving into fifth grade contemplated getting the kids iPhones before classes ended. Scott and I were against the idea. The majority of the other women were very passionate about the issue. They claimed that due to everyone's extended seasonal travel schedule, it was an essential purchase. Once the first phone was purchased, I had no choice but to cave and get my daughter one.

"See. Christie even sent pictures of their trip"—and Hayley showed me a photo of the girls on a sandy beach "They've all apologized, and I mostly forgive them."

I buried my face in my hands. "Hayley, why didn't you talk to me?"

"I knew you'd be angry I wasn't invited, and I didn't want to disappoint you, Mom."

I reached for her hands again and said, "You can never do anything to upset me. I love you, and I want the best for you. Please promise you won't try to protect me by lying or keeping secrets from me."

She bit her lip. "Okay, I promise." She scratched her chin. "But, can I still be friends with the girls?"

CHAPTER FORTY-FOUR
NOW
SEPTEMBER
Two Weeks Later

As ANTICIPATED, my fight with Donna spread through town like wildfire and fueled the Forest River rumor mill big time. Every mommy clambered to find out the inside scoop about what went down, and I couldn't wait for the notoriety to end. I even contemplated changing my phone number because, for the last two-and-a-half weeks, my phone hadn't stopped ringing, beeping, and buzzing from nosey bodies, but I settled on switching the ringtone. The other day at the dry cleaners, I heard my old alert, and my heart pounded so quickly, I feared I developed a minor case of PTSD.

The look of relief on Hayley's face when I told her she could still be friends with the girls nearly shattered my heart. It killed me that my daughter had suffered in silence for weeks because she worried about upsetting me as well as the ramifications from the other girls' thoughtless behavior.

I didn't hold any information back from my daughter. I felt it was important for her to know all the facts. I explained the reason her class was changed was because the girls' moms lied to the school and claimed that she was a bully. I promised her I would make sure they contacted the school to set the record straight.

As a mom, you're supposed to be the one to sculpt your child's mind and teach them the important lessons in life. But sometimes the tables are turned, and you end up becoming the student. I knew instantly I had to make some changes.

I walked away from my conversation with my daughter seeing things in a whole new light. With Hayley and Christie still friends, I knew I would be placed in an awkward position when they spent time together. There was no way I'd be able to avoid Donna. I promised myself I would not let my feelings affect my daughter.

After our little talk, Hayley had excused herself before I could get mushy. I gave her a little space, and then went up to her room. She didn't see me, but I heard her on the phone with her friends demanding their mothers apologize to me for what they did to both of us. In record speed, the mothers of the girls involved in the coup called me to make amends. But more importantly, they also said they would call the principal and the school psychologist to recant their claims against my daughter. Even the mastermind, Mia Montgomery, had phoned me with a half-assed apology for her actions. She rationalized her actions by saying she only wanted Melissa to be the most popular girl in the grade. Donna was the only one who never reached out.

Claire and the other PTA board moms had been a godsend to me during this challenging time. The sad realization that Donna was never my friend, who never deserved one drop of my time or compassion, shook me to my core. I truly believed she would have seen the error in her ways and would have begged my forgiveness, but I was wrong. I wasted enough time mourning the loss of the one-sided friendship. I knew it was high time for me to move forward, and I was determined to make great strides, even if I still cried a little bit every night.

Aimee offered to gather together all the first-grade carpool moms for me. At her suggestion, we went to La Petite Boulangerie and, over decadent macaroons and glasses of Ace of Spades champagne, we revamped the carpool schedule. Aimee convinced the ladies the change was imperative because it would be uncomfortable for me to have Julia, Donna's youngest daughter in my car. Don't get me wrong, I had nothing against the child, and I would never do anything to hurt her, *or any kid*, but I was thankful Aimee took a strong stand. It made me feel so much better knowing I wouldn't be forced to face Donna three mornings a week.

Revamping the schedule was no easy feat, especially so late in the game. Between long-standing manicure appointments, personal trainers, and yoga and Pilates classes, everyone's schedule already had been set. I worried we wouldn't be able to make the new line up work. It took a while, and I needed to pop a Xanax or two, but eventually, we sorted everything out.

There was only one big-ticket item left to handle, so I gathered the PTA board at my house for an impromptu meeting, about a week after the term began.

"Where is Stacey?" I asked everyone and no one in particular.

"She should know better than to be tardy." Trisha smirked.

Claire snuck a peek at her phone. I tried to keep our meetings technology-free. I couldn't stand it when someone was more focused on their device than our discussion. "I have a hunch she'll have an excellent reason."

As soon as the words were out of her mouth, my doorbell rang. "That's probably her now." As I walked to let Stacey in, I glanced around my house and felt Joan's presence. While I used to hate how she furnished my home, now, since she was gone, the decor gave me comfort. I felt like her strength was with me, and my girls, especially during challenging times like these.

As soon as I saw Stacey's bright smile, I knew her tardiness was well worth the wait. I gave her a quick hug and air kiss, and quickly ushered her into my den. I poured her a glass of Chardonnay as she said her hellos.

"Sorry, I'm late," Stacey said as soon as she took a swig of wine, her eyes dancing. "I had to pay someone a visit. I won't lie, it wasn't fun, but it was productive. Has anyone checked their emails since they arrived?"

Claire blushed slightly. "I did. Good job, you!"

Trisha, Aimee, and I reached for our phones and read.

To: Jackie Martin, Claire Conroy, Stacey Williams, Trisha Dickens, and Aimee Roberts
From: Donna Warren
CC: Forest River Elementary School Principal, Harrison Williams

Date: 9/10 @ 5:08 PM

Subject: Forest River PTA Resignation

Hello,

After much thought and consideration, I realize I must resign from my elected position of Forest River PTA Treasurer.

This decision wasn't easy for me. Leaving my post wasn't something I had intended but it is crystal clear how my resignation will be the best solution possible for the team. We know intimately how the "team" must take first priority.

Well, "team", I wish you the best of luck in your future endeavors, and all the challenges this year will bring each and every one of you.

Regards,
Donna Warren

I jumped up out of my wing chair and hugged Stacey. "You did this? Thank you."

"I told you I would," Stacey said. "I knew you doubted me, but I can be extremely persuasive when I need to be."

"Don't we know," Aimee added with a wink.

I waved my hand. "I never doubted your talents for a second. I thought Donna would refuse to do the right thing to spite me."

Stacey frowned. "Well, she didn't seem as hell-bent on holding onto her role as I thought she would be."

"Is it me?" Trisha asked. "Or is there something ominous about how she ended her note? 'Challenges to each and every one of you...'"

I speculated what Stacey had said to encourage Donna to resign, and I did wonder about Trisha's assessment. "I wouldn't put anything past Donna at this point. I certainly don't trust her as far as

I could throw her. We all need to be on guard in case she does anything else stupid."

Claire made a face. "In case? I think it would be a safer bet to wonder *when* she'll do something stupid."

"You're right. But we've wasted enough time on Donna Warren. It is time for us to move forward. We need to find her replacement! Who has made headway?" I asked.

I had hoped Donna would resign, and last week I had tasked the ladies in selecting a mom to bring into the PTA fold. The bylaws allowed us the flexibility to enlist a new member post-election without going through the rigmarole of nominations and holding a vote. The issue was finding someone who'd align with our vision and mission and would also be willing and able to work. Most Forest River moms loved to complain about the injustices at the school; unfortunately, when it was time to put the time and effort into making the school a better place for their children, no one was home.

One by one, the ladies tossed out names. There was an issue with every woman. Either someone didn't get along with her, they feared she'd be too laid back or domineering, or one of us knew she wouldn't be interested in public service. Somebody even mentioned the new Forest River mom, Colleen-somebody from Ohio, who I had met at Paired the day I learned about Donna's deception. I too was about to throw in the towel when an idea struck me.

CHAPTER FORTY-FIVE
NOW

Okay, fine. Inspiration didn't just hit me like a bolt of lightning. The idea crept into my brain at three o'clock in the morning a few days ago, when I woke up to pee and couldn't fall back to sleep. But what I was about to suggest was crazy and completely out my character. I had no clue how the women would react.

My eyes ping-ponged around the room as I asked, "What about Sydney Clayton?"

"Who is she?" Stacey scrunched her face.

Claire locked eyes with me and tapped her index finger against her lips as she seemed in deep in thought. "Hmm. That's an interesting choice."

Aimee added, "I don't know. Maybe?"

"Again, guys, who is this person? I've never even heard her name before," said Stacey.

"Her daughter is Amanda, and she's in the girls' first grade class," Trisha replied.

"And her babysitter is Sally," Aimee said.

Stacey said, "Okay, so I think I know the kid, and I definitely know the babysitter, but I don't think I've ever met the mom."

I stood up and started to pace around the room as I began to make my case. "Sydney is a CFO for a food importer, so she's clearly good with numbers. I bet she could handle the treasurer role in her sleep. She's been living in town since before her only child was born. Somehow, she manages to stay clear of all the drama and parental politics, and we all know how crazy kindergarten can be for a new mom."

The women all laughed as memories of our past flashed in our minds.

"I've only really spoken with her a handful of times," I said. "Usually, I interact with the babysitter Sally. The few times we spoke Sydney really impressed me. She was smart and funny."

"I actually like her, too," Claire added. "And the girls all love her daughter. But, Jackie, I don't know if she'd be reliable, though. Remember, Aimee, she was the only carpool mom who didn't come to your gathering?"

"She didn't even take a second to consider attending," Aimee said.

"Good point." Then I raised my index finger. "But I also remember she was the only mom who was reasonable and flexible. She sent me a private text message telling me to select a slot for her, and she'd make it work."

"Of course she was able to make anything work." Trisha rolled her eyes. "She didn't have to worry about juggling her schedule. She'd make her hired help handle all the heavy lifting for her."

It saddened me how resentful and judgmental people were when their situations changed. It was like they forgot the past. Every woman in this room at one time had either full-time or live-in childcare.

Stacey's eyes gleamed. "You know, she could be the perfect pick for us."

"What do you mean?" Aimee asked.

Stacey looked around the room at everyone and then locked eyes with me. "Okay, so I don't know this Sydney person, but I think Jackie is onto something. On paper, she'll look like a presentable option, which is important, as we all know. She'll also be a benign selection. Since she will be preoccupied with her career, we won't have to lose sleep worrying about her overpowering the PTA. I'm sure with the proper persuasion, we can even manage to motivate her enough to get her to contribute a bit of her time and energy when needed."

"Actually, that's not what I mean at all," I said softly.

"I disagree, Stacey." Claire put down her wine glass on a coaster. "I probably have interacted the most with Sydney. At the beginning of last term, Kevin insisted it was essential for him to get to know her attorney husband better. I arranged a couple of dinners before Kevin realized her spouse was of no use." Claire made no qualms about her distain for her husband's aggressive networking ways. "Sydney's no shrinking violet. If we welcome her into the fold, she won't be satisfied just taking a backseat and letting us run wild. She'd insist on being part. She may even force us to mix things up a bit."

"Well, that will never fly," Trisha said. Her and all the women's eyes were fixed on me.

"Why not?" I asked.

"Come on, Jackie." Stacey walked over to where I sat and squatted down next to me. She reached for my hands. "You know we all love you. And you know we'd all do anything for you, right?"

My affirmative reply was automatic even though I currently second-guessed everyone and everything. Getting stabbed in the back does wonders for destroying your confidence.

"I think inviting this woman into the group is a mistake. Sydney's a wild card. We have no idea how she'd behave or react. Are you really willing to take the risk?"

She didn't give me a chance to answer.

"Jackie, I don't need to remind you. You've scarified so much and killed yourself to get where you are." She pointed around the room. "All of us here would do anything for you and the school. We've supported every one of your crusades. We never once even thought of working against you. Can you say the same thing for this Sydney woman?"

"No," I said. "But I'm willing to take my chances."

"What?" Aimee and Claire asked in unison.

"I'm sick and tired of following the same script. For years, I've allowed pettiness, jealousy, and insecurity to define me. Look at everything we've been through together. There was no reason why we had to take such drastic measures to have our voices heard years ago. If only Pamela wasn't so worried about getting some competition, we could have been partners instead of adversaries."

"You're right," Claire said.

"I know I've made mistakes over the years. I put my trust in the wrong people. And I may be making the biggest mistake of my PTA career right now, but I think we need to take a chance on change. Sydney may completely overpower the PTA, or she might just be the right balance we need. Regardless of what we decide, I have no doubts we're in for one crazy school year. So what's a little more drama and uncertainty? What do you say? Should I call Sydney?"

"Yeah. Go for it. Go on, girl."

THE END

KEEP READING FOR AN EXCERPT OF
GO ON, GIRL

GO ON, GIRL

WHOEVER HAD THE IDIOTIC IDEA to invent text messages? If I could, I'd strangle them. Back in the day, when people had to rely on the telephone, they were forced to hold back their every insecurity and issue, even if only a bit. But now, with the ease of a few keystrokes, everyone was able to share their thoughts and opinions at breakneck speed, without any consideration for their reputations. Not to mention how it made other people feel.

"They're all freaking crazy!" Disgusted, I tossed my new iPhone with a bit too much force. It landed right on the edge of the kitchen table and dangled precariously, narrowly escaping a sudden death.

My husband, Craig, rescued the device and turned it face down in front of him. It beeped in frantic succession, alerting me to at least three new incoming texts. He picked up his coffee cup and calmly took a sip, completely unaware that during his five-mile run this morning my phone hadn't stopped beeping for one single second.

My pulse raced with every alert. "At this rate, I'm going to have to change my text tone, again." A few months back, after my phone had exploded from a similar incessant group text, I switched the sound because every time I heard the chime, it stressed me out.

Last week, I was in the supermarket, and the woman in front of me at the deli counter had the same melody on her phone I used to. When she'd received a text, I'd instantly had palpitations. It was like some technologically provoked post-traumatic stress disorder. "What's it this time?" my husband asked as he coated his pumpernickel bagel with jalapeño cream cheese.

"A major calamity, apparently." I rolled my eyes. "I never realized organizing a carpool could be so cutthroat. But that's what I'm dealing with."

Craig scratched the dark stubble on his chin before he frowned in sympathy. He'd heard different versions of this same story a hundred times during the last term. But he knew I needed to vent, and he would let me. The mothers of my daughter's classmates were catty and juvenile, constantly at each other's throats over petty situations. I missed out on most of their meltdowns because I wasn't part of the clique, thanks to my full-time job as CFO of a food importer. But sometimes, like now, I couldn't avoid the aftermath of an argument, because the turmoil trickled down to my day-to-day life and impacted my daughter and me.

"I don't understand what's wrong with people." I stood up and refilled my coffee cup. Before I returned to the table, I gazed out the back window. I stared at a cardinal that was perched on top of Amanda's swing set and imagined how wonderful it would feel to be able to fly away. "We're supposed to be adults, but everyone's acting like petulant children." I pointed at our six-year-old daughter, who was sitting cross-legged on the floor in the den. Her dark pig-tailed head was bowed, and she was deep in concentration. She intently colored, despite being surrounded by fifteen Barbie dolls, most of which were naked. "She has more maturity in her little pinky than most of the mothers of her classmates."

"She does take after me, you know." Craig beamed. He was five years my senior, and often acted far older than his forty-one years. He was very rational and levelheaded, perfect for his chosen profession, corporate law, which was how we'd met thirteen years before.

When the company I worked for had undergone their first merger, they had hired Craig's law firm to represent them. They'd assigned him to the case, and he and I had to work closely. I'd managed the finance side of the transaction, and the workload was intense. Craig and I had a bit of a bumpy start. I wasn't in the best state of mind since I was petrified about how the corporate change would affect my day-to-day job. But once the deal was signed, our relationship was sealed as well.

Craig's reasonable side suited me perfectly since I tended to get easily upset over insignificant events. My patience level was low for two reasons. First, I was always stretched so thin. I had more commitments and obligations than I could comfortably juggle, so I hated to waste one second. Also, I was a bit of a control freak who feared change. When situations, regardless of their magnitude, were out of my hands, I felt overwhelmed.

It took everything for me not to throw my spoon at him, and by the smirk on his face, I could tell he knew I was contemplating violence. I wasn't usually this angry and upset on a Sunday morning in the summer, but today my blood was boiling. My next-door neighbor, Suzanne, had warned me about this inevitable drama, but I didn't believe her. I figured she had to be exaggerating. I should have trusted her, though. While her kids were now in college, she did raise three of them in this superficial town where social status, appearances, and wealth meant more than morals, compassion, or real friendship.

"Come on, Sydney," Craig mumbled as he chewed his bagel. "Are you going to tell me what's eating at you?"

Before I could say a word, my phone exploded once again. "Ugh! Can these mothers stop it for five seconds? What would they do if they had a real issue?"

Craig picked up my phone and waved it in front of my face. "Don't you want to check what they said?"

I opened my mouth to reply but shook my head.

"Very well." He did what I should have done an hour ago. He silenced my phone and placed it face down on the table.

I took a deep breath. "School starts in only two weeks. Right before kindergarten ended a bunch of the moms organized a carpool schedule, which was no easy feat, mind you. Apparently, it is almost impossible to juggle long-standing manicure appointments, personal trainers, and yoga classes." I pointed at my chest. "I work, and I was the most flexible woman in the bunch! Eventually, even though it took about three weeks and probably numerous refills of Xanax, we managed to sort everything out. But now the plan's gone up in smoke because two of the moms, Donna and Jackie, got into a huge fight last week at a Pilates class."

"What does one thing have to do with another?" Craig tilted his head.

"It shouldn't. But after they had this knock-down screaming match, Jackie went home and called the other moms in the carpool and invited them over for lunch." I took a sip of coffee. I was so frustrated. I thought by agreeing to participate in a carpool this year, I would be able to eliminate some stress from my life. I couldn't have been more wrong. The entire experience had been nothing but aggravating.

I'd yank Amanda out of the schedule right now except I knew my little social butterfly was excited to ride back and forth to school with her classmates, and I didn't want her to miss out.

"Did you go?"

"Um, no. Unlike the other moms, I work for a living, remember?" I felt a small smile creep on my face as I thought about our babysitter, Sally. "I'm shocked Jackie didn't call Sally and invite her to the rant session. That way at least someone from the Clayton household could have represented."

"Sally would have enjoyed it." Craig smiled.

We both knew our babysitter was quite the gossip. Craig and I never worried about missing out on anything that happened in the neighborhood when Sally was around. She had the inside scoop on everyone and everything. In her mid-sixties, Sally spent the better part of her life devoted to caring for children living in this town. Although she'd never married or had kids of her own, she had no shortage of family. She was an instrumental part of so many homes in Forest River; the woman probably received more holiday invitations than the mayor.

"I know. So, anyway, Jackie filled them all in on the fight. She told them she wanted nothing more to do with Donna unless she apologized. She rallied the moms with macaroons from La Petite Boulangerie and Ace of Spades champagne. Of course, they all caved like a house of cards."

"What did Donna do anyway?"

I waved my hand in the air. "Believe me, you don't even want to know." I rolled my eyes. "It's all so petty and stupid." I hated that I was so invested in the drama, but I worried about my daughter. She was such an outgoing child, one who loved spending time with her friends. I didn't want to compromise her happiness in any way, especially since I knew firsthand how difficult life was when you didn't fit in as a kid.

"I know I'll regret this but tell me what happened."

I'd won the husband jackpot. Most men wouldn't have the patience for this type of nonsense, but Craig was different. He was a natural problem solver and loved to try to rectify a situation. He also knew it was in his best interest to let me babble right away about what bothered me than hear me harp about it later.

"Donna jumped on the bad-mouthing bandwagon. She and Jackie both have daughters who are entering the fifth grade, and they're part of a tight-knit clique. Right before the school year ended, Jackie's daughter got into a fight with one of the other girls in the group. Instead of letting the battle blow over, this girl's mother decided to make sure the girls weren't in the same class come September."

"How did she plan on managing that?" Craig asked with a mouthful of cookie.

"She apparently called the school psychologist and told him the girls were having issues and requested they be separated."

"That's not so terrible."

"No, it's not. She didn't stop there, though. This woman then called all the other mothers and offered to take their children on an expense-free Caribbean cruise. It's a blatant, conniving attempt to convince them to contact the school's psychologist as well and tell him their girls couldn't get along with Jackie's child either. The other mothers made the calls as quickly as they packed their kids' Louis Vuitton bags. This mother's manipulative tactics guaranteed her daughter was placed in the class with all her friends while Jackie's daughter was left out, alone."

"Nice way to treat a friend. No wonder she's upset."

"Yeah, I get it. I would be hurt too if the roles were reversed. But I'd be able to put things into perspective and move on. There would be no way I'd cause even more drama."

He cocked his head to the side and stared at me with unblinking eyes. "Really?"

I felt my face flush. "Well, I certainly wouldn't refuse to participate in a carpool because Donna's daughter was in it, which is what Jackie did. And of course, her posse is supporting her."

"They're all grown women. I'm sure they had reasons."

"Yeah, right, Craig." I stood up and kissed the top of his wavy jet-black hair. "Bless your heart. For someone who has such book smarts, you're naïve sometimes. I'd be shocked if half the women in Jackie's fan club would even be able to decide what to eat for lunch if their fearless leader wasn't there to direct them. I've seen these women in action. They all idolize her."

"Maybe they have reason to?"

I clenched my teeth.

"I'm simply saying, Syd, I think you're blowing this all out of proportion. It'll take some work, but you ladies will sort out the schedule once again."

Craig seemed ready to end the conversation. He'd rather be outside playing Frisbee with our daughter.

I put my elbows on the table and rested my head in my hands. "What do I do about Julia? Amanda's best friend." I sighed.

"I really couldn't care less if Julia's mom is," I made air quotes, "'out of the carpool,' but I do feel sorry for Julia. She didn't do anything wrong, and now she's going to have to pay the price because of her mother's actions. If the moms aren't accepting Julia into their cars because of this fight, will they invite the girl over for play dates, birthday parties, or sleepovers?" I got up and started to pace around the kitchen. "She and Amanda are in the same first-grade class. I know Amanda is going to want to pal around with her. Do we have to worry these other kids are going to shun her because of their mothers, who are clearly as mature as a toddler? What is wrong with people?"

"You've got me." He raised his arms over his head and stretched. "Unfortunately, I think things are only going to get worse."

"I know." I sat back down and took a bite of my cookie. "This town is so superficial. The people here don't share the same values as us. I worry about how it will effect Amanda growing up here."

"She doesn't have to."

"What do you mean?" My breath hitched in my throat, and I looked around our newly remodeled kitchen. "This is where we live. This is our home."

Craig pushed his plate away. "It doesn't have to be forever."

I blinked. "What are you talking about?"

He leaned in. "Maybe we should consider making a change, Syd."

I swallowed hard. "What kind of change?"

"A move."

"A move?" I felt my eyes bulge. "Why on earth would we move? We love our house and look at all the work we did. It's finally perfect."

Craig and I were renovation junkies. We'd spent years improving this house and did a lot of the work ourselves.

"I know." I followed his gaze as his green eyes scanned the room. "Our house is wonderful. But let's face it; we don't love this town anymore. Honestly, I'm not sure we ever really did."

Craig and I had decided to settle in Forest River ten years ago, right after we'd gotten married. One of the paralegals in his office grew up here and recommended we visit the community once she'd learned we were in the market to buy a home. We immediately fell in love with all the unique stores and restaurants located in the heart of town. Both Craig and I were lovers of water, so living so close to a lazy river was quite appealing to us.

I instantly regretted eating the cookie, which now sat like a lead weight in the pit of my stomach. "What are you talking about?"

"Come on, Syd. We never were part of this community. We've kept to ourselves, and it was wonderful until Amanda started school. You know as well as I do that the people here are not like us. We don't belong." He folded his arms across his chest. "You carried on all last year about how obnoxious and phony the mothers were. You kept fretting about how you were afraid Amanda would become spoiled by having to keep up with her classmates. This school year hasn't even started yet, and the drama is already in full force. Do we really want to raise our daughter in this type of environment?"

I shifted in my chair. Although he had some valid points, this was my home. "I don't know."

"Consider your commute for a minute. How many hours a week do you spend in your car?"

"Way too many." I frowned. One of the worst days of my career was when my boss announced he was moving our office. I'd even contemplated resigning as a result.

"If we moved closer to your office, you'd be able to spend more time with Amanda."

"That would be nice." I imagined my life without a two-and-a-half-hour daily ride in bumper-to-bumper traffic.

"You know what else would be nice?" Craig continued. "If we lived closer to your family."

Unlike Craig's siblings who'd dispersed across the country when his parents had retired and moved to Florida, my sister, Bethany, and I remained in New York. In fact, Bethany lived close to where we grew up, near the town where my parents still resided.

"Yes, it would be. I'd love to be able to pop over and visit them rather than always having to plan an excursion, especially now that Dad hasn't been well." My father had had a heart attack a few months before and needed a double bypass. While he was recovering nicely from surgery, it was a wake-up call for my sister and me about our parents' mortality. I stayed with my mom while he underwent the procedure, but it was difficult for me to return home afterward. I did wish I lived closer to them like my sister.

I picked at my cuticle. "But Craig, I love it here."

His eyes narrowed. "Do you really?"

I looked around the room once more. "Of course I do. Where is all this coming from anyway? We've lived here for ten years. Since when have you thought about moving?"

He bit his lip. "I really haven't. Last week I received an email from a local real estate agent. She has someone who's very interested in buying a house in this neighborhood. She asked if we'd consider showing ours. I didn't reply, but it's been gnawing at me ever since." He rubbed his forehead. "This town is very hot right now. People want to live here, and not many houses go up for sale. When they do go on the market, they sell pretty much instantly and usually for more than the asking price."

"I know. It's crazy." A family who'd lived down the street from us had put their house on the market a year ago, and after only a week they found themselves in a bidding war between two prospective buyers.

"Maybe we should consider it, Syd. We can probably get top dollar for this place. Then, we could move into an even bigger house in a more relaxed kind of town."

I picked up my phone. "Crap," I muttered as I scanned the twenty-five text messages I had missed. So much for the ladies sorting anything out. Relaxed they were not. Would I be able to survive a drama-filled term? Would we be better off living someplace else?

ACKNOWLEDGMENTS

Thank you so much for reading *Mom Boss*. This was the quickest book I ever wrote. I started to tell Jackie's story right before the world turned upside down. And then for weeks, as I was glued to the news about Covid-19 cases and death tolls, I struggled to type a word. I found it impossible to find anything funny in such a difficult time. But eventually, I turned back to my crazy ladies of Forest River. I allowed their antics to take my mind off of what was going on in the world around me. I hope Jackie, Donna, and Claire helped you as well.

To my mom, Loretta—I love you more than words can ever express. It has been so difficult not being able to see you, but I cherish our numerous phone calls each day. Thank you for always being my biggest cheerleader and the best Mom Boss any girl could wish for.

To my husband Marc—-Even after being in the house with you for six months straight and counting, I still like you a lot. Thank you for always making me laugh and being the inspiration for all the good men in my books.

To my amazing editor—Christina Boyd— I've considered you a friend for years. I always—thanks to you I know I overuse the word, but it fits here—wanted to work with you but never had the chance. I am so thankful for this opportunity. Your keen eye and insights pushed me and transformed this story. Oh, and you are fast too! I can't wait to meet you in real life!

Thank you to all my friends! Shout outs to authors Laura Heffernan, Tracy Krimmer, and Meredith Schorr as well as my always first readers Bethany Clark, Kathy Lewison, and Tiffany Maytum. A big hug to the real "Tania Wald" – I added a cameo character because Tania's real life mommy drama inspired this series. Also, her husband may be the doctor but Tania was my voice of reason during the scariest parts of the pandemic.

The biggest thank you goes out to book bloggers, bookgrammers and all my readers: Thank you so much for spending your precious free time with my characters. Your support and kind words mean the world to me. I love nothing more than reading your reviews and emails and seeing your posts on social media. I'm sending you huge virtual hugs.

If you enjoyed Mom Boss, it would mean the world to me if you left a short review on any retail website and/or Goodreads. And if you haven't already done so already please check out Sydney's story *(Go On, Girl)* and Claire's story *(Mom Genes)*. Donna's story *(Mom Rules)* is coming soon too and is available for pre-order.

I love to chat and stay connected to readers. You can find me on Twitter @feelingbeachie or Facebook as Hilary Grossman Author. My email is hilarygrossmanauthor@gmail.com. To find out about new releases, join my mailing list http://eepurl.com/brIroD

XOXO,
Hilary

Printed in Great Britain
by Amazon

52663739R00145